Journeys in the Dead Season

Spencer Jordan has worked as a software engineer and more recently as a lecturer at the University of Wales. He lives in Cardiff. *Journeys in the Dead Season* is his first novel.

SPENCER JORDAN

Journeys in the Dead Season

PAN BOOKS

First published 2005 by Pan Books
an imprint of Pan Macmillan Ltd
Pan Macmillan, 20 New Wharf Road, London N1 9RR
Basingstoke and Oxford
Associated companies throughout the world
www.panmacmillan.com

ISBN 0 330 44122 1

Copyright © Spencer Jordan 2005

The right of Spencer Jordan to be identified as the
author of this work has been asserted by him in accordance
with the Copyright, Designs and Patents Act 1988.

The events and characters in this book are fictitous.
Certain real locations and public figures are mentioned,
but all other characters and events described in the book
are totally imaginary.

All rights reserved. No part of this publication may be
reproduced, stored in or introduced into a retrieval system, or
transmitted, in any form, or by any means (electronic, mechanical,
photocopying, recording or otherwise) without the prior written
permission of the publisher. Any person who does any unauthorized
act in relation to this publication may be liable to criminal
prosecution and civil claims for damages.

1 3 5 7 9 8 6 4 2

A CIP catalogue record for this book is available from
the British Library.

Printed and bound in Great Britain by
Mackays of Chatham plc, Chatham, Kent

This book is sold subject to the condition that it shall not,
by way of trade or otherwise, be lent, re-sold, hired out,
or otherwise circulated without the publisher's prior consent
in any form of binding or cover other than that in which
it is published and without a similar condition including this
condition being imposed on the subsequent purchaser.

To Mr Atkins, English teacher

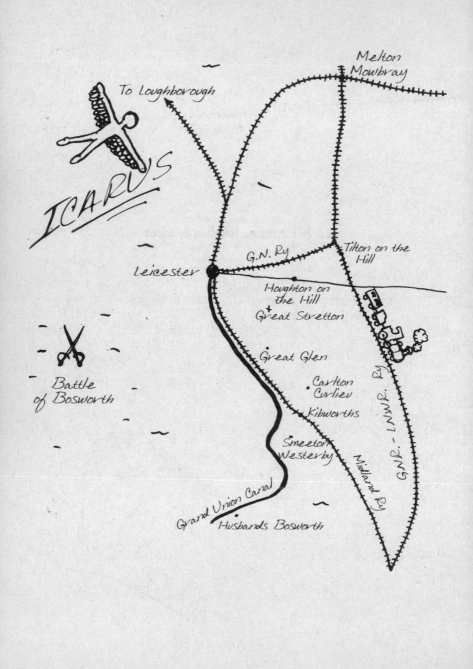

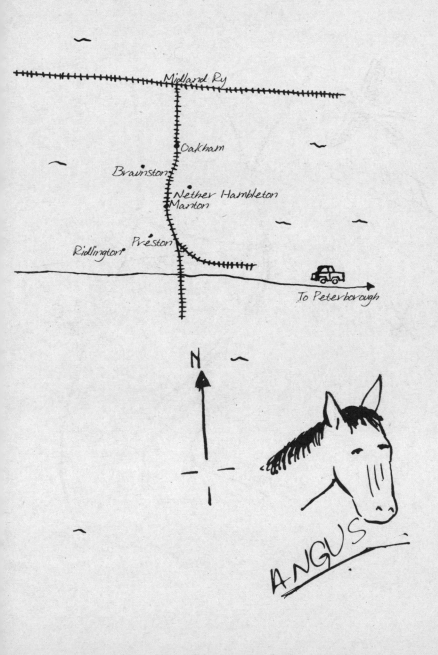

Midland Ry

Oakham

Brainston

Nether Hambleton
Manton

Preston

Ridlington

To Peterborough

N

ANGUS

PART ONE

Durham Category 'A' Prison

Present Day, Early Autumn

My guard, Anderson, is unaware of Greek history. Of Greek thought. Hellenistic was the word I used earlier this afternoon. He screwed up his face as though I had defecated on my bed.

What? he asked.

Hellenistic. Anything to do with Ancient Greece, I replied. He watched me get up from my desk. You asked me what I was doing and I merely replied that I was continuing with my Hellenistic studies. My studies of Ancient Greece. I placed the tattered prison library book down on the desk in front of me. Although a simple little tome, I am finding it an excellent introduction to the history of science and philosophy, just two of the many areas that are presently exercising my mind.

No bullshit. Hotplate now! As Anderson uttered these two fractured sentences he forced my metal door wide open, slamming it against the reinforced walls of the cell. The starkly lit corridor was revealed beyond.

A bundle of keys beneath a peaked cap – that's how I think of Anderson. Keys, peaked cap and those hard, hard, metal-capped boots slamming against the door. He is a big lad, a veritable Spartan no less.

What are you smiling at, dick shit? he asked as I walked towards him.

I was just thinking what an excellent Spartan guard you would have made.

Don't give me any lip, sunshine, otherwise you may find yourself back in the queue for Dr Hardacre.

A bit of Socratic debate never hurt anyone, surely, I replied.

The force with which I was evicted from the cell suggested that Anderson was less than impressed with my reasoning.

Though I have been here less than three weeks I have come to recognize that such ill-mannered behaviour is the norm. I am still shocked by the barbarism of this place. But do not fret too much; this is hardly Devil's Island. After all, I have a cell to myself, a very rare thing indeed. I realize of course that, in part, my solitude is recognition of my scholastic reputation, an acknowledgement by the authorities of my requirement for peace and quiet within which I can continue my academic studies. Certainly my present situation facilitates my work in several ways. Not only am I writing this diary, but I am also undertaking the construction of a series of web pages on tropical fish keeping – that is, when I am allowed access to the computers in the education centre. Only last Tuesday, at a moment of the interview that is still an unsettling memory, Dr Sanders asked me pointedly who I was. I can still recall exactly what I said in answer to this rather bizarre question: A fish keeper, of course, a professional aquarist. *I am devoted to the maintenance of life, however small.*

For some reason, this elicited nothing more than a smile from my interlocutor. A smile and the simple rejoinder, Go on.

And so I did, of course: The maintenance of life within an artificial or false environment can be highly complex. Although a living thing may seem to be a most wondrous creation, for the purposes of the hobbyist it should be viewed as nothing more than a highly structured machine, operating to clearly understood biological and psychological norms. In fact, for the hobbyist I would say that delight at sentient creation is quickly dispersed. It is not unhelpful to consider the living form as a rather inefficient converter of food stuffs, a bag of flesh into which solids are applied through one orifice and deposited from another. The safe conversion of such waste matter into less harmful substances is a key part of the science, as is temperature and the level of lighting. The hobbyist should try to imitate reality as closely as possible, switching the aquarium light off at night for instance, so that the diurnal patterns are maintained.

After a moment's thought I added that in many ways a prison is rather like a huge aquatic shop, with the prisoners as the fish within their individual aquariums. I could tell that Dr Sanders was impressed with my little philosophical lecture. I watched as he made some notes.

But, alas, it seems I have become distracted from what I had hoped to discuss with you, namely my activities within the prison. As well as my diary and web pages, I am continuing with my scientific studies, a process that has been greatly facilitated by the governor's permission to allow me access to one or two of my books. But despite these cognitive activities, activities that I doubt this place has seen the like of before, I cannot fool myself regarding the real reason for my solitude: protection. In short, it was felt that my safety could not be guaranteed if I shared a cell with another inmate. As I'm sure you know only too well, inmates associated with certain crimes, even remand prisoners such as me, are seen as fair game when it comes to private retribution. In here I am called the Beast and few opportunities are missed by the prisoners to remind me of it. When I first arrived I was told that the protection of the guards would be enough, but sadly this has not proved to be the case. Hence Anderson's reference to Dr Hardacre, a man who devoted much time to my unfortunate facial wound. But let's not dwell on these things – I have convinced myself that the attack was an aberration, a one off, as it were. And I would be wrong if I didn't state that the wound appears to be well on the way to an almost complete recovery now that the stitches have been removed. The twenty-four-hour surveillance of my cell has also been lifted, so you could say my life is beginning to return to some degree of, dare I say it, normality. This isn't normality in the sense that you would understand it, of course, unless you are reading these words from your own prison cell.

Rather, I use the term in a relative way to indicate that the provision of a simple desk, with pen, paper and assorted secondary material, has provided the foundation on which the essential academic flavour of my life can be restored.

I hear shouts outside the door. Although only early – not even nine o'clock! – it's almost time for lights out. It's the guards I can hear stomping heavily on the landing in anticipation. As always at this time of the day, the noise of the inmates increases, made restive by the thought of the long, dark hours they will have to spend sealed in their claustrophobic cubes. With dark thoughts crowding my head, perhaps it's best I lay down my pen, for it is moments such as this that I think of Bedlam, that madhouse of old, and the caged animal within us all. And I think of Jim, of course.

– 2 –

I was there when Jim discovered the web – the World Wide Web, www, the Internet (remember that capital 'I'). The Net. Call it what you will. I took him into my room and gave a demonstration, both of us sitting on hard wooden chairs. I take no delight in relating this detail to you, no sick pride. I merely state these things as fact. I was there. I was there as we peered at the flickering screen in the autumnal gloom. And, at that very moment, as Jim's fingers moved like slugs across the screen, depositing lingering trails of greasy slime, it was I who thought of Joseph Wright's Experiment with an Air Pump. There was Jim, the empty-headed enthusiast at the front of the proceedings, and I next to him, the great rationalist, holding centre stage, as the beautiful bird in the glass case slowly suffocates. Perhaps not the most fitting image, given what was to come.

I could see that Jim liked the Internet, or at least he liked what he saw on my nineteen-inch screen. About five minutes into the demonstration he started clicking his fingers, something he only does when he gets excited.

I'm sure it doesn't come as a surprise to you that I have

asked the governor if I could lead a workshop on using the Internet. Unfortunately, my request was turned down without a moment's thought. It is their loss, of course; I cannot but think that it is the only way the inmates will better themselves academically. Perhaps I shouldn't have asked for the return of my goggles as a quid pro quo. Dr Sanders did say that they were completely harmless. When he first brought them in, it was a bit of a shock, I can tell you. Dr Sanders is my psychiatrist. I see him every Tuesday morning at 10 a.m.

When you were caught by the police at Bosworth Battlefield you were wearing these. What are they? Such was Dr Sanders' opening gambit. Of course the police had asked these questions before but Dr Sanders was different. He placed my goggles on the table between us as though they were a gift.

They're my goggles, I replied. They're antique, very rare. Early flying goggles, the sort of thing you would have worn in the 1920s or 30s. I got them from ... As I said this I suddenly realized I couldn't remember how I had ended up with them.

Dr Sanders smiled reassuringly. Why do you wear them?

Why do I wear them? I secretly pondered. Oh, Dr Sanders, surely *you* have sneaked them on behind my back ...

On occasions, Dr Sanders has allowed me to wear the goggles during our little meetings. And then he has sat back and listened as I describe the wondrous things that were open to my eyes ...

– 3 –

It is early Sunday morning and I have been up many hours. I couldn't sleep after I was told. Some time next autumn, probably late October, my solicitor had said.

The date of our trial, Jim's and mine. Over a year away.

In an effort to distract my mind, I have spent the morning reading what I have written to date in this notebook. You must remember I am a man of letters, a writer of important academic tracts, and so it is easy for me to understand the shortcomings of what I have written thus far. And I am not afraid to admit them. In justification I can only reply that at the commencement of the diary I had not fully thought through its purpose. But this news of the trial has galvanized my mood and sense of purpose. All effort will now be expended on the defence of my innocence, a process that I freely admit will be both long and tumultuous. But this in no way should entail the prescriptive creation of propaganda, a vile falsification of the truth, if you will. For, as I have heard Dr Sanders state more than once to others, I cannot be held to blame for what occurred. Indeed, it seems that on reflection my role in the sordid events was at worst neutral and at best a positive check on the macabre activities of my companion. And this surely *is* the truth – that without me Jim would have sunk far lower, far quicker, than in fact he subsequently did.

The veracity of these words is for others to judge, of course, but at least I now know my true direction, for I am like St Paul on the road to Damascus. And like St Paul I must believe that the purity of my position will see me through in the end. The truth is my sword and I should wield it as best I can. For now, however, my humble diary must take the battle cry forward, until, in the forthcoming autumn, my campaign begins in earnest.

It has been some hours since I wrote the above paragraph, time in which I have had the opportunity to reflect on my previous thoughts. Sitting here in my small cell I have been reminded of the similarity in my circumstances to that experienced by Adolf Hitler in Lansberg prison. As you may be aware, Hitler wrote much of *Mein Kampf* while in prison, as well as copious other notes and jottings. As he was only too aware, his time would eventually come as well.

This may seem a strange thing to say, and perhaps I have shocked you. But as I said to the oaf not more than one hour ago, I think you'll find that my time will come. Of course my words were wasted in that particular case. Indeed, I can still recall the rather confused sneer that spread across his pock-marked face as he digested my response.

If I recall correctly (time has such an odd quality in here) it was only last week, as I was being led down to the canteen, or hotplate as the slang would have it, that I reflected that, even in the most unsettling of environments, it is interesting how one seeks solace in the mundane or the repetitive. It seems fair to say that in this madhouse the slow etching of routines onto our faceless existence appears to be one small way by which the inmates can exert a degree of stability on the chaos around us. In my own case, for instance, I have taken to sitting at a certain table for my meals. As is apparently customary for someone under a charge such as mine, the seats in my immediate vicinity are always left unoccupied, thereby allowing me far greater elbowroom than that enjoyed by my illustrious companions. But I have noticed that at my table, safely beyond the *cordon sanitaire* as it were, have sat a number of increasingly familiar men, one of whom I have only recently discovered is known, rather prosaically, as Mad Bob.

His presence can hardly be missed. He sits on his plastic chair like a Buddha, his stomachs and double chins flowing down to his knees in a corpulent tide. He holds his fork upright on the table in a clenched fist as if it is a trident and he Canute upon his throne on the open shore. He has a series of tattooed tears rolling down from his left eye and across his cratered cheek. Perhaps more a court jester, then. His eyes gleam out, their focus never leaving my face. At first I found this most disconcerting, even more so than the calls and shouts from the others. But Mad Bob says nothing, only offering me the cold gleam of his piggy eyes. On one occasion I believe I mentioned the panopticon to him in an attempt to break the ice. As I reached for the salt and looked up at him I said, Foucault was right after all: despite a free choice, we all sit in the same seats in the canteen every day.

I could see a degree of confusion flash across Mad Bob's face, a tear or two disappearing into folds of flesh as though they were molluscs seeking shelter from an oncoming storm.

I attempted to elucidate. We spend so much of our time under strict regimentation that whenever we're offered an open choice you would think we would delight in spontaneous anarchy. I coughed. Would you not? The piggy eyes refused to blink. I continued: Foucault's panopticon comes to mind of course . . .

But there was no point continuing. His saliva was already dribbling down my cheek. I should have known that such a high level of Socratic debate would have left my mute companion feeling distinctly inferior. I can only assume that since a verbal exchange was beyond him, the physical attack remained the only alternative. I, of course, silently wiped my cheek clean before returning to the baked beans and chips.

I think you'll find that my time will come.

I can reveal that I did not rehearse what I said but rather simply responded to a whim of the moment, to the impromptu calling of my more creative side. On reflection I am rather proud of the words: a trite monologue it certainly wasn't but rather a laser-guided missile straight in through the open window. A sentence that not only asserted my ultimate innocence but also whispered of the greater things ahead.

Let me tell you that while Hitler was in prison he received the most favourable treatment – he occupied a large room on the first floor with windows offering extensive views of the surrounding countryside. The room was amply furnished, including an expansive desk at which he did much of his work. Now none of this bears the remotest similarity to my own dismal quarters, except that I too have been given my own room with a desk at which to work. I appear to have been positively encouraged to continue my writing and researches. And most subtle of all, I have begun to notice the slightest signs of respect shown to me by the prison staff. A nod here and a smile there, a passing inquiry perhaps about the weighty complexities of my work. I cannot help but think that this bodes well for the forthcoming trial and what waits beyond. I have said as much to Dr Sanders (Ludendorff!), who nods with a knowing approbation. We are both professional men, you see, men of books and letters. He does not interject because my eloquence can defeat him. Yesterday he even let me wear the goggles again.

Dr Sanders is encouraging me to explore the past, to go over those events that have already occurred. To unearth those things that my mind may have subconsciously tried to bury away. A diary may help, may help focus your subconscious voice. They were Dr Sanders' very words. And such is the case. Though I cannot travel beyond the straitjacket of these four walls, in my mind I am as free to move through time as the most peripatetic of nomads. And like a traveller I have my diary to record these most exotic of experiences.

This morning, locked in my cell, I have had much time to explore those early days after I first met Jim. I do not know why that particular time has been bothering me. Perhaps I linger here for no other reason than it is the beginning. But perhaps there is something else, something more funda-mental, more profound, that I need to explore. Put simply it is this: did Jim have some great plan from the beginning in which I was but a helpless pawn or were there moments when an alternative path existed? And if so, when?

I cannot deny that from the start Jim had his plans. He told them to me soon after we first met. In turn I told him the importance of preparation, of planning, of strategy. Yes, strategy. I remember liking the word. I liked its sound, its connotations. Normal people don't have strategies, you see. Normal people have plans. But Jim and I, we had a strategy, like a government, like generals. Or Hitler. Like Napoleon when he invaded Russia. When he swept over the Nieman with 600,000 men and horses. What a sight that must have been! And the retreat – one of the great stories of warfare. Frozen rivers, frozen land, frozen men, frozen horses. Napoleon skidding away on his sledge, his infallibility broken for ever.

I would imagine you think you know Jim so well. No doubt you have seen his picture in the newspapers and have read the most intimate details in the reports. But listen, I know the truth. I knew Jim from the beginning, from that very first day when it all began; and so hush and listen to what I have to say. And let me say this: that more than anything, Jim was always the Other, the postmodernist Other (I told you that I read – never underestimate your enemy, my friend). He's Grendel, he's a Hobgoblin, a kobold, Big Foot, a werewolf. He's a Fabulous Creature, tuatha de danann. He's a Creature of Night. He's Rousseau's native, he's a Swift Yahoo, an Irishman, a Blackman, a Red under the bed. And of course he's you.

Yes, dear friend, you have made him too! But try to reach in and he retreats, pulling back, over the grass, over the Steppes, well beyond Moscow. You, the Grand Armée, can only turn back and retreat in disarray.

It is my contention that one should remain aloof from individual snipes or comments. For example, and as I have already written, in my present circumstances I am repeatedly called Beast, or worse, by the lowest form of inmate. I could easily reply to these men that I am on remand and therefore awaiting trial. I could mention that my role in events was of a singular kind that throws serious doubt, to say the least, on my ultimate culpability. I could mention that as Hitler drew the bourgeoisie about him, those with intelligence and insight, then so too do I, in the form of my guards, the governor, and Dr Sanders. And lastly I could state that a beast is an unthinking primitive creature, driven by the most savage of instincts, whereas I am cradled by the bosom of the Enlightenment, a man who even in such a dark place as my cell is capable of pursuing the most exotic of intellectual challenges. I could say all these things, but to do so would be to hand the advantage back to my accusers. And so I remain mute and leave the real beasts to rattle their cages in fury.

But occasionally certain comments are made that could

be called constructive. This very rarely happened with Jim of course. His constant attacks were nothing more than jealous outpourings – jealousy at my greater intellectual ability, jealousy at my higher capacity for strategic thought. But other things have been said to me, by other people, that have made me think. For instance I see no shame in revealing that only this morning Dr Sanders made a comment that even now has left my thoughts rather unsettled. The remark was made during our usual Tuesday morning meeting, an appointment I believe we now both look forward to with some professional anticipation. We were sat at the usual wooden table with two cups of tea between us. I do recall that Dr Sanders was stirring the contents of his cup with a red pencil as I once more held centre stage.

The piping in this place is truly dreadful. I am constantly aroused in the morning by the sound of my fellow inmates' plumbing as they go about their ablutions.

These may not have been my exact words, but the general thrust of the sentence is correct. The reaction of Dr Sanders surprised me. Rather than nod knowingly, as he often does when we discuss weighty issues, he cocked one eye up from the mini whirlpool in front of him and began to laugh. The shock on my face must have embarrassed him because he quickly regained control, before adding, Sorry. Do you have a sense of humour?

It has often been as an intrepid anthropologist that I have trooped through the canteen or stolen precious moments on the landing. And one of the things that my fieldwork is already beginning to isolate is the role of humour amongst the inmates. When I say humour I do not mean to imply that my companions are constantly exchanging puns and jokes as if they are professional comedians. Rather, it should be understood that humour in this particular environment is distilled into its more caustic form. By this I refer to sarcasm, irony and the more biting aspects of witticism. Although often meant as barbed attacks, I must admit a certain admiration of the humour through which many of the affronts are delivered.

Let me give you an example of the sort of thing I mean: Fred's gone to the vegetable garden, has he? Well at least he will have friends he can converse with. I heard this only a day or so ago at a nearby table in the canteen as we settled down for tea. My representation may not be strictly accurate but I hope it is enough to give you a sense of the comical character I am trying to explain. It was merely a throwaway line, said between two young men behind me. Although I did not turn round I must admit that I did smile as I ate my soup.

I have merely provided this background information so that you are not too alarmed, dear friend, when I admit that I spent most of the early part of this afternoon practising a little witticism that I thought I could use to dispel any 'difficult' situations that might arise in the near future. Dr Sanders' comments this morning have merely highlighted that an attuned sense of humour may not just be a matter of health and safety, but perhaps also of professional necessity. Locked as I was in my cell, I had few distractions.

At first I sat on my bed and wondered with some bemusement about how I should proceed. Witticisms and sarcastic comments are not my strong point but I was aware that they are often delivered spontaneously, seemingly with little preparation or rehearsal. Yet I felt that if I could have some pre-arranged material it might possibly act as a catalyst to further comic delivery. If nothing else I could use the material to practise both the timing and delivery of comical utterances.

Wondering where to start, I remembered the words that had so amused the good doctor. If they were good enough for him then surely they would be good enough for my erstwhile prison colleagues. With renewed enthusiasm in my quest, I began to recite the sentence that Dr Sanders had found so funny. Pacing the length of my cell, I played around with structure and imagery until confident that the little story was as entertaining as possible. And when Anderson unlocked my door to inquire on my state, I was more than ready for him.

Stepping from behind the door I began: Just the man! I find it most difficult to get to sleep at night what with all the noises coming from my inmates' plumbing! Perhaps you should not allow them so much tea!

Anderson, to be fair, was rather taken aback. All right, all right, just settle down there. He carefully inspected my room before asking me if I required any liquid sustenance. I said that a cup of tea would do nicely.

The whistles have been blown so it is only five minutes before lights out. I had better lay down my pen, although I doubt I will sleep. I have not yet had the opportunity of delivering the 'joke' to my colleagues but at least its first airing was not a complete disaster. It seems to me that even after this most tentative of trials humour can be a most effective weapon. Perhaps I should have used it with Jim. Maybe things would have been different if I had.

– 5 –

At Great Glen there are more great dogs than honest men.

I came across this quote during my extensive historical research. I include it now for your delectation and amusement. As I'm sure you know, both Jim and I live there.

When I close my eyes I can still easily picture it. Great Glen is one of those places that hovers between classifica-tions, situated as it is somewhere between a large village and a small town. Its population in 1999 was 3,222. Just large enough for anonymity. Just small enough for a sense of community, for those that want it. There's an old part, with the picturesque houses. Here there's a village green, with several pubs. Further out are some very large houses indeed – so large that they cannot be seen, such is the expanse of front garden. Elsewhere are the lesser dwellings – the red brick, the concrete, the bus stop, the sticky-floored supermarket. Pockets of post-war terraced housing, nests of mock-Tudor domesticity hidden on the commuter-friendly outskirts. Silver cars and big dogs, all spick and span, still as night.

According to my notes, at the time of the Roman

invasion this area was settled by the British tribe Coriel-tauvi, who had named the area glennos, meaning valley (in this case, the valley of the Sence River). The Domesday Book simply calls the village Glen, but by the late Middle Ages the village had taken the name of the Lords of the Manor and was known as Glen Martel.

Jim and I live (or lived) on the same street, in identically built houses. Only his looks very different. He's done a lot more to it, you see. He's very handy with his hands, good at DIY and that sort of thing. Has all the right tools, and the skills. Crazy paving and rockery in the front garden. Dwarf conifers and heathers cascading across the stone. He has a fine eye for detail. At the back of the house, more crazy paving, a greenhouse and pond with waterfall and fountain effects. Although the waterfall is created with fibreglass, he's managed to disguise it well. On summer nights he used to sit there in his chair listening to the frogs. Sometimes I would join him. He'd put on the garden lights.

Inside is different, too. Only not in a nice way. The inside always smelt of death. Like a hospital and church rolled into one. The shadows crushed you as you walked in. The air tasted so good when you emerged back outside you'd almost faint.

When I first met Jim his wife was dying. She sat and watched television and waved her hand to me. I waved back and asked her how things were. Less tired today or, Feeling a lot better, she'd say. She looked like death even then. Her eyes always returned to the TV screen as I was led away, past her bed. Lounge lizard installation art.

Upstairs in Jim's house we were never disturbed. The stairs were a point of demarcation – *on ne passe pas*. Further on up into the converted loft, with skylight. Pull up the loft ladder behind us, switch on the strip lighting and we were untouchable, safe in our tree house. Our Berchtesgaden. From here we made our plans. From here we surveyed the Empire, fired the cannons, co-ordinated our troops.

Jim had a large table in the centre of the room. It was covered with miniature hills and trees. Sometimes a shiny river or stream. A mansion, derelict church, barn or farm. Around us, on the shelves, sat sleeping armies, glinting, frozen in frenzied battle cry. Pikes, long bows, swords and spears bristling in the suburbs. There was a table and chair in the corner of the room with studio lights and tiny pots of paint. Thin slithers of brushes, micro hairs impossible to see with the naked eye.

I used to imagine Jim working there at night, like the cobbler or toy maker in the nursery rhymes, painting his creations. Creating life. How ironic of course, given what was to unfold.

I can sit and watch Jim now, in my mind's eye. It is many months ago. How many? I cannot say. But I can see him seated in the chair at his table. It is daylight but the harsh strip lighting is on. It hums like a fridge in summer. I sit in a deckchair on the other side of the covered table. I have a mug of tea on the carpet to my left. I can feel the hot steam on my naked arm. Involuntarily I move my fingers through the vapour.

Napoleon's 57th Regiment charges the Borodino Redoubt. Jim is thoughtful. Both of us have not spoken for some time. Our eyes have not met either. Only summer can be this quiet. There is bird dropping on the skylight.

We are forming our plans, our strategy. Goading ourselves. Seeing who will back down first.

Jim speaks. There is a fun fair this week in Leicester. I've seen the posters for it.

There is a line of cannons stretched across one side of the Redoubt. On the Russian expanses. The charging 57th stand no chance. The cannons have a cloud of cotton wool in front of them. They've just fired.

I have to take Julie into hospital Saturday morning. But I should be OK for the evening, Jim continues.

The cannon balls must be frozen in mid-air, somewhere on a parabola stretched between the open muzzles and the line of men. I squint but can't see them. I reach for my mug of tea.

I could pick you up at seven, he says.

I get up from my deckchair and follow Jim down the ladder to his landing, then down the stairs, past Julie, outside and across his crazy paving.

I'm thinking of digging this up, he tells me, pointing at the rockery with his foot.

I think of the dead soldiers of the Borodino Redoubt.

*

Jim took me in his car. A very new car. Julie needs a reliable car now, I remember him telling me as we both circled it on the car dealer's forecourt. She needs a bit of comfort. He bought it there and then.

We drove into Leicester as arranged. After parking, Jim got out and went to the boot. I watched him in the side mirror. He took his walking boots out of the back and put them on. After closing the boot, Jim leant into the front of the car, placing his shoes under the driver's seat. The walking boots were clean and probably freshly water-proofed.

It shouldn't be too muddy, I remember saying as I climbed out of the car and closed the door. He ignored me.

We had thought carefully about what we should wear. We had decided that jeans would be good, with a shirt, preferably a T-shirt, and jacket. Trainers were mentioned as ideal footwear. Jim had obviously decided against these plans. Perhaps he didn't have any trainers. I remember thinking that his walking boots could spoil things for us that evening. But then, perhaps in the crowds, no one would notice. And Jim was wearing a black T-shirt. He'd brushed his hair. I think he'd even used some gel. And he smelt. He smelt of some cheap aftershave. The car needed to be fumigated. Jim took his leather jacket from off the back seat. I took my anorak.

There were lots of people. Lots of young people. I remember noticing how we were the oldest by a long way. We stood out. There were gangs of teenagers moving towards the fair with us, and there were gangs moving away. But mostly they were walking in with us. What with the screams and shouts from the kids, and the music, I could hardly hear myself think.

We continued walking, Jim's boots wading through the burger wrappers and chip papers mercilessly. The green was just up ahead. There were hundreds of thousands of young people. There were millions of people – the whole of China had been sucked up in a tornado and precipitated down on to the green. Like locusts, like frogs.

The noise was unbearable; the lights were flashing. I hadn't expected such noise; I hadn't planned for such high volumes of background distortion. I feared that nothing would be heard. All my efforts would have been for nothing. I reached into my anorak's inner pocket and checked that the equipment was in position.

I think Jim speeded up – despite the crowds by the entrance, he actually managed to increase his speed. As we delved into the mountain of bodies, we were buffeted and rocked. We briefly separated as a gang of lads bore down on us like a shoal of piranhas, but we were safe and secure, and watched them pass by under our steel hulls.

I shouted across to Jim, Which way should we go? and Jim nodded his gelled head in the direction of a long row of burger bars. Over there.

Are you hungry already?

Yep. Jim moved off through the crowd. And I followed.

The queue in front of the burger place was long. We added ourselves to the back, and slowly started edging towards the sizzling grills. The smell of fried onion was overwhelming. I started to salivate profusely even though I'd already eaten.

Suddenly Jim, who was standing next to me in the queue, bent forward and asked the group of girls in front if they knew the cost of the cheeseburgers. The two nearest us shrugged their shoulders and turned back to their friends. And they carried on queuing. And we stood behind them. And nothing had changed. It was still all OK, it was still natural. We were just standing there waiting for our burgers. I reached up and instinctively checked my inner pocket.

We eventually got to the front. Jim ordered a cheeseburger and I a hot dog. We both had onions. We moved away and started to drift through the crowds. I couldn't get over the sea of faces, all screaming and shouting. Everyone talking, everyone swaying to the music that never stopped. Only Jim and I were silent as we walked with our food. Only Jim and I remained unmoved by the music. No one noticed us, I could make no eye contact. It was as if we were ghosts – shadows unable to pass over to the other side.

We stopped by the bumper cars. There were electric shrieks and horn sounds above the disco beat. It was a steel amphitheatre surrounded by Marlon Brandos. And young girls. Egging on the boy racers with their eyes.

Shall we hang around here a bit? Jim asked as he threw his sauce-stained napkin to the floor.

OK. Split up as arranged?

Jim nodded and strode off. I recall watching him as he forced his way through a crowd before leaning against the wooden rail as the bumper cars whirled in front of him beneath the flashing lights.

I began to circumnavigate the racetrack and while doing so switched on the recorder in my coat pocket. Jim didn't know about that yet. But he soon would. I remember all the words, even now. They are stored in my brain as imperviously as they are recorded on the magnetic tape.

Where's Jessica?

She said she's off to meet Dac.

She's a slag.

I think that skinny kid'll be there.

I ain't got no change for a can.

Have you been on the Death Wall?

Na, went on it last year and didn't think it were anything special.

Look, there's Melanie with Sam.

Don't look. She thinks she's so cool.

I think her brother's in prison.

Wouldn't surprise me.

If you listen to something enough it becomes something else. It takes on meanings it could never possibly have had originally when it was recorded.

The weeks following the fair I listened to those secretly recorded conversations again and again. Play, stop, rewind, stop, play. A different sort of music belting out of my hi-fi. A music muffled through my coat – can you hear my heart beat? The background noise – who is shouting about his leg? There's a sudden sound of thunder, it's my arm moving. Listen to those voices, though. Just listen. Listen and close your eyes.

– 6 –

This morning Anderson kindly informed me that I have mice. Or to be more exact that this wing of the prison is infested with the tiny rodents. If you hear any scuffling in the walls, that'll be them.

I smiled feebly as a prisoner brought in my lunch. The metal tray was lowered on top of a pile of library books resting at one end of my desk.

You OK? asked Anderson as the Red Band backed out of the cell.

I nodded. I was lying on my bunk reading a short pamphlet on tropical fish keeping.

Mad Bob has been up before the governor. He's in the Block for a month.

Anderson hovered by the door as if waiting for a tip for bringing me this news. I smiled again and nodded. He looked across the cell and out of my window, squinting his eyes, as though focusing on some curious aspect of the non-existent vista. Your mate was found trying to hang himself. A guard caught him just in time, strung up from the ceiling with his blanket. His face blown up blue like a fuckin' rotted pumpkin. Anderson's eyes returned to my face. You'd find out sooner or later, he said.

There was the briefest of moments again in which the guard's eyes refused to leave mine. I lowered the pamphlet and placed one hand against my chin, attempting to speak as I did so. You have no worries on that front with me, I said. I await my trial with a clear conscience. I just wish I wasn't confined to this cell for every hour of the day.

Anderson smiled in that curious way of his before a distracting shout from a fellow officer on the landing caught his attention. He quickly glanced about my cell before retreating. Once more there was the heavy sound of the lock turning.

Despite every intention of continuing with my studies once Anderson had gone, I must admit that I found it hard to concentrate on the complexities of under-gravel filtration. The thought of Jim's desperate attempt at freedom would not let me go. In a rather gruesome turn, I found Anderson's figurative description haunting my imagination, with Jim's blue, bulbous face, a decayed pumpkin head as the guard had so neatly observed, leering out of the page in front of me. What had driven Jim to undertake such a violent act was not hard to fathom, my own experiences here providing ample evidence of the strain that can be exerted. But whereas I can draw strength from my own marginal culpability, Jim, wherever he is, has no such escape. Blood is well and truly on his hands. Pacing my cell I began to wonder whether his conscience had at last begun to break, whether the memories of the things he did to that young girl had finally become too much to bear.

I would be wrong if I said that I had not considered suicide myself. The life of a remand prisoner, particularly one associated with such heinous events, is far from easy. But, as already stated, I have faith in my innocence, and in the ability of the British justice system to recognize and act upon this fact. Even my latest facial wound, with stitches, has not deterred me from this line of thought. Even now, as I sit writing these words, my jaw hurts whenever I attempt to move it. Two black eyes have also materialized, giving me the appearance of a heavyweight boxer whenever I happen to stumble across my reflection in the tiny mirror above the sink. Perhaps I should just be thankful I got out of the canteen alive.

It was certainly not how I intended things to be and I am still unsure of the exact reason for these events. It was all meant to be so different – my comical piece facilitating friendship, a flash of hilarity even, rather than provoking the orgiastic riot that ensued. But as one of the guards said to me as I was taken to the hospital in the van, this had been brewing for some time. I took this to mean that the event was nothing to do with me at all but was rather the product of deeper, older injustices within the prison.

Yet it did come as a surprise that when I leaned over to Mad Bob and said in my clearest public speaking voice, Rather noisy in here today. I hope they don't serve extra tea as I find it most difficult to get to sleep at night what with all the noises coming from my inmates' plumbing!, he reacted in the way that he did.

It was lunchtime and I was seated in my usual place. Mad Bob had joined me two seats away on the opposite side of the table. As always, I managed to keep the seats around me free. Mad Bob was staring in his usual manner, most of his food secretly throwing itself off his fork before returning to his plate via a round-the-world trip across his chins. The usual calls and exclamations from other inmates were surprisingly lacking, and as I settled onto the plastic chair and began to eat my mashed potato I recall thinking that my presence in the prison community was slowly becoming accepted. Thinking back, perhaps it was the extra confidence generated by this thought that encouraged me to deliver my comical piece. As you are aware, it was certainly something I had considered using on my colleagues at some point. And although it was now some days since I had tested it on Anderson, this original purpose was not forgotten. Indeed, at certain moments of the intervening days I had continued to go through the piece, refining timing and delivery. And so, as I was led down into the canteen for lunch yesterday, I was aware that I was as ready as I was ever going to be to utilize this newfound weapon.

As Mad Bob's eyes bulged and the chair fell away behind him I recall reflecting that his tattooed tears gave him a rather melancholy flavour, as though he were in permanent upset over the rotten hand that fate had continually played him. Sitting opposite me and of jocular girth, perhaps it was not surprising that the table began to list alarmingly as though it were the deck of the distraught *Titanic*. Mashed potato and baked beans nestled on my lap as a gnarled and scabbed fist hurtled towards my face with all the certainty of a cosmic cataclysm. As I fell backwards into those colleagues seated behind me, a number of inmates used the disturbance to begin further distractions. Collapsing to the ground under a barrage of kicks and punches, I couldn't help but notice several other tables being turned over, food and plates cascading to the floor. Whistles and shouts from the guards swirled around the chaos like banshee wails; and as my consciousness began to fall away, one of my last memories is of Mad Bob's shoe crashing down onto my head with the force of a lump hammer.

The down side of all this is that I am now confined to my cell, for my own safety you understand. I am to become the most Sensible of Sensibles. Still, the advantage of such solitude is that I have ample time to continue my academic studies and to complete my diary, which you are now reading. Perhaps it is best this way. On reflection I have come to the conclusion that my humour is obviously of a certain kind, suited only to those with the wit and intelligence to enjoy it. I have learnt that, like much else in life, it needs careful thought about its best deployment. Perhaps it will be something I keep only for Dr Sanders, although I have a suspicion I will leave the comical turn alone for the moment. I am suddenly very tired.

7

I am not used to this past tense, to this new way that I now have to write. About what I was, what I did. What I am – well, you know so much already – is a remand prisoner here in this tiny cell, shut up for all hours of the day. But what I was, that is a different matter.

Writing this diary is one way to reflect on the past. Dr Sanders has made that clear. In order to properly psycho-analyse me, the good doctor requires that those memories hidden away in the darkest corner of my mind be raised up into the light, to be given a full public performance on these very pages. I have made it clear to him that he will never see my diary. I simply will not let him. It is a private thing and you are my very special friend. I cannot share you! To be fair to him, he seems amenable to this, most certainly comforting himself that he can achieve his goal through the improved clarity of my mind when we meet face to face in the prison office.

Of course I fully understand what he is up to. I have read the necessary literature. Indeed, I have to admit to finding his approaches rather crude, dare I say outdated.

Yet I have gone along with his little game, as you can clearly testify. If nothing else, one needs something to reduce the boredom, and jumping through Dr Sanders' hoops is certainly an intellectual stimulant.

When you were working at the fish wholesalers, take me through a normal working day.

I can clearly hear Dr Sanders' voice even now, falling flat and empty to the floor, sucked of all life by the muted acoustics of that little room. Strange, I do not know why I denied working at the wholesalers. He had the evidence in front of him, of course. Neatly arranged in the paper file. Dr Sanders opened it and began to read from it: Claremont Fish stockists. On the A6. And with a smile, Fish Wholesalers to the Discerning. Dr Sanders had obviously seen the logo.

Asking for the goggles had been a ploy – if he wanted me to revisit the past then surely he could spare me a few precious minutes with my prized possession. But no. The goggles were not to be mentioned in this session.

You worked there for three years. Surely you can pick out just one day?

Three years? Was it really three years?

Just tell me the normal routine.

I'm glad I left Dr Sanders none the wiser. It is not right that he should interrogate in such a manner. A fellow professional requires a degree of respect. A knowing acquiescence. I was led back to the cell rather brusquely, our meeting ending far sooner than I or my guard had anticipated. Does Dr Sanders really think that I am fooled by his cerebral games? Does he think that a man of my training is not fully aware of the good doctor's agenda?

I must admit to being rather annoyed as I lay on my bed, perhaps as annoyed as Dr Sanders was with me. Ah, my dear doctor, exasperation will get you nowhere! But as I have thought more carefully about the meeting I must profess that a tiny seed has grown, a seed, I fully admit, planted by Dr Sanders. Recollections of the fish wholesalers have indeed blossomed in my mind. Without intention I have spent the last hour or two reflecting over that time, reliving key moments, events, smells and sensations. At times, if I close my eyes, it does feel as if I could step back into the darkness of that labyrinth. But I will not tell Dr Sanders. At least not yet.

My days were unexceptional then, that much I do recall. Indeed it is the simplicity of my life that hits me as I think back, seated at this tiny table under the harsh light from the single bulb. Such glorified plainness, even dullness.

I can see it clearly – it is early, there is little light and I am in my car. The drive to work was always something I enjoyed. Going as early as I did in the morning meant that I rarely hit any serious traffic. Up on the A6, through Leicester and Loughborough, towards Nottingham.

Fish Wholesalers to the Discerning. The building couldn't be a more unprepossessing construction if it tried: a grey concrete hanger on the edge of the A6. Wind blown, strewn with litter. No windows. No natural light in. No light out. A car park at the front and a blue door. Swish and you've driven past it. On towards Nottingham. Blink and you've missed it. Even if you don't blink you won't see it. It has no presence, no architectural gravitas. It sits like a black hole, only a black hole is visible because of the enormity of its nothingness. This building is invisible because of its very presence. Dark matter.

I park the car at the front and climb out. I can feel the cold air striking my lungs. There is a crunching sound beneath my feet. I lock the car and move towards the blue door. The metal handle sticks out like a bone, repulsing contact in the way that it protrudes through the splintered surface. The metal is cold to my touch, and I move inside.

Here, within the building, the air is always warm and damp, the tiny reception area as dark as night. Maria has not yet arrived. Her little desk and kettle lie idle in the shadows. I move quickly through another door that swings shut behind me.

And now we come to the strangest of nerve centres: surely I am no longer on the planet Earth, but rather have been transported into some remote corner of a distant galaxy, in a time long, long ago. There is darkness, but a darkness bisected by thick chasms of light, cubes of luminescence that strike out from lines of great vaulted corridors in front of me. Where can this be?

Listen, there is the sound of a million angels murmuring. The warm air smells of decomposing matter, a sweet fetidness that embroiders the shadows. From somewhere deep in the bowels of this place a shudder and moan can be felt as the great Minotaur in its labyrinthine lair awakens to my presence. I move tentatively forward over the wet concrete. Like Jason I should have brought a shield, a shiny bronze surface with which to avoid the eyes of the Medusa that surely lurks around the corner. Where are the stone effigies of other valiant adventurers that have gone before me?

Morning! Jonas flitters between the shafts of light like Hermes, wings on his cap and heels.

Morning, I respond, and move forward into the labyrinth.

As every morning, I shuffle around the perimeter of the room to a small, secret door. This leads to the grubby staff room, which consists of a table and four chairs. There's a sink and a kettle but not much else. I make myself a mug of coffee. As I do, Jonas enters the room.

I think the puffers are on the turn. Looks like Velvet. I stuck some methylene blue in the tank last night. But it's not looking good.

Have you lost any yet? I ask.

Not yet. Although lost a few of the blennies. They came in a few days ago and I thought they'd settle down really well.

The Lionfish look OK.

Yeh, they seem fine. I think Bob Crowther is coming in today. Wouldn't surprise me if he takes the lot.

Jonas walks out of the staff room and I follow.

Jonas is in charge of the marine part of the wholesalers, I take care of the tropicals. Phil, who's always the last to arrive, understudies for the coldwaters. Although the marine fish are the jewel in the crown so to speak, the bread and butter business of this place is done through the tropicals and coldwaters. The tropical section, what was my tropical section, is the largest – I had more species under my care than the other two put together. The coldwater section is mainly outside at the back, and the marine section is squeezed into one room at the rear of the building. The tropical section occupies centre stage through which everyone has to walk after coming past reception. If my section doesn't look good then everyone knows.

My first task, after making the coffee, is to check all my fish stocks. Overnight many things can happen and it is important to make sure that all stocks are healthy and ready for wholesale. I always take a net and a plastic bag with me so that any dead fish can be quickly disposed of.

There is a strict order to this process, a methodology that ensures all aquariums are inspected. I want you to follow carefully what I do. I always start down the central passageway. Here I have most of what I call the potboilers – the bestsellers, the cheap and cheerful. There are four columns of tanks on each side, and each column consists of three tanks. Twenty-four aquariums all lit and filled with life, bubbling and humming. Micro-worlds carefully stored away on wrought iron shelving. Press your nose against the warm glass and peer in.

Let's start with the tetras. Neon, black, Congo, emperor and glowlight. Lemon, serpae, cardinal and bloodfin. All classified and costed. All indexed and monitored. Little sticky labels on the glass for the uninformed. Mollies, platys and swordtails. Guppies, danios and barbs. My potboilers, my warm-up acts, appearing now in a child's aquarium near you. Moving on round (my plastic bag already becoming a slippery mass grave, you'll notice) we have the more specialized breeds. Here we find the cichlids, the angelfish, discus, oscars and the rest. Dwarf and rift lake. Gouramis, killifish, sharks and loaches. Bettas, the popular Siamese Fighting Fish – the males isolated in separate tanks, their long, flowing fins streaming out as they stalk the surface waters, the Gulf Streams of my little worlds. And occasionally the odd rarity – a freshwater pufferfish and stingray, and a large African Rope fish. Got to keep things interesting for the regulars.

After disposing of my bag of bodies out at the back it's time for general maintenance before the first customers arrive. Today there are no disasters so I can get on and clean a few of the aquariums, siphoning off excess waste and removing the patina of algae that has grown on the glass sides.

Customers always start to appear from about 8.30. Most of them own small aquatic shops but there are some bigger players – the larger garden centres can get through a lakeful of goldfish over a bank holiday weekend. There is also the odd collector or specialist keeper for whom we do business.

I have a few favourite customers and some of them can be quite entertaining, but most of them know nothing about fish. They wade through the tanks, nose pressed up against the glass, picking and choosing as though their life depended on it. If only they'd seen those fish two hours earlier, if only they'd seen them when they were delivered to us by the courier. Shut away in large foam crates, wallowing in inflated plastic bags, bathed in just an inch of water. Flown in over thousands of miles. Hundreds of them in one bag, more bubbles and fish slime than real water, wriggling as though frying on an African riverbed. If only they'd seen the fish as I netted them into our tanks and watched them as they dropped like depth charges to the bottom, more dead than alive, only the corpses eddying to the surface to be skimmed off later.

Jonas has a good story about a fish. I had forgotten all about it until my trip back to the wholesalers this afternoon. Standing there in the staffroom, watching Jonas flit from shadow to shadow, reminded me of so many things I had let slip from my memory. He used to tell it to any temps that came during our busy periods, or to new secretaries, or to me if he thought I looked bored. It concerns a fish. But the fish in this story wasn't any old fish. This was a big fish, a giant gourami. And Samson (the fish had a name) had indeed grown and grown. His body still thought he was swimming in the open Amazon where his brothers expand to prodigious lengths, swallowing men whole, capsizing boats and all that sort of thing. But it was unusual to see such a large specimen in captivity. In the beginning, Samson had started off by being just one of several fish in the aquatic idyll, but as he grew the other fish disappeared. At first the owner replaced the missing fish because he didn't want Samson to be alone in the aquarium. But the fish still kept disappearing so that eventually the owner stopped buying replacements and just left Samson to meditate by himself.

If the truth were told, the owner was quite fond of his solitary pet because Samson had become something of an attraction. The owner had a pub and Samson was in an aquarium that ran along the back of the bar, so that all the customers could wave to him and Samson could blow bubbles back. The tank was only two feet in length, and as Samson grew, all the ornaments and plants had to be taken out. By the time he was a foot long Samson was in there by himself with only the gravel for company. He was now so big he couldn't turn round. And still he grew.

Over the many years that both the owner and the fish sat behind the bar, a certain relationship developed between them, and when the owner had to go into hospital after a mild heart attack, he constantly asked his wife about Samson. So much so that while he was hospitalized, his wife, in conjunction with the locals of the bar, collected enough money to buy Samson a new, larger aquarium. This was four feet in length and came with new lighting and filtration systems. Samson's life was going to be transformed. The new tank was set up alongside the existing one until eventually the day came for the great removal. One of the locals volunteered, and after much splashing, Samson was netted and transferred into his new home. Samson seemed to settle in quickly, and the wife prepared for the arrival of her husband from the hospital the following day. Only, the next day when she got up, she found Samson dead, his huge body lying bloated on the surface. They say the shock killed the owner, because within three days of his return home, his naked, lifeless body was also found in his bed. He had taken an overdose.

Jonas can say it better than me. It is a comical piece is it not?

8

The constant question: what was he like?

How am I meant to respond to this? I have not yet found the words. The words do not exist. The darkness that lay behind his eyes. The latent threat of violence that forever swirled just beneath the surface. I can still see him going through the process of folding the loft ladder away. I watch as his great hands busy themselves with the dainty latches on the side of the ladder, how each stage of the process is undertaken with a calm, measured assurance, and finally how the hooked stick is used to swing the hatchway closed. The stick looks so small and pathetic in his hands – a brittle slither of wood along which his fleshy fingers dance like ballerinas. His special ability to bring out the vulnerability in things was always apparent, you see. It was not the act of violence itself that made him so feared but rather its suppression, its potential only, which exuded from his every pore.

Yet more recently, as I have started to think back over these terrible events, I have begun to sense something else, a more fundamental characteristic previously overlooked.

Perhaps it is only now, separated as we are by both time and space, that I am at last gaining a degree of perspective on our relationship. To put it into words is difficult – I have certainly not told Dr Sanders. But perhaps it can be best summarized by just one word: emptiness. Looking back, I can now see that above all, there was an all-consuming emotional void about Jim. Dare one say even a lack of humanity, any compassionate humanism, on which to cling? Perhaps I exaggerate.

Yet to suggest emptiness is also not quite right, for in one sense that was never true. Such was the emotional complexity of the man that one could also feel there to be a massive, yet invisible presence, a Black Hole perhaps, limitless matter, Dark Matter, undetectable, so crushed together, so impacted and condensed, that even light itself could not escape the vortex of destruction.

Hidden below the surface. Indescribable and unknowable.

I have to admit that in the midst of explaining the intricacies of filtration to Tuckman I clean forgot my own investigations into indigenous fungi. The limited amount of horticultural research I have already been allowed to undertake has hinted at the strangeness, even other-worldliness, of these bizarre creatures.

The more I read my little book on autumnal flora and fauna the more I begin to liken fungi to the diaphanous spirits of the underworld – those sea creatures that remain forever in the chasm of darkness at unfathomable depths.

Many have been the times recently when, sitting with the little book on the bed, I have felt as though submerged in a tiny capsule, peering out through the thickened glass as I descend down into the freezing eddies that coast like Kraken on the bottom of the world. Look, there are some polypores, sinister bracket-like growths that sprout from the bark of dead trees; there is a shoal of Chanterelles, their sightless trumpet-like bodies glinting yellow in the light from my cell; there, creeping amongst the detritus, are two boletes; and ahead, balanced on the edge of infinity, rippling like canvas in a summer's breeze, is the giant jellyfish agaric.

Just think of this – that most fungi grow beneath the soil and are themselves nothing more than microscopic filaments that extend and branch unseen to cover vast distances, the intricate lacework of the mycelium. Those things we think of as fungi are but ephemeral fruit, pushed up to the surface from the hidden depths, to lie exposed upon the shore of some quiet field beneath an alien sun like the carcass of a monstrous squid banished from the Deep.

The world of these creatures is strange indeed, suspended in the nether world that lies between plants and animals. Many are saprotrophs, living on the corpses of decaying matter; others form symbiotic associations with trees and plants (mycorrhizal fungi as they are properly known), effectively extending the host root system. It is estimated that over ninety per cent of plants have a fungus associated with their roots and that many would not survive without their fungal partner.

Perhaps you have surmised from the last two sentences that I have now managed to extend my reading beyond the few books that I was allowed to bring with me. This indeed is the case and Tuckman, the prison librarian, was instrumental in this process. Normally, of course, I would not have required anyone's assistance. But a prison library is not a normal place, sharing as it does the unconventionality of so much that goes on behind these high walls.

The library itself is on the first floor of the East wing, the oldest part of the prison, replete with the Victorian glazed tiles and tiny windows that I'm sure you have already pictured in your mind's eye. And unlike most other parts of the prison, the library wing has a rather pleasant smell, a heady aroma of varnish, gloss paint and cigarettes that rolls over your palate like a daydream. There is no fetid stench of vomit, piss or body odour. There are no shouts either, sudden expletives echoing, or missiles thrown by unseen hands. But it is the smell I always notice first. I come this way whenever I see Dr Sanders, you see. And there's something else – while most doors in the prison are thick metal things, blue and cold, the library door is maroon and wooden, a special timber portal that, like Alice, I try and squeeze through whenever I can.

Tuckman is always there, of course, suddenly appearing like a shopkeeper. Tuckman is a Category D. He has been given training as a librarian. A proper librarian is meant to come every so often from the local authority but I haven't seen her yet. There is only ever Tuckman, Tuckman and a thousand scruffy, unread books.

The first time I came to the library, a few days ago now, I quickly realized that this was no beacon shining out across the Mongol hordes. Tuckman merely opened his arms as though welcoming me to his bazaar. You'll find more here than you'd think, was his rather cryptic introduction as the door was locked behind me. The room is not large. Natural daylight enters through a series of four tiny windows that run high up along the length of the room. The harsh glow of the suspended strip lighting attempts rather forlornly to disperse the gloom created by the ranks of imposing wooden shelving, standing like teetering dominoes, or the monoliths of some primordial site. Tuckman followed me that first time as I walked between the rows of books, a knot of apprehension, nervously fingering the spines as though a curator awaiting a critic's judgement. I tried to ignore him completely, occasionally picking out a book to balance lightly in my palms. It was during this initial perambulation that the bleached green spine of the nature book fell into my hand. One of our oldest, Tuckman said. I ignored him of course, transported as I was into the mists of autumnal English fields by the black and white plates . . .

Then as now, most other prisoners are not allowed into the library when I am present. One hour a week is hardly conducive to my ongoing researches of course, but it has allowed some degree of progress. Thus it was that earlier today I again entered the library with the intention of continuing my research into the floral world and in particular that of indigenous fungi. As I have already alluded to, these good intentions were inadvertently hijacked by Tuckman, who I discovered reading *The Observer's Book of Tropical Fish* at his desk. Though he was not aware of my expertise in the area I was quickly able to enlighten him. It turned out that he was a fellow aquarist, although a mere dabbler. It was with some delight that I was able to show him a print-out of the web pages I was writing using the computers in the education centre. As recompense Tuckman was able to locate all those books on fungi that I had not yet been able to find. I couldn't help but notice that one of the books contained a series of plates showing native puffballs. Another spoke of the even stranger world of lichens, organisms created by the symbiotic relationship between fungi and algae. It seems I have much to learn.

Perambulations is very old, as Tuckman correctly noted, as are so many of the books in the prison library. Yet I cannot deny that this particular book, despite its crippled and faded spine, does offer a seductive escapism all of its own. Although not previously a gardener, I have found the book's descriptions of flora and fauna in the autumn and winter months offer great comfort. Perhaps this shouldn't be a surprise as it is all I can do to see the sky, let alone a great oak, owl or puffball. After so many days inside, I have naturally begun to lust after any evocation of the outside world, even if it is of a world long since gone. So much so that when the governor asked me about prison visitors I knew exactly how I was going to reply.

Unnecessary disturbance, Mr Carwardine, I said to him. He understood. I told him my wounds were getting much better. A bit of fresh air would help, I explained. I watched him light his cigarette with a match. Perhaps I could work on the prison garden, I suggested. I have been reading a library book about horticulture and I feel I would enjoy exercising some of my newfound theoretical expertise. Mr Carwardine wafted his match briskly before flicking it expertly into the plastic ashtray. He blew a cloud of smoke up into the stratosphere before looking at me with his usual watery smile. I was shown out.

PART TWO

PART TWO

Leicestershire

1922, Early Autumn

Perambulations of a Soldier: Autumn to Winter
by John Crowe

When embarking on an autumnal ramble one cannot help but ponder when this most elusive of seasons has its beginning and end. Scientists and other learned men locate its conception in the third week of September, when the day and night become equal in length, and then have autumn persisting until the equinox in late December. But the rambling naturalist knows that the dates of the seasons are not so set in stone.

For a closer approximation it is wise to watch the plants and animals that surround us. A few of those birds that come from foreign climes during our summer flee these shores long before an idle walker turns his mind to autumnal mists, but when the lapwings, swifts, martins and warblers have all gone, and the limes are thinning, the elms yellowing and the beeches browning, we know this most spectacular of seasons is almost upon us.

On cue a single lapwing dips and soars over our heads, its black and white body contrasting brilliantly against the blue of the sky. In its search for insects, fattening itself up ready for the long flight southwards, the bird provides us with a most breathtaking spectacle of aeronautical mastery, swooping low before rising almost vertically into the heavens. For a second I feel that if I stretch out my arms I too can fly away, high into the sun.

Over there by the gorse bush the grass is especially green

and long, and if we look carefully we can see that in the shade a most unusual object has taken up residence. You would be forgiven for thinking that I am pointing at nothing but a large white stone, but look again, for this is a fungus, a puffball no less (plate 1). As autumn advances and its skin turns black, the fungus will produce millions upon millions of spores to be released in thin milky clouds across the field. If I touch even this young specimen with my cane, notice how clouds of seed are blown into the air. Amazingly, the puffball is capable of generating its own contractions, sudden movements that send millions of spores off on their perilous journey.

It is still only early morning and I notice that the coppice on the hill is awash with light.

Rev Cecil Crowe,
The Vicarage,
Great Glen,
Leicestershire

10th October 1922

FROM: *Captain John Crowe, Canal Cottage,*
Husbands Bosworth, Leicestershire

My Dear Father,

I hope this letter finds you well. I cannot quite believe it is almost a month since my departure from Husbands Bosworth. Where has the time gone?

It feels so very strange to be in this little room again at the back of Aunt Beth and Uncle George's cottage, the growl of the trains on the Rugby to Stamford line, deep in its cutting alongside the canal, still waking me in the night as it did then when I stayed here as a child. As I write this letter I am sitting at that small desk and chair which I used all those years ago on our visits. It does seem such a long time ago. So much has changed of course, but here, in this room, watching the smoke rise above the trees from the trains, it appears that all is as it was twenty years ago.

As I look out through the opened window I can see both Aunt Beth and Uncle George pottering in the garden. At first I was shocked by how old they had become – before arriving I still saw them as they were many years ago, when I was last here. It seems the invisible hand of

Time is forever busy, but it is only at such moments as these, when one returns to the Past as it were, that one is made aware of how things are always in decay. They still have a little mooring on the canal bank, by the way, although there is now no boat. They sold off 'Mermaid' before the War and appear to have lost all desire for nautical adventure. I couldn't help but think of those expeditions Lizzy and I undertook in the long summer vacations, each of us pretending to swoop and soar above the water amidst the haze of swifts and lapwings that never left our wake.

Angus is safely ensconced in stables at the back of the Bell Hotel. It was on walking from the Bell after my arrival that I tried to recall when I last ventured down these leafy lanes. I came to the conclusion it must have been the summer of 1909 or perhaps 1910, at least two or three years before I went up to Cambridge. Much appears to be the same, although there is now a war memorial at the front of the church.

In fact, it was on this occasion, when first exploring the village, that the strange incident of the aeronautist occurred. Even now I find it difficult to describe the unusual emotions this rather comical event evokes. Perhaps certain aspects of it have been rather embellished by my memory, but when I think back it seems that all happened exactly as I remember it. It was such a bizarre happening that I hope you will indulge me with its retelling.

Whatever else, I recall that from the war memorial I moved away to the right, walking northwards away from All Saints and Bosworth Hall. Although it was never my intention to reach the canal, it now seems something of an inevitability that twenty minutes later there I was standing before its southern bank. The sun that had blessed the early part of the day was now gone, and I do believe the temperature had fallen by several degrees. To the west it looked very much like rain clouds were on their way. My visit to the village had left me rather melancholy, and the state of the empty, black waters of the Grand Union and the mournful vacancy of the railway line, stretching left and right into the middle distance beneath the darkening skies, seemed only to amplify my distress. In desperation I began to march along the towpath, hopeful of meeting a bargeman or two to lighten my spirits. But I saw no one.

Walking along the path with stick in hand, I had just reached the point at which I thought it safest to turn back home, given the now freshening wind, when what I can only call a singular sight caught my attention. In a field ahead, adjacent to the towpath, I could see the figure of a man running. He was a good five hundred yards ahead of me in the centre of a small field of low grass. However, it was not his precipitous movement alone that sought the eye, but rather the fact that he appeared to have large wings strapped on to each arm. These he endeavoured to flap as he ran, although the apparatus appeared to be rather ungainly, a fact that did not help his speed across the ground. Intermittently, he would suddenly crouch down, spread his wings out over the grass, letting them catch the remaining afternoon light, and lie motionless as if he were some exotic bird, pruning and sunning in the middle of the field.

My own motion along the towpath ceased abruptly, and

I believe I must have watched this bizarre scene for a good few minutes. My curiosity was completely aroused. As I have said, the scene certainly had a high comic turn, but there was also something strangely moving, beautiful, even tragic, as this little figure flapped his way across the grass. Eventually I was drawn to the hedgerow that formed the barrier between the field and the towpath, and thence, after finding an overgrown stile, into the field itself. At first I stood on the field's edge, as stiff and still as a scarecrow, until our erstwhile aeronautist spotted me. At this point he was on the opposite side of the field. He gave a cry of 'hello' followed by a particularly vigorous flapping of his wings, before making his way towards me. He still maintained the pattern of locomotion as before – periods of running with intense wing-flapping followed by a sudden drop to the ground into a crouching position, with the wings stretched out over the grass.

His progress, then, was not quick. I, for my part, waved in response to his salutation and watched as he bounded and crouched his way across the grass towards me. I quickly became impatient, however, at his lack of real progress and thought it best to meet him halfway, as it were. So off I set, stick swinging out in front of me and camera banging against my side, marching out to meet the fantastical creature from the other side, our paths supposedly converging at some equidistant point.

As we drew closer I noticed that the man was wearing a most unusual piece of headgear. It appeared at first to be a standard white pith helmet but as he lumbered, puffing, towards me, I could see that it had been blessed by a couple of remarkable attachments: two small wing-shaped finials placed on each side. Rather than sticking out at ninety degrees, however, they were carefully angled to point backwards, or rather over each shoulder. As I attempted to study these from afar, the birdman dropped down to the ground again. He was now only about thirty yards away and there was something in his body language that suggested he was not going to get up again in a hurry. I immediately speeded up and, indeed, that is how we eventually met – me striding forward and him lying crippled on the floor as though shot out of the air.

As I came close I offered a greeting, but my companion was so short of breath he could do little but look up and smile. His face was red with exhaustion, and sweat streamed down his forehead; the pith helmet was askance, and his wings lay stretched out on either side of him, seemingly immobile.

I recall studying carefully his wings draped before me. They appeared to consist of a wooden framework covered with canvas, and were each about five or six feet long.

'You must be wondering what on earth I'm doing. Nutty as a fruitcake I bet you're thinking!' My companion seemed to find the situation highly amusing. 'Just let me get out of the wings here, old chap.' And with that he began to slide his arms out from underneath the wooden frames where I could now see a series of leather straps secured to their underside.

'Need a hand?' I enquired.

'No, should be fine.' And indeed he was. Both arms were quickly released and then with some effort he rose to his feet, leaving the wings discarded on the ground.

Looking at him in that weak afternoon light, I surmised

he must have been about my age, perhaps slightly younger. He was a good six feet tall and, apart from his helmet, dressed rather as a country squire in the finest tweed.

'You're not a flying man by any chance are you?' he asked as he knocked the grass off his jacket.

'No, I'm afraid not.'

'Well, that's a shame. Seem to have a dearth of aeronauts in these parts, which is a pity since we get excellent wind conditions. Anyway, let me introduce myself. I'm Frederick Simms.'

I introduced myself and explained why I was down here in Husbands Bosworth. He explained that he knew the village very little. 'The age of technology, old chap! Flying will transform our society, you see. This is just the beginning. There'll be powered aeroplanes for long distance flights, but we'll also be able to use our own wings,' and here he glanced at the forlorn pair at his feet, 'for shorter flights around the estate, or whatever. Walking will become a thing of the past!'

When I failed to express my unequivocal support for his vision, he continued with his evangelism.

'I saw it in France. Not just the Sopwiths and Bristols but men flying under their own power. Apparently the French had a whole squadron of them that they used at Aisne. But the British won't develop the technology because of the threat to the Flying Corp. When I was in France I spoke to a French pilot who had actually flown using wings like these. In fact it was on his design recommendations that I constructed this equipment.'

Frederick then went on to explain some of the technicalities of the design, most of which I failed to understand. He seemed especially proud of his pith helmet, which was ceremoniously removed and held out in front of him.

'The French quickly discovered you needed frontal uplift to complement that achieved through the wings. It ensures balance in the air and can be used as a simple way of steering. Like so.' And here Frederick gently turned the helmet to the left and to the right. 'All you need to do is turn your head in the direction you wish to travel. Simple!'

And simple it all seemed although when I asked him if he had flown himself, he appeared suddenly circumspect. 'I've had a number of difficulties. The smaller fields here are a problem, but I also think my wings might not have the correct curvature. They might be a degree or two out. There have been moments when my feet have almost lifted off the ground. But either because of insufficient ground speed or because of the wing design, I haven't been able to get any further. But,' and here he placed the helmet on the grass, 'I do have a solution which should enable me to gain altitude.'

Frederick led me across the grass to one side of the field. Here, running along the ground, were two wooden tracks that had been secured into the soil by pegs. The end of both tracks rose off the ground by about three feet, supported by a simple construction of wooden scaffolding.

'This idea came to me in a dream. It's all about building up enough speed to get off the ground. I know that once I'm off the ground I'll be away. All I'll need then is good arm muscles to sustain the flight for as long as possible.

That's what I've been doing today, a bit of arm training ready for the big one. Anyway, in this dream I saw a racehorse running along, pulling behind him a man tied to a large kite, and eventually the kite took off and the man was up in the air. Well, I thought I could adopt that idea for my own purposes here.' He walked up to one of the tracks and tapped it with his foot. 'I'm having some skis made which will run inside the tracks. I'll then be attached to a horse that will be run like fury across the field. I'll be pulled along the tracks which, at the end there' – he pointed to the scaffolding – 'will provide a suitable launch for me to get into the air. The reins will detach leaving me to fly off under my own power.'

I remember asking him what would happen to the skis.

'Good point. I haven't made them yet but ideally I'll be able to knock them off my boots once I'm in flight. Or I could just drop the entire boot.' And at this his eyes fixed into the middle distance.

The rain was now coming down. Rather optimistically I asked Frederick if he would mind me taking a picture of him. He was more than willing and even insisted on wearing both the pith helmet and the wings. We trudged back to the centre of the field through the rain. As I looked through the viewfinder, Frederick extended his arms, forcing the wings to rise up over his head in a most dramatic display reminiscent of a peacock. When I had replaced the camera in its leather case I could sense that Frederick was going to stay in the field for some time to come. His wings had dropped off his arms and lay on the ground. As his head bowed and legs collapsed, a stream of water fell from off the rim of his hat and splashed onto his boots. I offered my farewells to his crumpled form before hurriedly returning from whence I had come, leaving my new found Icarus to face the gathering storm alone.

It may have been on returning from this strange episode out in the Leicestershire countryside that I found Aunt Beth back at the cottage reading *Perambulations of a Soldier: Spring to Summer*. She even asked me to sign the first page. I felt like Dickens as we seated ourselves at the table! Indeed, Uncle George is of the opinion that the *Autumn to Winter* edition will have as much, if not more, interest for the naturalist as my *Spring to Summer*, to which sentiments I wholeheartedly agree. Perhaps it was at that moment he mentioned the pond.

I should say before continuing that the countryside here is an undoubted feast for any naturalist, and I feel I have now more than enough notes for at least two books and numerous rolls of film! Inspired by the unseasonably warm weather, I have found myself out amongst the fields and coppices of South Leicestershire with my notebook and Kodak. I have already penned what I think to be a satisfactory opening chapter, much of which came to me as I sat atop a coppice-crowned hill on a particularly dank dark morning, a position that normally would have offered fine views over Husbands Bosworth, the railway and the Grand Union Canal. The spires of Theddingworth, Marston Trussell and North Kilworth loomed out of the misty rain like despondent sentries as I placed the viewfinder to my eye.

The chapter begins with an opening discussion of when autumn is considered to begin, and then moves on to examine some of the flora most associated with this time of year. I was particularly lucky to find a large puffball growing close to a hedgerow that I was able to examine in some detail and photograph. Unfortunately about a quarter of it appeared to be diseased in some way and thoroughly rotten.

But to return to the pond. I'm sure it was on that first day that Uncle George mentioned it, as though it was something that had been uppermost in his mind since my arrival. Yet despite his enthusiasm, it was only last week that I actually found myself in Wyndham's wood, in the grounds of Bosworth Hall – a place to the south of the village that Lizzy and I used to visit all those summers ago. I have a faint recollection that it may well have been Uncle George who had first taken us there. Then as now the wood consists of birch trees, with the occasional stout oak growing amongst them. Almost in the centre of the wood is a dip or hollow, at the bottom of which is the place.

As a child Lizzy and I had often stood by the water's edge, clutching our net and jam jars. Then the pond had swarmed with fish – dark, wild fish that were straight from the uncharted depths of the Yangtze! In the speckled light they sloughed like whales, their dorsal fins breaking the treacly meniscus, eddying leaves and flies, before slipping back without a sound. Our nets, however, were not for them but rather the smaller life that swarmed in the shallows – perhaps a tadpole or one of the strange black beetles that glinted like florins in the muddy depths. While in France, these memories often came back to me as I lay awake at night, and the memory of them, and those gloriously hot afternoons of childhood, undoubtedly sustained me in those wretched times.

Yet, last week, standing before the pond with my camera after all those years, I could not see any fish. Indeed, there was little evidence of any aquatic life, and the hollow itself had shrunk considerably, as had the wood that enclosed it. I walked round its muddy perimeter several times but failed to see any signs that those fish were still there. From the most complementary angle, I took out my camera and peered down into the viewfinder to take a picture. I profess that, in some way, I hoped the instrument would allow me to recover an image of how the pond used to look, as it appeared in my memory at that moment. But the scene through the lens was even more miserable, and although I took a picture, I could only bring myself to etch on to the film, 'Dismal Pond 6/10/22'.

On speaking to Uncle George of this on my return, he explained that the hollow in Wyndham's wood only flooded in winter, and that during the spring and summer it always dried out. When I explained about the fish that Lizzy and I used to watch, he suggested that I must be referring to another pond, but as to where that could be he had no idea.

This mystery of the disappearing pond has not left my mind. A certain melancholic temper has gripped me that I know from experience can be difficult to shake. I keep thinking back to those summers I spent with Lizzy, a time in my life that until recently was practically forgotten. Perhaps the recent letter has not helped.

It arrived several days ago. Apparently Lizzy is still in France but has now moved back to Paris where she has rented a small apartment in the 2nd arrondissement.

She has met an officer who knew Robert, and he has been able to give Lizzy fuller details about Robert's last months. I have not heard of this officer myself, he being in the Queen's Own Oxfordshire Hussars, but I am sure he is an honest and decent fellow.

My melancholy may in part be due to the time of the year, the coming of the 'dead season' as I have heard it called more than once before. But I also think it would be true to admit that Lizzy's epistle has also acted as some sort of catalyst, in a way that is only just resolving itself. For a few days after the arrival of her letter I could not sleep, although neither, should I say, could Uncle and Aunty. This house, with all its associations and memories, can act like a great boiler, feeding and accelerating the merest thoughts that race through the brain.

It was in this vein that, two days ago, laying my pen down after completing further notes on *Perambulations* late into the night, a sudden thought came to me, a thought I knew immediately would provide the answer to my melancholy. Its genesis can easily be seen in Lizzy's own process of reconciliation in France, and it is such a simple idea that it is a great wonder I haven't considered it before. You see, Father, it occurred to me that night, as I sat at my table staring out across the lawn, that from this very position, if one was to draw a circle of fifty miles radius, with myself at the centre, then some of my fondest companions from D Company of the 2nd Leicesters 5th Battalion would be included within its modest boundary. Almost a stone's throw, as they say. Comrades I haven't seen since my discharge in 1918. And this really was a paradox that took me some time to digest, because for so long I have placed those wartime memories where they could safely be forgotten. Yet the realization that tomorrow I, if so inclined, could walk from this house and up the front gardens of those men with whom I had fought side-by-side, was a truly startling, even ecstatic one.

And so my plan was born. Do not think this foolish, Father, but rather offer your support on something that I value intently. The purpose, of course, is to visit my companions while I still have the chance, and to this end I intend to leave the cottage in the next day or two. I realize this may seem a hare-brained scheme but it has many advantages. In terms of writing, I require perambulations, and a series of visits to my colleagues living across the county will serve admirably as a necessary pretext. You may recall my first walking tour – that of early 1918 at the request of Dr Worthington at Quex hospital. It is my intention that a similarly remedial action will allow me to expunge feelings that have been growing in the darkest corners of my mind over the last four years.

This must all seem like madness, but by Christmas I expect my perambulations to be over, with my book completed and a purging of my mind to a degree that I have not yet been able to achieve. I shall write regularly so that you are kept fully informed of events. But above all do not worry – I feel that I am doing something worthwhile, at last.

Your devoted son,
John

PART THREE

Durham Category 'A' Prison

Present Day, Mid October

I have again informed the governor of my horticultural interests. I have written him a letter in which I told him that I have been reading much about the great outdoors, particularly in autumn. More than ever I now understand how the great cyclical patterns control our wonderful countryside, the diurnal turn of the seasons, and that even amongst the newest shoots, the Shadow of Death is ever present.

There is an old adage that says you only appreciate something once it has been taken away. My enforced incarceration has certainly taught me the value of personal liberty, and as I write these words my body longs to be lost amid the expanses of a dank, dark oak forest. It must surely be one of life's cruel paradoxes that it is only when sealed within this tiny cell that I have come to value the majesty of the great outdoors. So little natural light falls into my cell, and I have such a limited view from my window, that at times I feel as though I am entombed within a coffin, buried deep below the ground, and that like some lost spirit, I torment myself with jealous gnawing at the world above. Down here, deep within the soil, I must content myself with mental excursions only, tripping beneath the canopies of forests that exist solely in the mind, ruminating on flora that are mine and mine alone.

It was while trying to pull up a large hydrangea in my front garden that I first got to speak to Jim. He was walking past on the opposite side of the road. But he could see that I was struggling.

That's been there a few years. You'll have trouble getting rid of that, he called over.

Indeed he was right. The hydrangea had been in the front garden since I could remember. In its early life it had been neatly clipped and tidied. In the last years of my mother's life, however, things had been left to go bad, and the hydrangea, along with almost everything else in the garden, and in the house for that matter, took on a dissolute, wild appearance. When I first came back after my mother's death the hydrangea was waiting for me. It was the first thing that I saw as I walked up the road. As I approached the house I could see that it was no longer the domesticated pet I had last seen twenty years before. When I was a child my mother had cut off its flower blooms and placed them in a blue-glass vase that sat on the dining-room table. In its heyday she had saved tea bags in an old margarine container under the sink, eventually to be brought out like some sacrificial offering and placed around the roots. But those times had gone.

You'll need a fork to get at the roots, said Jim as he

walked across the road to stand bending over the short wall that ran along the edge of the front garden.

I was using my bare hands because I had nothing else. All I found in the shed was a collection of plastic pots and a small hand trowel.

Do you want to borrow a fork? I've got plenty of garden tools that you're more than welcome to use.

I walked back with him to his house and was led through into his garage. There was a pushbike and a ladder resting horizontally on wall brackets. Tins of paint lined the Formica shelving and a chest freezer squatted beneath the window. Yet this was no normal outhouse: the place was pristine; there wasn't a single speck of dirt on anything. It felt more like an intensive care unit than someone's garage. He must have seen my look. It's Julie, my wife. She hates dirt. I keep it clean for her, he explained. It was then he told me about his wife and her cancer. I stood holding onto his fork and spade as I stared through the window at a cat walking along the wooden fence that ran along the side of Jim's house. So did my mother, I remember saying. Perhaps it was then that the rain came down and I decided that the hydrangea had won a reprieve.

It was Jim who finally helped me clear the front and back gardens. One morning, completely unannounced, he simply drew up with a wheelbarrow stacked high with garden implements, shouting out that the cavalry had arrived. There was little I could do but welcome him.

As he moved around my garden I realized that though

he was an older, more established figure, he shared my sense of loneliness. Indeed, he seemed to relish the opportunity to come across and lose himself amongst my weeds. And afterwards we shared a beer in the kitchen and gazed out at the results of our work.

It was on such occasions that Jim told me about Julie. The cancer had spread and the doctors had given her no more than six months. He took her regularly to the hospital but given the prognosis, Jim said it was more important to keep her comfortable at home. Jim said all these things with a deadpan expression, as though discussing a faulty carburettor. It was only later I saw his face truly animated.

As a treat Jim brought Julie over one Sunday. I remember that it was in early March. It was the first spring-like day of the year and in the sun it was warm, T-shirt weather almost. But in the shade it was as cold as ice. Julie had on a blue fleece jacket and a red bobble hat, and she hobbled over the road on the arm of her husband.

Julie must have known my mother quite well but she said very little. She had large sunken eyes that I found studying my face surreptitiously on more than one occasion. She may have had many questions, but she didn't ask them. Or at least Julie didn't ask the ones that mattered. Instead, she made appropriate comments about the garden, noting with interest the tamed hydrangea, the trimmed box and the pruned apple tree. Julie even said that she had stood under the apple tree once before, many years ago when my mother invited several neighbours over for tea. For some reason I found it strange to think that the two ladies had met, just as we were doing at that moment, separated only by time.

I brought tea and biscuits out on a tray. We all sat on wooden chairs taken from the lounge. The legs sank into the waterlogged lawn. Julie looked withered, like the stark branches of the trees that rustled around us. Jim was loud and spoke about many things. I sat with my face inclined to the sun, eyes shut. These days should be savoured, I remember thinking.

2

Conducting a search is a skilled business. It shouldn't be taken lightly. It requires careful thought and consideration. It's an academic exercise, an exercise of the mind. I tried to explain this to Jim, but of course he failed to appreciate these finer details.

I remember how we both sat by the side of platform two at Leicester station. I had a coffee, Jim a can of beer. This was obviously not appropriate to the occasion – a clear head is a must for this sort of activity. I had a copy of the *Times* open on my lap while Jim kept his copy of the *Sun* neatly folded in the pocket of his coat. The essence of an operation like this is to remain as invisible as possible, I explained while pointedly glancing at the can in his hand. We're like the tiger in the long grass, slowly moving up to the herd. One sight of us and our chance is gone.

I'm off to the toilets. Here, hold this. And with that Jim had lumbered along to the end of the platform.

I remember thinking even in this earliest period that such strategic insights were wasted on my colleague. As he barged through the toilet doors, the image of his podgy fingers hammering down on my keyboard like chisel blows came to mind. Sitting next to him in my study I had tried to outline the details of good Internet search techniques.

It's no use just putting in a word, I explained. My fingers flickered across the keys and entered a string of text. If I search now I will end up with hundreds of web pages. I hit the enter key with a degree of theatricality. Sure enough, the search engine returned over 500 pages. I turned to look triumphantly at Jim but found him squinting painfully at the screen. Jim's fingers smashing down on my keyboard was a motif for that first trip together from Leicester station. It was early spring. Early spring this year. Is that possible?

When Jim returned from the toilets, we both sat and watched as people scurried around us. I suddenly felt very vulnerable with Jim next to me. I remember suggesting to him that we should both go back home. But Jim urged me on. He said that we had to see this through, that we had to continue to the end. I remember he turned away from me and gazed back at the bodies moving past him on the platform. He had that same squint that I had seen in front of my computer monitor the first time I had shown him.

Selection is everything. Rather than a single string, why not use multiple words. Form these into a powerful algorithm – a net of individual search terms held together by Boolean operators. Cast this out into the Web. Then watch. And wait. Boolean operators and search engines were, of course, something Jim failed to grasp. His searching methodology was highly deficient. One minute he was sitting next to me at the station and the next he was up on his feet, with the words, Come on, let's go.

A train had just pulled alongside our platform and there was now a rush of activity around us. I looked up at my companion. What is it? I asked.

Don't worry. Just follow me.

And like a fool I did. We both moved through the crowds and got on to the train. As we shuffled through into the carriage I asked him who we were following.

Just sit down here. Jim pointed to two free seats. As we made ourselves comfortable, he looked across the carriage and got out his paper.

Well? I pointedly asked as the train pulled away from the station.

She's over there, half way along on the right. Jim's eyes didn't even lift from the newsprint.

With some concern I surveyed the sweaty faces strung out along the carriage in front of me. Since this was a Saturday morning the usual influx of commuters was absent. In their place had come – well, all sorts of other people. I looked where Jim had directed me. And, sure enough, there she was. There was Jim's girl. It was all so obvious.

Jim looked up from his newspaper and stared straight at me. OK?

I watched as the ticket collector entered our carriage. OK.

The train was crowded – full of hot, spent breath. The conductor asked us for our tickets and Jim instantly replied that he wanted a return to Birmingham. I had to do the same, of course. Jim's girl got off at Hinckley, a town to the south-west of Leicester. She walked down the aisle and Jim moved to get up. I didn't want to follow, I do remember that. I felt exposed. But Jim forced me to my feet and practically frogmarched me onto the platform. A cold wind blew along the station, quickly dispersing the few passengers that got off the train. We both hurried out onto the main road. The girl was not far ahead. She was walking purposefully, as though short of time. I remember the girl's blonde hair streaming out. I looked up at Jim's face and saw the hard, unrelenting gleam of his eyes. They focused straight ahead and I could tell nothing was going to distract him. I could only admire his determination.

The girl walked into the centre of Hinckley and began to shop. It was a busy Saturday, and although we lost her on several occasions, the blonde hair was never far away. At one point she stopped to sit on a small wooden bench by the side of a pedestrianized road. The girl placed the two or three bags that she was holding on the floor at her feet and got out her mobile phone. At the end of the call she agreed to meet her friend by a place called 'Mosaic's'. We followed, of course.

Mosaic's turned out to be a small café in the centre of Hinckley frequented by teenagers. Both girls went in. We remained outside and watched as they sat down at a table and ordered two chocolate milkshakes.

I suggested that perhaps we should now go: that, as a preliminary exercise, our little excursion had reached a natural conclusion. Jim simply shook his head and bit into the hot dog he had bought from a mobile stall. This is getting interesting, was his only comment. The girls emerged after thirty-four minutes and immediately separated, our target walking past Jim and me as she progressed further along the busy thoroughfare. Crowds can make it difficult to track individuals but conversely, they also provide ideal cover by which one can remain in close proximity. Jim quickly realized this and was practically tripping the girl over as he marched behind her. I stayed behind him.

It was clear that the girl was on her way home. At least it was clear to me. She was racing past all the shops, cutting through the crowds like the bow of a yacht. There was no way she was going to be distracted. Where else could she be going but home? I doubt whether Jim was considering these options at this time, he was simply in pursuit, like a bloodhound. As we moved away from the centre of Hinckley the crowds thinned and our presence became more and more obvious. Jim dropped back and although the girl continued as before, I began to suspect that she was aware of our presence. I said as much to Jim.

What should we do? he asked.

We could cross over the road.

Teamwork is the key. Intuitive. Something that can't be rehearsed or practised. It comes from a subconscious empathy between certain individuals. Jim and I – we were like that. At least in some ways. It was quite remarkable. This was the first time I became aware of it. The girl turning round was the trigger.

In that situation what do you do? The girl had been about ten metres in front of us and had suddenly stopped and turned round. Her hair was still blowing in the breeze. The bags in her hands swayed and rustled. She was standing, staring at us.

I think I almost faltered. Perhaps there was a slight change in the rhythm of my footsteps, as though I had just walked into a wall. But Jim kept going. In fact if anything he speeded up. He walked right up to her. I was now behind him. I couldn't believe what he was doing. There was no time for talk. This was all intuitive. This was teamwork.

He said he was a policeman. Can you believe that? He walked right up to the girl and told her we were undercover officers. From somewhere he produced a card with his picture. He flashed it in the wintry sun like a sheriff's badge. A momentary gleam of Perspex, a digitized imprint, an official stamp. The card was replaced in his pocket. The girl stood bug-eyed in front of us.

We have reason to believe you're carrying class 'A' drugs. Would you mind if we quickly searched your bags?

I could hardly believe what I was hearing! Class 'A' drugs – where did he get that from? The girl's mouth dropped open. I thought she was going to cry.

And then this is where I came in. This was my bit. This was where my experience counted. I quickly looked up and down the street. We were alone. The road was built up with small red-brick terraced houses interspersed with garages and shops. In front of us, a small passageway separated a row of housing and a hairdresser's. I seized my moment. We needed to be off the road, in a place where I could protect her.

Please, let's just stand off the main street.

I led my companions into the passageway. It was a disused strip of land, muddy and full of litter. We walked a few feet along it, the girl in between Jim and me. She was saying something but I wasn't listening.

I pretended to search her bags, giving her time. Run, run! Jim talked to her about things. She watched me bring out the gloves and T-shirts, the book and pencils. I handed the bags back. For God's sake, get out now!

She tried to scream but Jim was on her in an instant. Hand over mouth. His full body pressed against hers. Her coat made a screeching sound on the wall as her body moved in time to the flicker of Jim's other hand.

PART FOUR

Leicestershire

1922, Mid October

Perambulations of a Soldier: Autumn to Winter
by John Crowe

A strange and unexpected depression in the ground is always worth further study of course but what is most noticeable to us is that it is without the oaks. Perhaps the undue dampness of the hollow is not to their liking, or perhaps the old trees were felled when this piece of land had its other, more mysterious, use. Only the birch grows here. As we move down through the maze of white trunks we catch the gleam of water, for there, at the very bottom of the site, is a pond.

Moving forwards toward it, we quickly notice that the ground is becoming increasingly boggy; in fact it is impossible to get close to the water's edge. Yet even from this distance the occasional sight of the few dark fish that molest the surface water gives one a thrill. Their slow, ponderous movements are in stark contrast to those of the ubiquitous pond-skaters and water-measurers, darting maniacally across the fragile meniscus, avoiding the detritus spinning with them. The play of light upon the water of such a pond can make a most startling effect at this time of the year, something our great artists have known for many years! And so it is with some reluctance that we move on away from the hypnotic beauty of this little scene.

Leaving the birches, we enter the oak wood proper again at a part where there are some of the oldest and finest trees. Over here, for example, is a most interesting specimen. High up in its branches is one of our largest wild birds, fast asleep after a hectic night on the hunt. Such is the colouring of the tawny owl that many might fail to distinguish it from the tree, perhaps mistaking it for a mis-shapen branch. We creep by, making sure not to disturb the tree's daylight guest.

But look, the light is disappearing from the sky as night closes in, and so it is to home that we tired ramblers must turn, leaving the wood to the pond-skaters and tawny owls.

Rev Cecil Crowe,
The Vicarage,
Great Glen,
Leicestershire

14th October 1922

FROM: *Captain John Crowe, Black Horse Inn,*
Houghton-on-the-Hill

My Dear Father,

   I trust this letter reaches you in good health. I am well
if tired after my recent sojourns. As you can see from my
present address, I am safely ensconced in the Black Horse
Inn, a charming public house in the centre of Houghton.
As I look back over the few days since I last corresponded
with you, so much has happened that I feel quite
overwhelmed. My optimism remains high as ever, but I
would be lying to suggest that the recent events have not
been tinged with sadness, and that as I hold my pen before
me, I am not unduly engulfed in a bleakness that I felt
confident my journey would dissipate. But it is late, and
perhaps the wind howling outside through the deserted
village high street has led to an unnatural inclemency of
character! I also realize, dear Father, that I am getting
ahead of myself in my story.

   As I informed you in my previous letter, I had decided
to leave Husbands Bosworth to undertake a journey
across the county that would enable me to visit some of

my old comrades in arms while affording excellent opportunities for the research of the autumn to winter edition of *Perambulations*. A growing restlessness lay at the heart of this scheme, restlessness both at my imposed inactivity at the cottage and a less tangible emotion that even now lies beyond adequate human description. Please understand that I am not putting the blame for my departure from Husbands Bosworth at the door of Uncle George and Aunt Beth. They remain admirable hosts, and I can honestly conclude that the visit was both timely and beneficial. However, I had been there for over a month – yes, can you believe it! – and although in many ways it would have been lovely to stay and luxuriate as their guest, I felt I needed to move on. As you yourself might say, the next phase of convalescence must begin. Only now, the remedy is less certain and, although I have every faith in my plan, the outcome cannot be foreseen. Alas, the bleakness of this weary hour corrupts my thoughts again.

Following my decision to leave the cottage, I informed Uncle George and Aunt Beth over breakfast the next morning. They were naturally rather surprised, particularly when I explained what I would be doing. However, after our conversation, I was of the opinion that, though sorry to see me depart, they sympathized with my motives. And of course, being the fine motivators that they are, they wholeheartedly agreed that the journey presented an unparalleled occasion to complete much of the autumn material for *Perambulations*. When I explained that I intended to leave early the following morning they were of course shocked at the suddenness. I explained, with some justification, that it was appropriate to set out before the rains of winter made the lanes impassable, and that, given the present fair conditions, it was best I left as early as possible. It was some consolation to them when I explained that I was not intending to go far, and that I would never be further than a day's ride away. I did promise that I would return immediately after I had completed my visits.

I spent much of the afternoon packing. Aunt Beth kept popping into my little room to make sure that I was not too melancholy. She suggested I packed Khartoum, a brown, moth-eaten teddy that I had apparently left behind one summer long ago and that had now made his home on one of the shelves in my room. Do you remember him? He made no impression on me whatsoever, although even if he had, poor thing, there would have been no room for him in the saddlebags.

I left early the next morning. There was a slight fog rolling over the village as I led Angus back to the cottage. He seems to have enjoyed his time at the Bell and although I had been riding out on him, I recognized in his poise a keenness for the chase. Aunt Beth and Uncle George provided an emotional farewell as they stood outside their front door. Aunty could not hold back the tears, despite my protestations that I would soon return once my journeying had been concluded. I have certainly had a wonderful time at Husbands Bosworth but Angus's stamping in the cold morning fog reminded me of the task that lay ahead. After a final embrace, I mounted

Angus and slowly advanced down the street. The fog quickly enveloped the huddled forms of my hosts, although their voices carried long after I had lost sight of them.

Beyond the village the fog was both thicker and colder. The breath from Angus streamed out before me, and I remember pulling up the collars on my long coat. The journey ahead was not necessarily arduous, taking no more than a few hours at a gentle canter. Although Angus was more than capable of faster speeds, I was in no particular hurry since I presumed that Albert Furrows would be at work until at least late afternoon. I had also intended to take in the joy of the Leicestershire countryside and thereby propagate further material for my book. There was now hardly any sound, save that made by Angus and me. It really did feel as though we were the only creatures remaining in the world.

I have heard it said that the Leicestershire country is both flat and unvaried. I can only think that those who have made such comments have not journeyed across it. Certainly there are no great hills or gradients as other counties can boast. Yet the land is hardly flat. Riding out from Husbands Bosworth one had the sensation of piloting a boat in a modest squall, the sea ruffled and flummoxed in the most unexpected ways. At times a level approach could indeed be plotted, and one could take a hand off the tiller and stare out at the becalmed waters of the Sargasso. Then suddenly, from out of nowhere, a great wave would be upon me and my little boat would climb precipitously, the bow riding blind over the crest before splashing down into the shadowy trough.

On leaving Saddington the lane descended steeply to the desolate Grand Union Canal. It was at this point, as we traversed a small bridge, that a black Humber suddenly appeared in front of us with lights blazing. It raced past at great speed, the single occupant waving and screaming. Angus was most alarmed by the suddenness of the intrusion and promptly reared up with dramatic effect. It was all I could do to pacify the beast once the motorcar had disappeared.

After an arduous ascent, we stopped for a break in the village of Smeeton Westerby, which lies just beyond the crossing of the Grand Union as it bends round to the west from Debdale Wharf. I dismounted in front of the public house and let Angus drink from the stone trough standing on the opposite side of the street. This tiny village appeared to be deserted, and as I stood beside dear old Angus, listening to him lap up the water, I began to lose faith in my trip. Perhaps I was no more than a fool to embark on such a journey, visiting friends with whom I had lost contact for so long. As a nation we have all moved on from those sad events, placing a veil of restraint over our memories and experiences. It is right, of course, that we do so, grasping the potential that the Modern Age has to offer our great Empire. Yet, despite these fine and proper sentiments, I still longed for one last drink with my old comrades. Given the messiness of our parting, and my consequent stay at Quex Park in Kent, I considered that my full recovery could be sustained only through such action. It could not be denied then that this journey was a voyage back in time with Angus inexorably leading me to those darkest of hours. Indeed, it would be true to say that from the moment I had left Husbands Bosworth in the fog, this sense of regression had weighed heavy on my shoulders. With Angus refreshed, I continued on silently through the village. We met no one save a young lad who stared at me as if I were a Bolshevik.

Not far from Smeeton lie the two red brick villages of Kibworth Beauchamp and Kibworth Harcourt, separated only by the Leicester and London railway line. Compared to Smeeton, Kibworth Beauchamp proved a veritable hive of activity, its mix of agricultural and hosiery workers providing much needed interest. At one point on our journey along the main street Angus and I moved past a hosiery factory – a small, red building shut up tight against the sun and air. Inside, the whine and clatter of metallic machines throbbed through the pavement and into our bones while shadowy figures darted like ghouls across the frosted windows in attendance on the new technology.

Further on, as Angus and I passed over the line on the bridge, we could see a train pulling out from the station below us on the left, the smoke and steam mingling with the mist that swirled along the platforms. The shrill of the whistle pierced the air as we went on through Kibworth Harcourt, glimpsing the wooden windmill standing resolutely on the outskirts of the village to our right.

As we headed due north, I suddenly recalled the existence of the 'motte and bailey' just off the main street. Although I do not recall ever visiting the Kibworths, a small detour quickly located it. As I'm sure you are aware, despite numerous excavations, little is known of this ancient and mystifying site with its small tumulus and ditch. Certain educated guesses suggest that it is the burial place of a Bronze Age king, a certain Kibbeus, but I have also heard, although from whom I cannot remember, that this is simply a nineteenth-century fable inspired by the overzealous landowner.

Angus and I stood and watched for some time as the mist slowly writhed within the tiny circular ditch before setting off once more. Back in the open air the fog was now beginning to lift, and as we rode on, the sun began to burn through the low, grey clouds. My mood started to rise and I think Angus too began to enjoy himself for we started to race along the little country lanes. I made infrequent stops to take a closer look at any vegetation that caught the eye although the camera remained safely in its case.

My route had been carefully thought through with Uncle George, and although I had nothing written down, the directions had been committed to memory. At times, however, my usual navigational sense deserted me, and I was unsure in which direction I should turn. About two miles beyond Kibworth Harcourt I had such a moment of confusion. Erroneously I left the gentle road on which I was proceeding and instead headed due north along a narrower lane. Unfortunately this took me into Carlton Curlieu, a tiny village I was not expecting to pass. As you may know, Father, there is not much here but a church with a large sequoia, a few cottages, a fine old hall, and a disused moat of unknown antiquity. I was saved by a farm hand who happened to be standing outside the entrance to Carlton Curlieu Hall. The hall appeared to be a seventeenth-century country house, solid and square as you would say, but with an elegant simplicity that reminded me of Quex Park. When I explained that I intended to reach Gartree Road and thence to make my way to Houghton, the young man kindly suggested a short cut across open fields that would bring me out by Carlton Curlieu Manor House. This indeed proved to be the case, my path being an ancient byway that took Angus and me across several fields of mud. The going was heavy and when we finally intersected Gartree Road I dismounted and let Angus rest for several minutes.

Opposite us, on the other side of the road, was the Manor House, as predicted by my guide. The road itself was quiet. The fog was now all but gone and a strong autumnal sun was beating down on the sodden ground. I estimated that we were more than half way through our journey, and it was only one o'clock.

Gartree Road is an old Roman road, of course. Standing there next to Angus as he nibbled at the grass on the verge, it was easy to imagine the Pretorian Guard marching off from their garrison in Ratae. Your knowledge of these things is greater than mine, but as I stood there by the roadside, Father, I could not remember where the Roman Road actually led. My memory of walking along it is that it just seems to fade away five or six miles out of Leicester, not far from the village of Medbourne. But surely the Via Divana was a more majestic enterprise – your descriptions of a bustling Roman thoroughfare have stayed with me and it was with some disappointment that I looked upon the tranquil but deserted road before me.

Along the Gartree Road Angus and I headed west towards the city. To our left the magnificent church of St John the Baptist at King's Norton could be clearly seen, dominating the countryside like a miniature York Minster. Not far after the turning to Little Stretton but before the deserted village of Great Stretton with its stark, lone church, we turned right onto the Houghton lane. From here I knew that we were less than forty-five minutes from the village, and so it was with some leisure that we climbed away from the Gartree Road, occasionally glimpsing the sprawling metropolis of Leicester in the valley of the Soar to my left.

The ironstone spire of St Catherine's is a veritable beacon in these parts, rising majestically from the distant bank of trees. The lane on which I travelled led straight towards it, past the slight depression to the south of the church that could be interpreted as some forgotten earthwork. Apart from this there was little distraction to take my eyes from the stone structure before me. Yet, as I advanced, it would be true to say that doubts about my journey once more returned. The growing church spire of Houghton brought home my sudden approximation to Albert Furrows, and at once I started to feel uncomfortable. Why was I disturbing Albert's life here in this tranquil part of the world? What claim had I on a companionship that had been neglected almost four years? I imagined Albert's face as I drew up in front of his house, his stoical expressions contorted as the memories suddenly returned. He had a right to peace like everyone else.

To ease my discomfort I tried to recollect as many
details about Albert's present situation as I could. Although
I assumed Albert to be a close friend, I realized on
reflection that I did not know as much about him as I
presumed. Indeed, it surprised me the degree to which he
had the quality of a stranger. One fact did spring to mind,
however: he had often spoken of his sweetheart back in
Houghton when we were at the Front. Perhaps they were
now married and perhaps he even had a small family.
I must confess that this thought shocked me – in my eyes
Albert was the baby-faced recruit, a lad fresh from the
fields, with all the gangling incompetence of any teenager.
As I drew up to the outskirts of the village I realized that
many things could have changed.

The approach to St Catherine's is circuitous and
narrow, the tiny lane winding past the school house and
rectory before finally reaching the church. I stopped
outside the gate and drew from my greatcoat pocket the
letter that Albert had sent me while I was at Quex. I
looked at my watch – it was only half past two. Albert
would presumably be hard at it in the fields somewhere –
that is if he was still a farm hand. The afternoon had
become warm and Angus and I were covered in sweat.
We both required rest and sustenance.

Houghton is a most quaint little village. The houses are
arranged higgledy-piggledy around the lane, which
meanders to and fro in a most pleasant manner. I would
suggest that the majority of the buildings date from the
late eighteenth and early nineteenth centuries. Red brick
predominates of course, but some of the older cottages
have ironstone parts with whitewashed brickwork or

roughcast above. There are even a few thatched roofs to be seen. As Angus and I progressed into the village we soon found the inn. As I dismounted, the landlord hailed me from an open window on the ground floor. I explained that I would require stabling for Angus and a room for the night. He explained that I should take the horse round the back where I could leave him with his son, who would be waiting for me. This I found to be the case, the son being a lad of no more than fifteen with a fringe of black hair that swept straight over his eyes. The landlord appeared and took me to my room. As we climbed the stairs to the first floor, he asked if I had come for the festivities. Apparently there was to be a wedding on the Saturday, and a weekend of merriment had been planned. When I explained that I was here to meet Albert Furrows, he nodded solemnly.

My room was bright and cheerful, with a wonderful view of the high street. After the usual particulars, I decided to take advantage of the landlord's local knowledge by asking him a few questions about Albert. At first I asked where he lived and got more than adequate directions; I then asked if he still worked on a farm and whether he was married or not. The landlord looked rather puzzled at this line of questioning so I explained that I had not seen Albert since the War, when we served together in the 2nd Leicesters.

'Ah. Of course, sir. Well now, Albert is indeed a farm hand with George Whatling as far as I remember. He's certainly married – married last year or the year before if memory serves. Lovely girl. From Evington way if I'm not mistaken. Shall I get some hot water brought up for you?'

Once washed, I went down to see that Angus was

content and to collect my saddlebags. After depositing the bags in my room and throwing the camera over my back, I returned through the bar and once more entered the high street. The afternoon was turning out to be an exceedingly warm one, the autumnal sun was hot and there was hardly a cloud in the sky. As I emerged from the shadows of the bar, it seemed as though I had stepped back in time by several months to those scorching days of early June when I helped you cut down the oak tree.

My presence caused some excitement amongst the locals. Given the warmth of the weather, most of the populace appeared out on the street, and so were in a perfect position to monitor the progress of any 'stranger'. Further down the thoroughfare I passed the village shop, outside of which stood a number of old ladies taking advantage of the shade offered by the awnings. As I passed, I raised my cap in a gentlemanly way and offered a salutation. This had the effect of ceasing their conversation, but instead of a reciprocal greeting, they merely stared as though frozen in stone.

Dingwell Cottage was not far from this provisionist's. It was one of a row of small labourers' cottages standing directly on the high street. The red brick abodes were hard to tell apart although I could see that each one had a name etched into the door mantle. Dingwell Cottage was in the middle of the row. With the eyes of those ladies still burning my back, I walked slowly past the front door, half-expecting old Albert to come rushing out to greet me. But of course he didn't. The door stayed shut and the heavy net curtains remained unmoved across the little front window.

At a loss what to do I continued walking along the row of cottages and onwards until the end of the village. Near the main Peterborough Road I came across a small circle of grass in the centre of which a war memorial had been recently erected. At its base were two large millstones. I read some of the names before turning to face the road. Here was certainly a symbol of the Modern Age, replete as it was with the frequent passing of both motorized cars and bicycles. The few carts that could be seen were certainly a visible anachronism as the traffic sped down into the valley and on to the outer reaches of Leicester, that bright new metropolis that calls itself the richest city in the Empire!

Casting my eyes across the road, I saw a number of figures moving in the fields and I wondered if one of these could be Albert. They appeared to be loading several horse-drawn carts with straw, throwing the grass high into the air with their pitchforks. Even from this distance I could hear their voices above the din of the traffic, the high pitch of the female workers contrasting starkly with the low rumble of their male counterparts. The rhythm of their work was mesmerizing and I must have stood stationary for some time, struck by the contrast with the high-speed activity on the highway. I remember taking a picture of the scene with my camera. I called it 'Janus-face of the modern age', perhaps rather melodramatically.

As I have said, I spent a few minutes watching these various scenes, wondering what I should do. It appeared that I had at least another two or three hours before Albert's return from the fields. I could return to my room and wait or try and alert Albert to my arrival so that he could finish his labours as early as possible. But, in order to do that, I needed to know his location. I looked again at those figures over the Peterborough Road. If I knocked at Dingwell, maybe his wife would be home and I would be able to ask her?

It was with this notion that I turned away from the fields before me with the strange circular tumulus just south of the road, and once more returned to the row of small cottages. The old ladies outside the village shop had been transformed into a large carthorse that stood whishing his great tail in the afternoon heat. For a moment I hesitated, my hand raised over the door and my eyes scrutinizing the net curtains in the front window. It was still not too late even now to return home. I banged at the door and stood back. After some commotion I heard a female voice from within the house shout, 'The door's open.'

I peered more closely at the inscrutable glare of the netted window. Given the situation, I considered it highly inappropriate to simply walk into the house. The woman was most probably of the opinion that the caller was a female village acquaintance and not an old comrade of her husband's. Thus I rather hesitated before once more tapping lightly at the door. Again, there was a similar demand to enter, expressed with a degree of exasperation, to which I again responded by knocking. This produced the sound of echoing footsteps, after which the door was suddenly flung inwards. There before me, in the darkness of the passageway, stood a small, slight woman of no more than twenty-five years. Her hair was down, and, in the heat, appeared stuck to her face, while the sleeves of her dress were rolled up above the elbows. Although you would have found her a most contrary heroine, Father, she immediately struck one as a hard-working country girl rather than a devoted Pankhurstite! This indeed would be borne out by subsequent events, but as the door swung open, the light yawning across the darkness within, she let out a most undignified exclamation.

'Lord have mercy on me,' she screeched, and appeared to collapse against one wall. I realized immediately that I presented a most startling image to the young lady, standing there on her doorstep in full army coat, collars up of course, with regimental cap sitting askance over my forehead. I remember whipping the latter off and perhaps even holding my other hand out to her in reassurance.

'Oh, I'm terribly sorry. Please forgive this intrusion . . .'

I recollect faltering badly at this early stage of our introduction. To be perfectly honest, the young lady had recoiled to some degree into the safety of the shadows. As I placed the cap under my arm, I discerned the aimless babble of a baby from behind her while a steady breeze caressed my sweaty face, suggesting that the back door of the house was open. This giddy sense of domesticity, a sensation long forgotten but as pungent as any gas, almost sent me collapsing to the pavement. Perhaps the young lady saw a flash of bewilderment sweep across my face, or perhaps it was her general sense of propriety, but either way, she emerged back into the light and surveyed me with deeper interest.

'Are you here to see Albert?'

'Yes, yes, that's right. I'm a friend of his from the War. Captain Crowe.'

Although there was still suspicion in her eyes, the young lady appeared suddenly more relaxed. I could not help noticing that she was a most attractive woman, despite evidence of her domestic labours. Indeed, it was those little evidences – the rolled up sleeves on her crinoline dress, the hair hanging freely and the red spots of exertion upon her cheeks – that were curiously her most disarming features, recalling the diligent nurses at Quex. As for myself, I was hardly the officer gent as I had imagined when setting out on this journey! Although I had washed at the lodgings, my shirt was damp with sweat and my long coat smelt far too much of Angus. Together, I suppose we made a fine pair – that is, my old coat and me, and the camera slung across it. In other situations, the front door would have been justifiably slammed in my face.

There was a scream from the baby, and the woman's head immediately turned to face the darkened interior. She looked back quickly at me. 'Albert's not here yet. He'll be working until six.' There was a slight pause as the young woman stared hard at me. 'Would you like to come in for a minute? I must see to Johnny.'

My eyes quickly adapted to the cool darkness of the cottage. Immediately off to the left of the passageway was a closed door that must have led to the front room. There were then the stairs disappearing precipitously off to the left, and at the end of the short passageway was the back room itself. Like everything else in workers' cottages, all was small and rather cramped, at least to my eyes, but the general ambience was one of peace and feminine charm.

I quickly concluded that Albert had got himself a fine

wife and together they had made a most comfortable nest. I noticed the small fire burning contentedly in the grate, a mantelpiece crowded with mugs and other ceramic features, a small table and vase displaying an assortment of rural flora, and a little window which overlooked the back garden. On the chimney breast was displayed a framed photograph of Albert in full military attire taken, judging by the youthfulness of its subject, not many days after first gaining his uniform. The pride in his eyes was difficult to avoid.

'Please come through.' The young woman looked rather embarrassed but it was I who felt grossly out of place in such a domestic setting. 'Would you like to remove your coat and hat?'

'Thank you, but no. I won't be stopping.'

I was taken through into the cramped kitchen. A door from the kitchen led out into the tiny back garden. I say 'tiny', but in all honesty the strip was as much as a man might need, and Albert had obviously been busy tending the various flowers and shrubs that grew in the adequately stocked borders. A clothes mangle stood by the side of the back door, while a line of washing stretched off to the end of the garden, obscuring the fine views obtained across the county. From the bottom of the garden came the sound of cooing. I remembered Albert's love of pigeons.

In the shade of the adjoining wall was a well-sprung pram in which Johnny could be heard screaming. The young woman removed the piece of netting and pulled out a very rosy-faced child, wrapped loosely in a cotton sheet.

'This is John, Albert's son.'

John! I moved over to touch the child's little nose. All

of a sudden he stopped crying and looked up at me: his eyes were exactly those of Albert's and, for a moment, I was transfixed. I informed the mother of my observation.

'Yes, others have said as much as well. As long as Johnny doesn't have his father's stubbornness. Albert doesn't talk much about his days away. He's mentioned one or two names. He occasionally has a drink with Willie Jones when he's in Leicester.'

My spirits rose immediately. So I was not alone in my endeavours to seek out old companions! Others were driven by equal desires. My tentative and precursory voyage suddenly became part of a saner, more rationalized movement of which I was just one component. Willie had joined the regiment just before my enforced stay in hospital and was nothing more than a vague memory. He would have been a year or two younger than Albert. Albert would have taken care of him.

'Has he ever mentioned me?' I asked with some hesitation.

'Are you the captain that went to hospital?'

'Yes, indeed.' Again there was a quizzical look that had become so common since leaving Quex. 'My own wounds were of the mind, as you might say, although I was wounded in the leg. Albert wrote to me when I was in the ward. I am staying at the Black Horse. Perhaps if you could inform Albert I . . . might meet him there, if that is acceptable to him.'

'Albert's got a new life here. I don't want him being upset by the past. He,' and here she paused slightly, 'he isn't as strong as some.'

*

I returned to my room and flung my coat, cap and camera onto the bed. It was now just after four in the afternoon and the heat was at its greatest. A subdued quietude hung over the village, the busy high street almost deserted save for one or two pedestrians. I ordered food, which was duly brought up to my room by the landlord's wife. After eating I returned downstairs, where I found a free table by the window overlooking the high street. The landlord came over with a pint of ale. He stretched out one of his great paws. 'My name is William Potter, landlord of this wonderful little world.'

I shook his hand. 'John Crowe, ex-captain of the 2nd Leicester's, 5th Battalion.'

'A few of our lads enlisted, and more than one or two didn't return.' Mr Potter took a sip of his beer. 'Albert's one of several here with memories of the Front. He's a hard-working lad and has a lovely wife.'

I explained that I had had the good fortune to meet her.

'Ah, indeed. And a lovely baby to keep them company. Mind you,' and here he drew closer, 'there are one or two rumours floating around. I've heard it—' The rather unseemly turn in conversation was suddenly halted by a customer banging his empty mug on the unattended bar. Mr Potter scowled. 'Be with you in a moment, Jack.' Then, turning to me, 'Excuse me while I serve the old duffer.'

Suddenly, as I sat back to enjoy my solitude, the front door of the bar creaked open and in walked Albert. He was dressed in the garb of any field worker, his shirt open, sleeves rolled high, with soiled trousers and boots. As the late afternoon sun slanted in across the room, plumes of dust could be seen rising from his clothes. Yet he stood straight and true as any oak, striding to the bar with that indefatigable English steadfastness. Was it merely fancy thoughts, or was there still a military precision with which he removed his cloth cap on confronting the grinning Mr Potter?

''Cuse me, Mr Potter, but I have been told that a certain English gent is staying here tonight.'

His voice was deeper than I remembered it, and those shoulders broader. Of course he was a man now. When I had last seen him he was still no more than a boy, a boy in the midst of Hell.

In the sunlight Albert appeared bronzed and lean, the sweat and mud drying to his face in visible rivulets. Certainly his face was still youthful, much as I remembered it, but there was a hardness there now, a rigidity, that was almost disconcerting, sitting like a mask across a visage that at one point I had read only too well. 'I'm sorry if my visit has caused you some distress. I did intend to write but I had no time. This whole madcap idea just ballooned from nothing.'

We were sitting at my small table in the large bay window at the front of the pub. It was only after Mr Potter had brought over two pints of bitter that I began to tell Albert the full details of my odyssey, how it was my intention to visit the friends I had left behind in September 1917. I brought out the letter he had written to me while I was at Quex. 'You foolishly left your address on this.'

Albert picked it up. 'My parents' address, just round the

corner. You must have seen that address a thousand times with all the letters I wrote back home.'

'I suppose so, although I have few memories of that. But then other things are so very vivid.'

Albert looked away. The dark turn of this conversation was obviously not to his liking.

'I wasn't expecting you until much later,' I said.

'Mary sent Lewis, the boy next door, into the fields to get me. She mentioned a hat and coat.' Albert smiled nervously before gulping down mouthfuls of the ale.

I nodded. He must be referring to my regimental cap and long coat that were presently upstairs in my room. 'I hear you've seen Willie Jones?' I said after another awkward pause. My companion explained that he did indeed meet up with a few old Leicesters, but with Willie most often, who was part of a workers' co-operative in the centre of the city.

There was a certain pause as we both finished our drinks. 'You certainly have yourself a lovely wife and home, Albert. And a son as well. You have a wonderful future ahead.' At this it would be no exaggeration to say that Albert's face beamed, and he began a long monologue on both his wedding and the birth of his son that had occurred less than two months previously.

I listened with much interest to this detail, ordering another round of drinks in the process. But the more he talked, the more I realized the parameters within which his life was now set. There was to be no looking back, no open remorse or sadness. Listening to him, I began to experience those familiar sensations that I had felt so often during my rehabilitation at Quex and the subsequent walking tour of 1918. Albert's eloquence belied a fundamental sense of repression, and, as he spoke, the metaphor of the pillow returned, that thick, heavy pillow pressing down on those things that had once been.

You remember, Father, those few poems I sent to you while at Quex Park. Although I might not have told you, I also wrote several to Albert, inspired, no doubt, by his kind words in that letter of his which arrived within my first week or two at the hospital. Since I had not heard from him after that first epistle, I began by asking whether he still remembered fondly the few stanzas that I had foolishly sent him. My strategy was simple, of course – by such an introduction I intended to reveal the literary string that was now firmly tied to my bow, what with *Perambulations* and all.

However, as soon as I mentioned the poems it became clear that Albert was getting even more uncomfortable. To make matters worse, Mr Potter had removed himself from the bar, and was now seated on an adjacent table, smoking a rather bulbous clay pipe. The proximity of such a character appeared to further the discomfort of my companion. Yet I persisted, despite the unpropitious circumstances. Apart from your good self, Father, I have informed very few of my experiences since sustaining the injuries at Ypres that forced me from the Front. Through my treatment at Quex Park, and the subsequent walking tour, I made some headway in banishing those demons that had previously caused me such pain and debilitation. Indeed, the first volume of *Perambulations* should be seen as a tangible by-product of my recovery, as you are aware.

Certainly the practice of Dr Worthington at Quex Park, and those specialists I subsequently attended, was of the highest quality and enabled me to regain what Dr Worthington termed a 'neuropathic equilibrium', from a most fraught situation. However, as I have often written to you since, this 'equilibrium' was a most delicate state, and my symptoms could all too easily return with the veritable drop of a hat. You can count yourself fortunate, Father, that you have not witnessed such attacks on your son.

As you might imagine, having familiarized myself with the recent theories of repression and dissociation over the last two years, I had invested much thought into the process by which the full 'psychological' origins of my malady could be laid bare. Yet, although I had often scrutinized my memories, when it came to finally speaking of these things, I found myself more than a little tongue-tied.

Albert was hardly the most supportive of companions in this endeavour. He seemed initially uninterested in my experiences at Quex, and I suppose it was in an attempt to entertain him that I described the extraordinary antics of Major Percy Powell Cotton who, as you will recall, was the owner of the Quex country house. My stay in 'B' Ward, with its screened-off dioramas and its numerous skulls and heads mounted on the walls, still returns in my dreams, as does the figure of Major Cotton himself, set in the centre of the gallery, organizing the removal of those thick wooden screens and the repositioning of the beds. Albert was most interested in these experiences and I do believe our barman drew his chair an inch or two closer.

Thus it was that I explained the history of Quex Park
Auxiliary Military Hospital, or as much as I had been able
to pick up during my four months stay there.

The hospital consisted of three wards, the first of
which, 'A' ward, was actually based within the oriental-
styled drawing room of the house itself. The two other
wards, 'B' and 'C', were museum galleries, contained
within a specially constructed pavilion close to the house.
These galleries had been built by Major Cotton to house
the large number of exhibits and trophies brought back
from his many trips around the Empire and beyond. The
centrepieces of the collection were several large dioramas
specially designed and constructed to the Major's
specifications, and around which, after 1914, the injured
were situated in their beds. These dioramas were
monstrous glass cases, stretching from floor to ceiling,
a good fifteen to twenty feet in length, within which a
multitude of stuffed fauna were presented to the eye. In
one of the most memorable, a herd of horned deer or
other such creatures appears grazing in front of a family of
giraffes while, in the right hand corner, on a large rocky
outcrop, a lion sits and watches for easy prey. With the
painted backdrop and appropriately situated flora, the
effect when standing before such creations is to
undoubtedly transport you to the African wilderness from
which the content came.

After Major Cotton offered the services of Quex Park
to the Red Cross in 1914, large wooden screens were used
to protect these glass cases, but occasionally the Major
would order them to be removed, and those patients that
were capable would assemble in the galleries, or just prop

themselves up on beds moved to one side for the occasion, and listen to his lecture on the strange and wonderful lives of the Congolese man and beast.

'Dear God, sir, were the animals not shot through with holes?' asked Mr Potter, who was staring transfixed through his veil of blue smoke.

'No, they had been preserved to the highest order and were so lifelike that one almost felt the beasts could leap from their savannah scrubland and onto your bed.'

'Seems a strange thing to do, although certainly educational for us that will never see such things. Like Noah in reverse, if you take my meaning.'

Albert and I both stared at our uninvited guest. He smiled and returned to the bar where a customer had fortuitously appeared.

I used this opportunity to move the conversation on to my walking tour, which I undertook in the first few months of 1918. This was obviously a most sensitive subject but one that I had been keen to air. Although the tour was undertaken upon the advice of Quex's medical officer, and was seen as a key aspect of my treatment, allowing me the space and isolation to come to terms with my suppressed emotions and memories, I was still filled with guilt that while my boys had been at the Front I had been lost amid the Central Shires. Many of those days upon the tour are no more than a blur to me and I see them as an endless procession of rural images, spinning across my vision as if in a dream. Not only did I not write to you during this time, Father, but I fear that, to a certain degree, I lost contact with much of what could be called reality. However, through my horticultural activity at 'The

Bothy', I was in a position to commence preliminary drafts of the first volume of *Perambulations: Spring and Summer* during that tour. Somehow my grey exercise book became filled with meticulous notes and diagrams of flora and fauna that I encountered, although even now the document and its finely detailed scribble remain a great mystery to me. The pictures that I took come from another age. Yet it was this document that certainly saved me from ultimate despair, so that as the skies began to clear and I was finally discharged by the Medical Board in May, I could set about finalizing the publication. But such behaviour seems highly out of the ordinary when faced with a man who spent those months in the Boche's teeth. Perhaps it is not surprising then that Albert remained quiet during my revelations, only allowing himself a grin when I informed him of the success of *Perambulations*. Yet as to my general psychological state, and the breakdown that ensued, he said nothing at all but merely turned his empty pint glass round and round in the evening sun.

'Was it like shell shock then?' he asked at last, without looking up.

When they dug me out of the ground I was insane. That much is certain, Father. I collapsed mentally. I couldn't function. I could hardly move or speak at first. If that is shell shock then Albert's diagnosis is correct. But my suffering was not like a wound on a leg that heals – it's there with you at all times. I had to be taught how to face those things, those memories and thoughts, how to grapple with them and then hide them firmly in the darkest, deepest corner of my mind. That's what Quex Park was all about: its isolation ward, its doses of chloroform,

hypnotism, and faradic shock treatment. That's what Dr
Worthington wanted when he talked about my
'neuropathic equilibrium', and that's what I was meant to
attain on my walking tour in the spring of 1918. I have not
mentioned these things before, Father, even to you. But
you should know that they happened, that this was the
extent of my treatment.

We ordered more drinks and Albert told me about his
transference to the 11th Leicesters. 'We spent most of
February and March on trench work and road repairs at
Fremicourt. It was blasted cold but quiet, as I remember it.
We all just dug like moles for two months for we knew
what was coming. At midnight on the 21st March we
received orders to 'Stand to' along the Vaulx-Morchies
line. I remember the line was already under heavy
bombardment as we took position. They came at us hard –
we lost a number of men; Dickey and Bill Watson both
bought it. Word came down that Sergeant Barrett was
taking over command of 'D' Company because all officers
were gone. We withdrew to a camp by Longeast Woods,
but it was all a mess. We lost Jimmy Fenton that day too.'

These names meant much to me. The Watson brothers
and Fenton had all been with me since the beginning.
Indeed, my memory of Jimmy Fenton will always be at the
Ballsbridge cattle show where, despite the danger from
rooftop Fenian snipers, he rounded up two escaped sheep,
his long arms waving the Lee-Enfield above his head. I
reminded Albert of this incident and noticed it brought a
smile to his otherwise dour features.

With the German push in the spring, the boys
undoubtedly had it bad. They were transported to Belgium

again but forced to retreat. The Pioneers were then taken
to France, from where they began the process of
extricating the Germans in a process that eventually saw
the signing of the Armistice. After a long march into
Germany, the 6th Division was finally disbanded in March
1919. All this was said in Albert's deadpan tone. I asked
many questions, but Albert seemed reticent in his replies.
Then he suddenly said, 'There's not a day goes by without
me thinking about those duck boards floating on the mud
at Wieltje.'

'Number five mule track.'

He nodded slowly. 'When I walk along the pavement I
still feel the boards sinking beneath my feet.'

'Even now I'm always walking behind the creeping
barrage on Hill thirty-seven. The shouts and screams, the
whiz overhead, the piston-pump explosion of air—'

'That murderous gunfire from Pond Farm. I was lying
in a shell hole and I could see our lads just dropping to
their knees.'

I remember a shell landing close by as we stormed those
pills. Two lads took a direct hit and I was thrown to the
floor. My arm was covered in blood and it was only
afterwards I realized that it wasn't my own. I recall
laughing hysterically and dropping to my knees as Albert
described.

We drank up. On an impulse I asked Albert if I could
take his picture. He seemed more than willing, and so I
quickly rushed upstairs for my Kodak Autograph. The bar
was now rather dark but I trusted that there was enough
illumination offered by the electric light under which we

sat. Albert raised his empty glass in a defiant gesture, a broad smile on his lips. The glass sparkled in the manufactured light, its luminescence heightened by the impenetrable blackness of the window that formed the most startling of backdrops in my viewfinder. I remained seated on my stool on the other side of our little table. I remember scribbling the date onto the film from the back of the camera: 'Albert Furrows, 13/10/22'.

I left the camera behind the bar and we both moved outside. It was now dark and cold. Albert looked nervous but said that I should come back with him. I was unsure as I felt I would be less than welcome. But Albert was insistent, and so it was that we both returned to his little cottage, hat and coatless.

On entering we found that his wife had already gone to bed. Albert led me through into the kitchen, where he prepared himself a large cheese sandwich. It was then, to my surprise, that he opened the kitchen door and whispered, 'Come this way.'

The pigeon coop was quiet, all the birds resting on their perches under the bright stars. The coop was situated on top of a small shed, and it was into this shed that Albert crept through a short door. Inside was dark as pitch, the ceiling so low one could not stand up straight. I heard Albert scrabbling momentarily, followed by the strike of a match, and two candles were lit. I could now see that I had come into a most wondrous and secret place. Although the shed was only tiny, Albert had used every available space within his domain. A camp bed ran along one wall, beside which stood a small chest of drawers with the two candles upon it. The floor was covered with old carpet, and once the door was closed, the place had a most intimate and homely air.

'We can talk openly here without fear of disturbing Mary and Johnny.'

Above us the pigeons could be heard moving, their claws scraping on the perches that now ran over our heads, above the low wooden ceiling.

Albert sat on the bed and leaned back against the wall. I took up a similar posture, sitting on the carpet. My companion leaned forward, opened the top drawer of the chest of drawers and drew out a bottle of spirits and two small glasses. 'This will keep the cold away.'

Outside there was not a sound to be heard. I took a glass and had a sip of its contents. 'This reminds me of Brigade Camp at St Albans. One night it was as quiet as this, and I went out to look at the sky and there, far above me, was a Zeppelin moving across the stars. It made no sound but just drifted like an enormous cloud. I watched it until it had disappeared in the west.' I paused. 'Uncle George seems convinced that now peace has descended upon the world, Count Zeppelin will put his efforts to more worthy operations, constructing, so Uncle George would have it, a large fleet of dirigibles capable of carrying their passengers across the Empire in the lap of luxury. Uncle George foresees huge floating hotels, drifting in the clouds, with swimming pools, bars, libraries, and even motorized automobiles taking the effort out of footwork. An unseen world of opulence afloat miles above us, only occasionally letting down the tiny observation car, like a spider from its web, to seek direction and communication with the world below! A crow's nest in reverse, on a galleon floating amidst the stars! Do you sleep here?'

Albert stared into his drink. 'Now that we have Johnny we need the space. I find I sleep better out here. I don't disturb Mary.'

Albert told me about his pigeons. He has five hens and five cocks. Just a small flock, but they're racing pigeons so he regularly takes them out in his basket that he puts on the front of his bike, or perhaps even on a train.

'They swirl off into the sky and by the time I get home they're all here waiting to be fed. I don't race them properly; it's enough to watch them circle the sun and head for home.'

A small newspaper cutting pasted onto the wall close to where I sat told the sad tale of the passenger pigeon. At its peak in the early nineteenth century, its total population may have reached five million, the most abundant bird ever to have graced the skies. But during the nineteenth century mass hunting parties decimated the population, the new telegraph system allowing the easy tracking of the flocks across the Northern States of America. By the 1880s it seemed that the species had entered a vortex of extinction from which no degree of preservation could prove a success. Albert's cutting referred to the fate of the last known passenger, a specimen born and bred in Cincinnati Zoo. Martha, as she was known, became a popular tourist attraction while scientists frantically searched for a mate. This was in vain for Martha was indeed the last of a once mighty breed, and on 1st September 1914, the bird was found dead at the bottom of her cage. Her body was stuffed and put on display in a museum of national history. The last wild passenger pigeon is reputed to have been shot by a boy in Sargents, Ohio, several years before.

The pigeons above us stirred as an owl hooted from a nearby tree. I had another drink with Albert, but it appeared that the drink had affected him disconcertingly, and so it was that I left him gently sobbing on his bed, blowing out the two candles before crawling through the miniature wooden door, closing it quietly behind me as though I were Alice leaving a secret world.

Back on the main thoroughfare of the village all was still and at peace. The experience in the shed had left me rather distressed and so I found myself slowly marching northwards, out of the village and across the Peterborough Road. I continued along a small country lane, the moon and stars providing enough light for me to see by. The trees rustled in the breeze but all else was still and silent, bar the occasional shout that echoed out across the night from the village behind me. Albert had been right when he said that he felt as if his whole time at the Front had been spent digging through mud. Lying prostrate on the darkened road, I was once more slithering through the slime, feeding out wire from the reel, inching ever nearer to the advance posts somewhere out there in the black: the Ashby, Loughborough and Coalville as we called them at Ypres, the Hinckley, Great Glen, and all the others at the Somme.

Ahead of me a train appeared where the Great Northern Line rose out from a deep cutting and ran along a high embankment. The lights from the carriages shone with spectacular brilliance in the night sky, their speed and elevation mimicking the blazing trail of a celestial shooting star, a comet foretelling the greatest of births! I watched as the train disappeared into a cutting, only to reappear a mile or two further down the line towards Leicester.

Lying there, with the train in the distance, I could now see that there was a large house in front of the railway embankment ahead. This I have since been told is Ingarsby Old Hall. Its lights must have beckoned me for I found myself wandering over a most uneven field, with rubble and stonework sticking out rudely from the soil like well-grounded molars. Sheep stood silent and ghastly in the sickened moonlight, hardly stirring as I brushed past them. I crawled over into a small cattle shed in the corner of the field, the night air now strangely filled with the sound of music and singing. Fearing discovery, I rolled up into the corner of the empty shed and fell straight asleep.

Of course I do not believe in ghosts or the supernatural, Father, although I have met many that profess a certain interest. The farm lad who eventually woke me early in the morning was kind enough to explain, after his preliminary inquiries, that the field was in fact the site of the old village of Ingarsby, a settlement that has been derelict for many hundreds of years. The sound of busy activity that chased me into the shed during the night must have been no more than an acoustic trick played upon the ear by the cuttings and embankments of the Great Northern Line.

My state of dress was such that when I finally returned to the Black Horse Mr Potter was most alarmed and suspected that I had been involved in a terrible accident. I immediately put him at his ease by explaining that I had gone for a midnight stroll and had got lost in the pitch black of the night. I had thus found shelter in a disused barn. Although less than convincing, I managed to retreat to my own room where I immediately collapsed on the bed and slept until mid afternoon, when Mrs Potter woke me with a cup of tea and some biscuits. She was relieved to find that I was much recovered.

As I sit and write these final words it is now well past midnight and I feel tiredness is at last catching up with me. I am unsure what I will do tomorrow. Perhaps what I am attempting is mere folly and I should be homeward bound like one of Albert's pigeons. It certainly seems the most attractive of options. But I have promised that I shall not decide anything until tomorrow, after one of Mrs Potter's hearty breakfasts.

And so to bed. I leave you in the knowledge that I am safe and well and trust that you are the same.

All my love,
John

PART FIVE

Durham Category 'A' Prison

Present Day, Late October

—1—

I do not talk about my mother. I have told this to Dr Sanders many times, of course, but still he persists. I assume he thinks my relationship with my mother holds the key to breaking down the blankness he is faced with every Tuesday. It is all a game, and I know the rules. Yet, despite the challenges, I am sure he enjoys the opportunity to spar with an intellectual equal. He must have to deal with some particularly inferior specimens. But Dr Sanders and I are men of the academic world, something he practically admitted this morning. I recall watching his head as it nodded in a seemingly involuntary way to the changing cadence of my voice.

Of course, only with a pink elephant.

Dr Sanders stopped doodling in his notebook and at last raised his eyes to mine. I beg your pardon, he said.

I did not reply but merely returned his gaze with a quizzical look that I know can be most effective.

I'm sorry. I didn't mean to give the impression that I wasn't listening. On the contrary, I value these little talks of ours enormously.

Those were his very words: *I value these little talks of ours enormously*. Now you may think that this in itself is nothing, a mere pleasantry perhaps, an empty gesture. But I can assure you that Dr Sanders does not work with such clichés.

Sometimes I'm not sure who is analysing whom at these sessions. Dr Sanders is very much aware of my abilities and this gives our interaction a certain frisson. For instance, I know that Dr Sanders is married, but I would suggest unhappily. He has a dog and at least two children. Though naturally conservative in nature, he has a rebellious, almost school-boyish quality that again indicates a repressed relationship at home. He, too, is interested in history. I do not know why he brought in the pictures this morning. Photographs I had never seen. History. I like history, Dr Sanders. I remember telling him so distinctly as I pushed the photographs away.

Tell me about them.

The past is all around us, Dr Sanders. Walk across any field and you will be standing on the flotsam and jetsam of two thousand years of history. Strange barrows and earth-works undulate the surface; flint arrow and axe heads rub shoulders with Roman pottery and Anglo Saxon coins. It's all there in the dirt, just scratch away at the surface, wash away the grime and there it is. The artefact in all its glory.

Who took these?

Perhaps I shouldn't have mentioned Great Stretton. I certainly think it caught Dr Sanders off guard. To tell the truth I had forgotten its current notoriety. In my mind

Great Stretton is still an abandoned village lost in the obscurity of the rolling fields of the East Midlands. It's still the village that I used to visit on those rare occasions. It's hard to imagine the tiny church of St Giles swarming with police and journalists, their hardened faces peering through those tiny windows. I had forgotten that since the body was found the image of St Giles has become iconic, appearing in all the papers, the stout Saxon tower sticking up mournfully into the grey clouds. I'm sure I do not need to tell you that it was my idea to place the girl there.

You left your mother when you were sixteen. Where did you go? Were you on the streets?

Let's not dwell on such unpleasantness. The church at Great Stretton of course has fascinated local historians, such as me, for many years. Indeed, deserted medieval villages in general have gained something of a celebrity status within the world of medieval and archaeological studies. Leicestershire has its fair share of these. Hamilton comes to mind of course, but perhaps one of the best known is Ingarsby, on the road from Houghton-on-the-Hill to Hungarton. A renowned expert, whose books I have read, once described Ingarsby as the best lost village in the county. Indeed, the high, uneven fields do make the village's layout easier to reconstruct, although this is certainly best done from the air. As you may know, Ingarsby was founded by Danish settlers in the ninth century, close to a Bronze Age highway, and at one point could boast a castle that must have dominated the ancient road that ran close by from Leicester to Stamford. Perhaps the village failed to recover from the ravages of the Black Death, but in 1469 the end was finally reached when Ingarsby was officially enclosed for pastureland. Depopulation followed.

There's no record of you ever working until your job at the fish wholesalers. There's no record of you at all between the ages of sixteen and thirty-seven. Who were you with? What did you do? Did you attack girls then?

You must understand that for much of the succeeding four hundred years there was little to suggest that a village had existed on this isolated spot, apart from the Old Hall, a three-storey Tudor house built on the site of the Roman camp that pre-dated the Danish period. The village was given a brief reincarnation when a small railway station appeared just to the north. The Ingarsby and Houghton station did little more than serve the surrounding villages and quickly disappeared in the Beeching cutbacks of the early 1960s. Yet even today there is still a lonely signpost that points to the station, as if, at any moment, a steam train might emerge from the cuttings and its whistle ring out across the buried ruins of the lost village of Ingarsby.

The small, squat church of St Giles, Great Stretton, is not far away, no more than a couple of miles to the south-west. Its village has long since crumbled into the Leicestershire clay but the church remains. Close by is the old Roman road, Via Devana, running as straight as a train line through the gently rolling hills. I have never found this road's beginning or end, but have often thought of all the people that would have passed by in ages past, looking up at St Giles and its huddle of surrounding houses, shining out in the gloom of a winter's storm. Those houses are now gone, of course, and they have been gone for many centuries. Why the village sank into the earth, no one appears to know.

You only came back to Great Glen once your mother was dead. What do these pictures make you think?

I assume Dr Sanders knew that only a few hundred metres away to the south lies another lost village, that of Stretton Magna, where its most famous son, Robert de Stretton, who rose to become Bishop of Coventry and Lichfield, established a chantry in 1378. Nothing remains of this site.

Great Glen lies about a mile to the south of these forgotten pieces of Leicestershire's history. There is a little-known path that leads from the north-western tip of Great Glen, running parallel to the River Sense, past the lost village of Stretton Magna. This path eventually meets Gartree Road, the old Roman road, but it is easy enough to leave the path to the left before this point and climb the short hillock on which St Giles rests.

Although the church is situated within its own tiny field gilded by a protective hedge, one can slip through into the enclosure and wander among the remaining headstones that sprout like mushrooms within the dark, bleak shadow of St Giles. The grass has grown long, and many headstones have either fallen down to be suffocated by vegetation or have acquired oblique angles, curiously refuting the perpendicular of its sheltering tower. Not far from the church, to the south, lies a strange earthwork, a series of

undulations that suggests the one-time existence of a large
moated area enclosing an island. Above this area, towards
the church, there still exists the large pond which must
have supplied the moat with water, while below it can be
found a smaller depression, which would have been used
for drainage purposes. Research suggests that this was the
site of a medieval hall, possibly connected with the Stret-
tons or Herricks, but no one really knows.

Early one morning, not long after my return to Great
Glen, I was able to make a full survey of the site, which
included listing all the names on the gravestones. Some of
these had lost all their inscriptions, of course, washed
away over countless winters, while others were ambiguous
enough to warrant their omission from my census. But on
that cold spring morning I was able to collect nineteen
names, together with assorted detail, including age, year of
death and marital status.

It was while undertaking this survey that I discovered
a means of entering the church. I had always assumed of
course that since the church door was kept firmly sealed,
the interior of St Giles would always remain out of reach.
It was therefore with great delight that I found the means
of my illicit entry. Let me state immediately that although
I would not condone such an approach by the general
public, there is certainly a case to be made that professional
researchers should never be held to ransom by a heavy lock
and key. Of course, trained experts have the skills to ensure
that the integrity of any site is not compromised; and so
when I discovered the wooden board, it was with some

justification that I immediately began to lift it from the position it had obviously kept for many undisturbed years.

The discovery of the board was completely serendipitous. I think I first stood on it accidentally as I was moving through the churchyard. It splintered and cracked under my weight. I remember tearing at the long grass to reveal its full form: a wooden panel, three feet along each side, sunk to ground level about five feet from the eastern wall of the nave. Levering it out of its position was not easy but it eventually succumbed, revealing a dark, alluring hole. Bending down, it was possible to see that the cover had been protecting entry into a small subterranean chamber. From the limited light, I could see that the walls were hewn from stone, and, apart from a layer of soil and other debris, the mysterious room appeared empty.

It was with some trepidation that I dropped down into the chamber, slowly lowering myself from the edge of the portal until the final moment when I fell the remaining three feet. I landed with a muffled thud and gasp. For a moment or two I stayed crouching as the damp, fetid air enveloped me. I recall that noises from the world above were strangely absent, and indeed the sound of my own heavy breathing simply withered within the ponderous atmosphere of this black cube. As my eyes grew more accustomed to the feeble light, not helped by the overgrown grass that smothered the gap above me, I began to make out a few distinctive features. The room itself was a perfect square, the walls constructed from rough blocks of stone which equally lined both floor and ceiling. Indeed, my entrance appeared to be no more than an attempt to secure an area of the roof where the stonework had collapsed. As I gazed at the ceiling, running my eye over the trailing roots that poked through the masonry like stalactites, I came across a small black void on the far side of the chamber, closest to the church. Moving towards it, I quickly realized that it could only lead up into the nave of St Giles itself.

It was only when I was standing beneath this second hole that I felt the silent movement of air, the softest of expellations running against my skin, as though the church itself was stirring into life. Looking up, I could discern the barest striations of light and dark as the morning sun crept into the barren nave above me.

It did not take much effort to pull myself up. The edge of the tiny gap was easy enough to hold on to, although it was with some relief that I eventually collapsed onto the ancient stone floor of the church. The first thing I noticed was the sound of my heavy breathing falling limply to the floor, muffled by a silence that had been undisturbed for many years; that, and the limited light that struggled through the single triangular windows on either side of the nave. The stone floor was covered with dust and dirt and so it was in some haste that I clambered to my feet.

The church itself had a most simple structure, consisting of nothing more than a small nave and chancel to the south. The two windows, as I have said, were located on the east and west walls of the nave. There were no pews or altar or indeed any ecclesiastical adornment. Rather, St Giles existed as nothing more than an empty stone shell, a theatrical medieval prop raised up upon a hill, steadfastly guarding its tiny brood of broken gravestones. I slowly walked round the darkened nave, running my hand over the crude surface of the walls. They were ice cold. The small windows were set deep within the stonework and offered poor views across the Leicestershire countryside. The wooden door at the far side of the nave was firmly sealed. I turned round and looked back at the chancel, wondering how many people had crowded into this small, hallowed place. All those people buried outside must at some point have come through that very church door and stood upon this floor just as I was now doing. I felt strangely moved by the sudden intimacy with the inhabitants of this lost village, and I do believe I shed several tears before moving back to the black hole in the floor.

I left as carefully as I had entered, making sure that the wooden board was securely replaced and covered with grass as though it had never been disturbed. I looked about but could see no one. The fields were empty, as was Gartree Road meandering close by. Far off I could see the spire of the church in Great Glen, and it was towards this that I eventually set off through the early morning sunshine.

I have told Dr Sanders that I took much solace from my early visits to the church.

2

The first time Jim came over to my house there were no fish tanks and few books. Over the months, however, things changed, and by the time of Jim's next visit he was particularly fascinated with the aquariums that I had put in each room. I remember him crouching in the lounge before the four-foot tropical that had only just been set up. The plants were green and luscious, the fish bright-eyed and active, and there wasn't a trace of algae or brown scum. All was fresh and new. I watched as he placed his great blubbery finger on the glass, trying to summon the fish as if he were Neptune.

Jim and I didn't see each other for some time after Hinckley. I carried on as best I could but of course things were now very different. I studied the papers and watched the television. I searched the Internet. I maintained vigilance by the window. But nothing happened. There was no word of what we had done. There was a silence, a void into which we had dropped, a challenge to continue as before.

It was some weeks before he appeared one day at my

back door, in full battle dress. I let him in. He placed his spear and shield on the kitchen table by the fruit bowl. His metal helmet sported a fine red crest. His feet were in sandals and a small dagger was slung around his midriff. He wore a red tunic that I had often seen in history books. Jim explained that he was Petronius Fulvius. I watched as he lifted off his helmet, placing it under his arm before running fingers through his damp hair. It was a warm day and he looked tired.

Jim explained that he was a member of a re-enactment society. There was to be a Roman skirmish at Bosworth Battlefield Country Park. Such things proved popular with the tourists during the holiday weekend. His was to be just one small re-enactment among many. The highlight would be the Wars of the Roses, with a 'Have a Go Archery' session run by the Bowmen of Bosworth. I invited him to sit down at the kitchen table. I pulled out a chair and watched as he placed his shiny helmet on top of his shield. His tunic rose above his knees, revealing gnarled, hairy legs.

He asked what I had been doing since our last encounter. I shrugged my shoulders and simply stated that I had been keeping my head down.

I haven't heard anything. It wasn't reported anywhere, he said. Jim looked earnestly at me.

I've heard nothing, I replied.

I watched as he replaced the helmet, picked up his shield and spear, and marched out of the house, down the driveway, his sandals making no sound on the gravel.

*

It would be true to say that Jim became fascinated with the Internet. He would come over and spend hours in front of my computer, occasionally clicking the mouse that so easily disappeared in his huge sweaty palm. At first it was just images and text. Searches, that sort of thing. Sometimes he would print out a few pages on my inkjet and take them away with him. As he got used to it I was able to leave him alone.

On reflection this was a mistake. However, one can never foresee all eventualities. Not with someone like Jim. It was a Saturday morning, I do remember that. It was a week or two after we had started meeting up again after Hinckley. Jim had come over to my house and was upstairs on the computer. Since it was Saturday I was cleaning out the smaller of the tropicals in the lounge when I heard a roar of laughter explode from upstairs and the stamp of excited feet thumping exuberantly on the floorboards of the spare room. In an instant I knew what was happening. Maybe in some perverse way I had been secretly waiting for this moment. As I ran up the stairs I do recall thinking that perhaps it was a surprise this moment had been so long in coming.

From the landing I could see Jim at the desk through the open door of the spare room. He did not look up as I entered but hunched closer to the screen, chuckling.

What are you doing? I enquired, my voice belying nervous tension. I was now behind him. Although his head and shoulders partly obscured my view, I could see that the screen was empty apart from one small area.

I'm speaking to Diamond Lucy. Apparently she thinks I'm someone called Smiler. That wouldn't be you, by any chance, would it? Jim turned round and gave me one of his cruel leers.

I pulled over the spare chair and sat next to him. I was eager to read what he had been writing on the screen. After all, Diamond Lucy was a friend that I'd cultivated over many weeks and I certainly didn't want such friendship ruined by a sordid inquisition from Jim.

Diamond Lucy: Hi there Smiler! U R up early!

Diamond Lucy: R U OK? Didn't get a response.

Smiler: I AM FINE.

Diamond Lucy: Where R U? Things R slow.

Smiler: AT HOME. WHERE ARE YOU?

Diamond Lucy: @ home. Every1s gone out! Wish u were here!

It was at this point that Jim had let out his depraved squeal. Diamond Lucy's comment had not received a reply and the cursor was blinking expectantly on the line below.

What should I say, Smiler? Jim was now watching me closely as though observing me for the first time.

Just be careful. This is not a joke.

Oh really! And can I ask who exactly Diamond Lucy is?

She's just a friend. I met her online.

Of course this was guaranteed to confuse our erstwhile cyber-surfer. The Internet he had obtained some primitive grasp of, but as for online chat rooms and discussion groups, such things had yet to fall within his realm of consciousness.

And how exactly did you do that?

Diamond Lucy: R U OK? R U still there?

Just through a normal chat room. You know, the sort of thing you get anywhere on the Internet.

This was rather cruel, as I knew Jim would have little idea about such things. I grabbed the mouse and moved the keyboard onto my lap. Let's take the caps off, shall we?

Smiler: I am fine. Am missing u.

Jim watched with amusement as my words appeared on the screen. How does it work? he asked. Is she seeing what you type?

Of course. That's the whole point. Look, it even tells me when she's typing her reply.

We both watched and waited. Sure enough, after about fifteen seconds, a reply magically appeared on the screen.

Diamond Lucy: Am missing U 2 ☹. What R U doing?

Does she write like that to save time? Jim asked.

You do it if you want to be cool online. The same goes for the emoticons. I pointed to the smiley face on the screen.

This is amazing. I remember Jim shaking his head, seemingly in disbelief. Then he turned round to face me while placing his hand on the back of my chair. But who is she? How did you meet her?

Smiler: I am working on homework ☺. What R U doing 2day?

I first met her in a different chat room. You've got to understand that what you're seeing here is a private communication between Lucy and me. When I first met her, however, I was in a public chat room that I happened to be exploring one evening.

So what happened? Jim rocked back on his chair while his eyes anchored themselves to my face. He looked like a recalcitrant schoolboy, wallowing in smut.

Well, it's hard to explain if you don't understand chat rooms . . .

I understand them all right. It's not exactly nuclear physics is it, Einstein.

He may not have called me Einstein on that occasion – my memory is not unusual in that it can be guilty of rare mistakes. However, it became Jim's habit to call me by this name whenever he wished to belittle my academic training and insight. Whether he used the name at that moment or not, it was certainly during such occasions that he often did. I, of course, tried hard to ignore his childish games. The very fact that he used the term was itself a victory – recognition, if you will, of my de facto intellectual abilities. However, I would be lying if I said that it did not leave some unpleasantness between us.

Well, since you're the expert I see little need to go into much detail. Suffice it to say that Lucy and I met in this public chat room and decided that we should establish a more private form of communication via proprietary chat room software. To this end I set up this facility you see before you, which allows me to talk online to her directly.

But who is she?

Diamond Lucy: Not much. Parents gone out shopping. Will stay home and watch videos. R U alone?

I recall finding this line of questioning unsettling and, frankly, unnecessarily intrusive. Although I had tried to remain calm, Jim's uncouth behaviour was rather galling, made worse by the fact that he was in my home using my equipment. Jim must have seen something of these thoughts flash across my face.

Come on. You can tell me, he coaxed.

I'm not sure I should. Lucy deserves some privacy and respect.

Oh yes, of course she does, smirked my companion. I shouldn't have told him but in the end I did. Jim was always expert at extricating information. He could suffocate you with his presence. But before I gave him the details, I had to make sure that he was aware of the subtle differences that existed between real and virtual personalities.

Online you can be whoever you want to be. It's not cool to be yourself. This is not just about email but about moving to an alternative plane.

Thinking back, I seriously doubt Jim understood the implications of my address. His smirk faded and his forehead became furrowed. I continued: Normally, all I would know about Diamond Lucy is what she decided to tell me, and that could be anything.

And the same applies to you, which is where your little game begins.

Jim's coarse retort still echoes in my mind. It was an ugly sentence conjuring up such a miserable picture that for a second or two I do believe I was stunned into silence.

Well, not quite. This is all quite innocent.

Smiler: Yes ☺. Wish U were here with me.

I recall vividly that Jim refused to believe any protestations of innocence, prising out, with the experience of an inquisitor, the detail he sought. Diamond Lucy was a schoolgirl called Lucy Hetherington. She lived in Stamford and was fifteen years old. She was currently studying for her GCSEs. She was very good at foreign languages, especially French. She had a brother called Jonathon and a sister Charlotte. They lived in a big house and often went on holidays abroad. She also liked history.

Jim listened to this with a deadpan expression. The smirk had now totally disappeared and the four legs of his chair stayed firmly rooted to the carpet.

And who does she think you are?

Diamond Lucy: Can U fall in love online?

I placed the keyboard and mouse back on the table in front of the monitor. You've got to remember it's like a game. This is all a bit of fun – it's not serious.

You said yourself you can be anyone online. So who do I see before me: a young heart-throb, an all-action hero, a Hollywood star?

Jim enjoyed being cruel and this was a situation ideal for him. He could give his sadism full rein.

It was neither here nor there that Lucy was under the impression I was a seventeen-year-old boy named John. As I have repeatedly tried to explain, normal conventions do not apply to the virtual world of the Internet. In this sense my actions were not those of an impostor or fraud but simply someone who was using the Internet in the most appropriate manner. This I tried to explain to Jim who, despite my vigorous lecture, appeared unable to grasp the implications.

What else does she think you do?

Maybe I went too far by showing him the file. But at this point I do believe a certain amount of professional pride drove me onwards. Looking back, I can fully understand my actions. After all, now that Jim had been introduced to Lucy, it was necessary to make him aware of the methodology underpinning the rather simplistic communication he saw flashing across the screen.

The computer file contained no more than certain biographical details about 'Smiler' that had developed over the few weeks Lucy and I had been communicating. As I explained to Jim, such recording was necessary so that a catastrophic mistake would not be made during the course of any communication. There's no need here to be troubled with the full contents of that document. Suffice it to say that Jim, in his own way, was once again struck dumb by the precision of my modus operandi.

Before I could intervene, Jim's hands were working across the keyboard.

Smiler: I love you. I think of you all the time.

You shouldn't have sent that. Smiler would never have said anything so crass, I explained.

This was the case, of course. Smiler was a character created over many hours of interaction. My biographical file was the 'double helix' holding his short life together. Yet Smiler was far more than that. He was also the words and sentences that appeared on the screen. Indeed, for Lucy in Stamford, this was all that Smiler ever was. Although Jim didn't understand, I had developed a style for my character, certain words and phrases, grammatical fingerprints if you will, that were as individualistic as a wink of an eye or a roguish grin. In this sense my on-screen characterization was done with the finest of paintbrushes, drawing out that indefinable detail upon which perceptions of reality rest. As I watched Jim's fist descend onto the return button to send his message, I felt the anguish that an artist must feel when he has caught an apprentice using a cake slice to daub paint on his masterpiece.

Well, let's just see what happens, shall we? Jim leaned back, his hands folded behind his head as though he really were an artist, critically analysing his creation.

I found myself doing exactly the same. Both of us sat and watched as the cursor flashed with the divine certainty of a pulsar. How would Lucy respond to this crude epistle?

Diamond Lucy is writing appeared on the screen.

It looks like we're going to get a response at least, observed Jim with obvious delight.

I shook my head. Once again I had allowed Jim to take over. Although one does not like to recall such things, I distinctly remember suffering a comparable sense of impotence during the Hinckley debacle. Here I was once more, pushed to one side, watching Jim manipulate and distort my life for his pleasure. I thought of Lucy sitting in her bedroom in Stamford. The house was empty, maybe there was a cup of tea by the computer. A cat on her lap? No, rather a big black dog outside, running round the large, open garden.

Jim laughed out loud and rubbed his hands. I looked at the screen.

Diamond Lucy: I think of U 2. I have fallen in love with U!

What a pair of lovesick birds we've got here, eh? bellowed Jim as he slapped me on the back. What shall we do with them? Get them to have Internet sex?

I cringed at the coarseness of Jim's humour. Perhaps it's best we sign off now. You've already advanced the character much further than I had intended.

Don't be ridiculous. This is just getting interesting. This Lucy is a fascinating girl. Jim's fingers began to hammer across the keyboard and all eyes once more returned to the screen.

Smiler: I want to meet you. I want to see your lovely eyes.

What are you doing? Why have you mentioned her eyes?

Smiler's in love and that's what you do when you're in

love. Jim turned to give me one of his winks: Not that you'd know of course.

What if she says she wants to meet him? What do we do then?

Then we arrange for her to meet him. Smiler's very keen for a meeting, you know. And then he said something that started alarm bells ringing: It's lucky I found out about this, otherwise you would have had Smiler languishing in his bedsit for ever.

That feeling of impotence was now overwhelming. Jim must have read my feelings because he immediately placed the keyboard on his lap, far away from the reach of my own fingers. Look, Lucy is responding, he said.

Shortly after, her reply appeared on the screen.

Diamond Lucy: OK. Where?

Well, what do you think, Batman? asked Jim, turning to me.

I must admit I was rather surprised by the enthusiasm implicit in Lucy's reply. I had expected her to show far more reticence. Indeed, it was such circumspection that had typified our communication up until Jim's intrusion and had acted as a natural foundation upon which the relationship had been built.

Where does Smiler live?

In Leicester, I responded. Jim's fingers immediately set to work.

Smiler: I could come to Stamford.

I suppose Smiler and Lucy were always destined to meet at some point, but I would have hoped for a more romantic Cupid than the ogre who was now orchestrating proceedings.

I looked at the screen. Lucy was not writing a response yet. Obviously the suggestion was less than straightforward.

She might want to meet on neutral territory, as it were.

Jim looked at me. That might be wise anyway, he said.

She did mention a trip to Rutland Water once. I remember because she said how much she had enjoyed it. She went alone and walked around the reservoir. She told me all about it the next day. She may even have said that I should have been there with her.

Well, that's it then. We'll meet her at Rutland Water.

Jim went quiet. I could see that he had turned to gaze out of the window. I suppose the issue is exactly where, I suggested.

Indeed. We need to pick a place that's appropriate for us.

That term, *appropriate for us*, sent a shiver down my spine. Once again the veiled crudity of Jim's enthusiasm came to the fore. I recall wondering exactly what Jim had in mind. I had already seen what he was capable of, and I was concerned that he was once more gearing himself up for another attack. This need not have been the case, of course, and maybe at this early stage I was able to quickly assuage my concerns by believing that Jim had nothing more in mind than a simple track and follow. I find it hard to stop subsequent events from colouring my recollection

of these occurrences, but I do believe that at this preliminary stage the full depravity of Jim's intentions had not
materialized. This is not to completely exonerate my part
in what subsequently happened. I would not be so churlish
as to suggest such a thing. However, I do believe my actions
should be judged by degrees – my role was one that
developed over time and was not something fashioned in
the fires of that first instance. You may know by now the
power that Jim can hold over people – it was a surprise to
learn that I was not the first. Although not a justification, I
should say that on reflection I was like a fly in a monstrous
web: the more I wriggled the more I found myself held
tight before the advancing spider.

Diamond Lucy: OK. We could meet by the river.

Smiler: I have a better plan. What about we meet at Rutland
Water?

Diamond Lucy: Gr8 idea! I could get the bus. Where shall we
meet?

Smiler: What about by Normanton church, say ten o'clock on
Saturday?

Diamond Lucy: OK. C U then. HsAKs.

Jim of course was exceedingly pleased with his morning's work. I remember that in the evening we had a drink
at the local pub. All evening he talked about nothing else.
He wanted to know about the technology that allowed
people to communicate in this way; he wanted to know

how easy it would be for him to join a chat room. This line of questioning greatly alarmed me, of course. At least when he was operating on my computer I was able to keep a careful watch on his activities. However, I do remember that it was during this particular evening that he first mentioned the possibility of getting a computer himself. I spent some time trying to put him off the idea. I may well have inflated both the costs and the complexity of the installation.

Unlike Jim, I was far more alarmed about what had been set in motion. In particular, I was keen to review the developing game plan for possible weaknesses and flaws. To put it bluntly, as I did to Jim on that very evening, it was necessary for us to ensure that, whatever happened, we would be able to evade culpability. Thus it was that Wednesday afternoon saw me driving from the fish wholesalers to Rutland Water.

The purpose of this journey was clear: I needed to draw up a feasibility study for Saturday's operations. Perhaps foolishly I parked in one of the main car parks, it only occurring to me as I climbed out to check for hidden security cameras. There weren't any, something that I did not fail to note on my miniature tape recorder. From the car park I carefully made my way to the tiny Normanton Tower that sits on the water's edge, not far from Normanton Park Hotel. As I stood before the tower, I fished around in my plastic bag for a certain book that was just one of several academic monographs I had brought with me. The book in question was called *Leicestershire Past and Present* and had become a most important intellectual crutch to me over the last few days of frenzied research. I have it here in front of me now, the book being one of the few possessions that I have been allowed to take with me into this dungeon.

I turn to page eighty-three as I did then. By the early eighteenth century Sir Gilbert Heathcote was one of the most successful merchants this country had seen. He had numerous trading ventures across the world, being an early supporter of the new East India Company and one of the founders of the Bank of England. In 1702 he became an Alderman of the City of London and finally Lord Mayor in 1711, being the last Lord Mayor to ride on horseback in his procession! Although a man of fabulous wealth, he was renowned for his parsimony, to the extent that his flouting of the charitable act drew comment from the Pope. Even Voltaire could not resist using Sir Gilbert as an archetype of the opulent merchant in his critique of the Royal Society of London.

In the early eighteenth century Sir Gilbert bought a large estate in the County of Rutland from the Mackworth family. The village of Normanton stood close by, and so it was here, in the small church of St Matthew's, that the great mogul was eventually laid to rest in 1733. However, in 1764 the village of Normanton was destroyed as Sir Gilbert's son extended the estate and its parkland. The church remained, but the village that had once flourished around it was removed for ever.

I recall looking up from this very page and walking along the little causeway that led up to the church, sticking out as it does on a promontory into the lake. When the waters came in the 1970s, Normanton Church was found to lie just below the proposed water level. A great rescue operation was undertaken that saw the church raised up on a plinth of rock and soil, allowing the waters of the reservoir to lap safely around its foundations. The long-forgotten remains of the village, however, disappeared beneath the tide.

By this time, of course, the great estate of the Heathcotes had long gone. After years of decline the estate had been eventually sold off in 1924 and Normanton Hall, standing for so long on the hill overlooking the valley, was demolished in 1926, save the stable block, which is now part of Normanton Park Hotel. Normanton church thus became the sole survivor of both village and estate. Peace and quietude returned to the valley until the surveyors arrived, brandishing their theodolites. And only then did the sleeping bones of Sir Gilbert, and the other inhabitants of Normanton, stir as they were gathered together and removed before the rising waters consumed them for ever.

The church, or Normanton Tower as the de-consecrated building is now called, includes a small display that tells the history of Rutland Reservoir. I paid the entrance fee and wandered slowly around the various displays, which included the bones of an Anglo-Saxon skeleton found during excavation. At the very back of the tower was an enclosed area in which a short video was shown in a continual loop. It described how the reservoir was built, and there was footage of huge mechanical diggers driven by long-haired men in hard hats over a limitless sea of mud.

I left the tower and wandered further along the water's edge. I brought out my digital camera and started preserving a few of the images around me. Rutland Water is now the largest man-made lake in Britain, comprising thirty thousand million gallons covering approximately 3,100 acres. It was located on the site of what once was the Gwash valley. In 1976 the Gwash was dammed, and more water pumped in from the Rivers Welland and Nene. Thousands of acres disappeared beneath the advancing waters. Lanes and cottages. Paddocks and garden sheds. Nether Hambleton was completely lost, Middle Hambleton only partially so. Upper Hambleton survives, forced out on a thin peninsula across the reservoir.

As I looked out across to Upper Hambleton, there were a number of small boats bobbing up and down on the waters. I could only just make out the tiny figures struggling to control them. I watched as they skidded over the glittering surface, the sails flapping prodigiously in the breeze. I estimated that these boats could well be circling over the submerged hamlet of Nether Hambleton. What strange flying craft they were, gathering like starlings over the silted roof tops and frozen trees below, uplifted on nothing more than the great tide of History.

I moved further on around the darkening water. There were few people and so I was able to go about my business with little or no interruption. Quickly speaking into the microphone, I made a note of cafés, car parks and toilets.

I made notes on the various walks around the reservoir and the woods and coppices through which they passed. I recorded notable flora and fauna, taking pictures of all-important features and specimens, as though I were writing my very own *Perambulations*.

3

Jim wanted to meet me at his house on the Friday evening. I had already decided not to tell him about my subsequent communication with Lucy. It was enough that I had spoken to her and had confirmed that she was still intending to meet me.

When I arrived at Jim's I was immediately led upstairs into the loft. As I passed through the house, I caught sight of Julie sitting on a chair in the back garden, enjoying the evening sun. She didn't hear us as we walked through the lounge and disappeared upstairs.

The table was covered with miniature figures. As the neon tube buzzed overhead and the floorboards creaked beneath our feet, I peered carefully at the figures and saw that they were a collection of mounted knights, archers, pikemen and foot soldiers. I picked one of these up at random. It weighed almost nothing as I held it between my thumb and index finger.

Fancy a game?

I looked up. I don't know how.

It's simple. It'll test your tactical abilities. Who do you want to be?

I must have looked rather bemused because Jim moved forwards and took the small mounted figure from my fingers and placed it back on top of a mound under the green tablecloth. Well, that's Richard III, he said.

And so it was that Bosworth Field appeared before me. I was to be Henry Tudor, with the three armies of the Earl of Oxford, Sir John Savage and Sir Gilbert Talbot strung out in a line across Redmoor Plain. On Albion Hill stood the forces of Richard III: the pikemen, archers and field guns of the Duke of Norfolk; the 3,000 heavy cavalry and foot commanded by Richard III himself; and the 3,000-strong force of the Earl of Northumberland. Jim was to be Richard III.

We stood at opposite ends of the table. Jim rolled some dice down Albion Hill that were chased by the forces of the Duke of Norfolk. More dice were thrown, maps and books consulted and calculations compiled. The weather carefully gauged. Men were moved with minute precision, the parabola of cannon balls carefully calculated against the strength of the easterly wind.

And then suddenly, as men lay dying across the hillside and on the heavier soils of the plain, Jim spurred his household cavalry into action in a desperate bid to revert defeat. Thundering through the grass, a glittering array of some 1,500 mounted knights at his side, Jim mortally smashed the forces of Henry in the last great cavalry charge of the medieval era. Henry is cut in two and Richard is declared King of England!

When Jim returned with two cups of tea I began to expound the results of my research. With my army lying destroyed at my feet, I realized that this was the one battle I had to win: the word is mightier than the sword, after all. And so I began to describe to Jim the necessity for planning and strategy. I explained that the good tactician left nothing, absolutely nothing to chance. As I progressed through my conclusions, a vivid image entered my mind. The picture was probably nothing more than an after-effect of the war game, but I do recall that as I began to relate the importance of strategy to Jim, a huge army of knights entered my mind, which, upon the cry of the Crowned King, began to thunder forwards across the plain to the broken ranks of the enemy.

I left my house at 8.30 a.m. I turned the radio off and as I stepped outside I remember hearing the fridge click into life. I placed my bag at my feet and locked the front door, sealing in the faint smell of burning. I walked down to the end of the front garden.

I had spent some time thinking about what I should wear. I had to be as anonymous as possible. I should not be traceable through my attire. These things were all very clear to me. I had written a list of actions. The selection of appropriate garb was near the top, third down in fact, after geographical familiarity and mental preparedness. In the top left-hand corner I had written 'to be destroyed'. One of the first things I had done after getting up was to burn that list.

I was wearing my anorak, a black sweatshirt, a pair of black jeans and white trainers. Nothing to attract attention. I remember thinking that in these clothes I was frictionless. The anorak offered the hood as an item of ultimate disguise. It also had a series of deep pockets within which I could keep my things. I needed my hands free.

I walked across to Jim's house and tapped quietly at his front door. As I did so I realized it was already open. The door swung ajar and I tentatively stepped inside. Jim poked his head round from the kitchen.

All ready to go, then? he said, or something like that. Jim was not whispering.

I nodded. Yes, I think so, I whispered.

I had planned to run through operational tactics with him before we left his house. But standing there in his hallway I realized I just wanted to get into the car and go. I looked nervously round for Julie. Perhaps she was still in bed in the corner of the lounge.

Jim's head had disappeared back into the kitchen. There was the sound of crockery being placed in the sink. I made out a few words, obviously directed towards Julie, and then Jim appeared in the hallway.

OK, he stated as he closed the lounge door behind him. He was wearing his black leather jacket, blue jeans and brown leather shoes. From somewhere he had also found a baseball cap, and this was now stuck incongruously on his head. There was the tinkle of keys in his hand. I thought of reindeers in the snow.

OK, I whispered back.

We both got into the car without a word. Jim put the key into the ignition and turned. As he did so I remember thinking that if the car starts first time we'll be successful. The engine turned over and fired up instantly. I sat back in my seat and let Jim lead me to the water.

I do believe the governor is relenting. I have told him that my enforced quarantine in the cell is beginning to have adverse psychological effects. I am convinced that this has been verified by Dr Sanders. I have asked for the goggles, of course. With them my solitary confinement would be bearable but instead I am cast adrift with nothing but the slow march of time to keep me company. As you know I am allowed an occasional visit to the library where I spend valuable moments reading and undertaking research, but the available resources are very poor for a man of my intellectual calibre. It has been suggested again that I should receive a prison visitor. Once more I have turned the offer down. I see no point in entertaining a complete stranger. I would rather have no one. As I said to the governor, just let me tend the garden is all I ask. We'll see, was his response, certainly a more positive reply than I have had previously. Maybe if you start to co-operate with Dr Sanders? So that's his game, is it? We should be thinking of bulbs for the spring, was my rejoinder, bringing a slight smile to the governor's lips.

We arrived at the car park at 9.00 a.m. We had hardly said a word to each other during the journey. Jim had even switched the radio on, an obvious sop to conventionality. I couldn't listen to the words, but instead stared out at the passing countryside. Unusually Jim drove far too quickly.

As the engine shuddered into silence we both sat frozen in our seats. I remember moving my arm. The artificial ruffle made by the anorak was as shocking as splintering glass. Around us moaned the gloom of an empty car park. Jim wound down his window. It made a repetitive squeak as though a mouse was trapped somewhere inside the mechanism.

Looks like it's going to be OK. Jim was staring up at the sky, the front of his cap banging against the cushioned upholstery of the roof.

I looked up and saw that the grey clouds were beginning to disperse. A few splodges of blue were clearly visible. Yes, could be a nice day, I replied.

There was a long silence again. I recall that we both watched another car, I think it was a silver Volvo, pull into the car park. It came to a halt not far from us, and we watched as the owners took out three huge dogs and led them away towards the reservoir. My pulse was now racing.

By 9.45 the car park was still relatively empty. This was a great relief to me and, I would imagine, Jim. I checked the contents of my pockets. I'm going to make a move, I said.

OK, I'll come with you.

I had expected this.

We both emerged onto the path that wound its way around the lake. I could see Normanton Tower in the distance to my right. There appeared to be no one near it. The path was also deserted. I argued that these were ideal conditions, although in the master plan I had always envisaged lots more people. I remember feeling very exposed.

We shouldn't be seen together. Lucy won't come if she thinks I'm with you.

OK, I'll drop back. But I won't be far away. For God's sake, put your hood down. She's not going to do anything if you look like Andy Pandy.

I moved forwards towards the tower. Jim hung back. I didn't turn round but presumed he remained at an appropriate distance from me. I could see that one or two people were now walking around the causeway. I was very nervous but didn't stop until I was at the tower. I saw at once that Lucy was not there: there was no sixteen-year-old girl wearing denim. Instead, two middle-aged couples. I remember the relief that flooded through me. Perhaps Lucy wouldn't arrive and we could all go home. I turned round and saw Jim standing by the water just to the side of the causeway. He was watching me closely. His stare was urging me on.

As I walked round the causeway I wondered from which direction she would come. From the end of the causeway I looked along the edge of the lake to see if I could spot her approaching. There were certainly a number of people heading in our direction. It was only then that I considered the possibility that Lucy might not be Lucy at all. Just as Jim and I were playing a game of deception, then so too might Lucy, or Lucy's creator. Why should Lucy be who she says she is any more than Smiler? I looked at my watch. It was almost ten o'clock. Jim was still standing in the same spot. I don't think he had looked away for a moment. I glanced out at the boats. Perhaps Lucy, whoever she was, really wasn't coming.

The museum in the tower was now open. I peered through one of the windows to see if Lucy had gone inside. I couldn't see her but caught sight of the Anglo-Saxon bones in the display unit. I continued round to the front of the tower where I found Jim waiting for me. Like the idiot he was, he had decided to come and speak to me. I looked nervously around in case Lucy was close by but I still couldn't see her.

Try not to look too suspicious. You're pacing. This was Jim talking to me!

There's nothing more likely to cause suspicion than you coming over to speak to me!

Don't worry. She's not here yet. Jim turned round and peered at the main pathway along which we had come. Although this might be her, he quickly added.

Instinctively I turned to look. I immediately realized I shouldn't have done, of course, but it was an involuntary action. It was difficult to make out sufficient detail to be sure. You'd better get back to the shoreline again, I replied.

Yeh, OK. Although I think I fancy another look at the tower first.

And with that Jim walked off along the causeway, looking as though he was just any other tourist. This was in contravention of the Strategic Plan of course. For a moment I stood aghast and wondered whether I should just return to the car. But as I looked back towards the car park, something changed my mind. A girl in denim could now be clearly seen walking briskly towards me.

She came along the lakeside and started to head up the causeway. Her beauty transfixed me. She was just as I had imagined. Her brown hair was blowing in the wind and she had a mesmerizing radiance that, if I close my eyes, I can still feel today. I couldn't move but stood watching her, and waited. She strode right up to me. A delicate cloud of perfume enveloped us. She walked up to me and then past me. The perfume was quickly dispersed by the wind.

It seems foolish, of course. We had never met in the flesh so there was no logical reason why she would recognize me. She was expecting a young, attractive man, the veritable Smiler. But I was Smiler, and it would be misleading of me if I didn't say that I was struck with disappointment as she walked past me for someone else.

It was with some restraint that I held back from putting on the goggles at this moment. My hand may have reached for the pocket, it may even have clasped the optical instruments themselves, but there they remained, in my anorak pocket, at least for the moment. I recall being unable to move for a second or two but when at last I was able to turn round I saw that the girl had stopped just beyond me, at the front of Normanton Tower and was looking back towards the shoreline in the direction from which she had just come. Jim was behind her, leaning nonchalantly against the side of the tower like a fat, ageing James Dean. I started to move towards the girl. She looked at me and smiled. I thought of the goggles. I smiled back and moved on past her. Jim threw his cigarette to the floor and beckoned me round to the side of the tower.

What are you doing? Why didn't you say something to her? I presume that's her.

I guess it is. I peered back at the girl from our position. She still had her back to us, her hair streaming out in the wind.

This is it. You've got to do it now. There are few people around at the moment. It's perfect.

OK. I whispered this.

As I moved away from Jim I reached for the goggles. I shuffled the leather strap down the back of my head. A hand slammed down on my shoulder.

For God's sake, take those bloody things off! You don't want to scare her to death!

Jim didn't understand. He didn't understand the special qualities that the goggles gave, give, me. With them on I knew that Lucy would come with us and that I would be protected. I wanted to explain these things to him but an immense wave of nausea passed over me. I recall simply pulling the goggles from my head and replacing them in the pocket. I turned to face Lucy but she had gone.

She must be round the other side of the church. You'd better go round after her. Jim pushed me back towards the front of the tower that jutted out into the reservoir. As I moved round I felt my anorak fill up with air at this more exposed part of the causeway. Jim was creeping along behind me. Although I didn't look round I could feel his presence. I found Lucy on the other side of the tower, on the eastern edge of the causeway. She was looking plaintively out across the waters. There was no one else on this side. As Jim said, conditions were excellent.

Slowly I edged towards her again. Once more, as I approached, she turned round and smiled.

Excuse me, but are you Lucy?

It's difficult to recollect these things, but I'm sure this is how it all began. Thinking back, I'm not sure what else I could have said. However, I do remember the concern that immediately spread across her face. I remember thinking that she looked so young and innocent.

Yes. Who are you? There was suspicion in her eyes.

I'm Smiler's brother. He's told me to come and meet you. There's been a change of plan.

It is quite possible that I was blurting these sentences out. Stuttering out the words. In fact, thinking more carefully about these events, I am sure this is what happened. I can take no responsibility for this, of course. Without the goggles I was left defenceless.

The plan is now that he will meet you in Oakham instead. He thinks it's a better place. He wants me to give you a lift in my car.

I remember the girl showed some confusion but I was surprised by how easily she took the bait. I even recall feeling sorry for Lucy as her face screwed up with disappointment.

He wants to take you out for lunch. He mentioned something about your birthday. He wants to do things properly.

And so it was that without much encouragement I found myself leading Lucy back along the causeway towards the shore. I saw Jim lurking behind us. He signalled the thumbs-up sign. I quickly looked away.

This walk towards the car is something I will never forget. My heart was pumping frantically, of course, while at the same time I was aware of the strained relationship with my companion. Lucy walked just behind me, making communication rather difficult. I remember turning to talk to her about a number of things, including the wonderful pine trees, but she seemed reticent and rather shy. The wind didn't help, now blowing at such a speed that I was obliged to pull my hood up. As we walked into the car park I mentioned the sunflowers that she had planted in the early spring. She was rather surprised that I knew of such things, but I casually informed her that John was so much in love he had told me all about her.

It was then that Jim came up and pushed her into the back of the car. Things happened very quickly. The Strategic Plan was torn to shreds in an instant. The Schlieffen Plan. Only give me a strong right wing. His dying words, words I thought of as Jim forced her to lie on the back seat. His huge knuckled right hand came down over her mouth. He peeled off his leather jacket just as von Kluck peeled south-east too early, leaving Paris for another time. Fatal! There was no one around us. Jim told me to close the door behind him. I slammed it shut and watched through the glass at his frantic hands.

A car must have rumbled across the gravel because my next memory is of watching a blue mini come towards us. The army of taxis from Paris had arrived! I could see two young men inside. There was a black dog in the back. The mini came closer and closer and stopped next to Jim's. The men were laughing and pointing. Was it at me or at Jim's lumbering form? I'm not sure if I put my goggles on at this point or whether I had done so earlier. But it was certainly through the protective shield of the lenses that I watched Lucy being thrown from the car as Jim lurched into the driver's seat. Lucy lay sprawled on the gravel, but the men in the mini didn't see her because Jim's car lay in between. It was only as Jim drove away that the girl became visible.

I could feel my hood expand in the breeze, cut in half by the leather goggle strap that went around it. I watched the black dog run over and lick Lucy. I walked over to the edge of the car park and disappeared into the bushes, as a line of trenches sprang up from the North Sea to Switzerland.

> O-o-o-h we don't give a fuck
> for old von Kluck
> And all his German
> army . . .

With the goggles on I knew I was safe. Their power was something I had never questioned. But it was during this most inauspicious period that I came to see that, if anything, I had underestimated their potency. For the goggles are a most magical artefact, offering the wearer not only a shield and the power of insight, but also a window on Time itself!

As I ran through the bushes from the car park I sensed this new force surge through me. I was now outside of Time, as you would understand it, for the passing of worldly events was but a blur. I stopped and watched as a tree rose up from a small seed, a great Scots Pine splintering through the canopy hundreds of feet high. There were no people visible through the goggles – as I pushed on through the undergrowth I realized that their lives had no meaning as centuries turned into seconds. The sun had set many times when I came upon Normanton Park Hotel, only now it was Normanton Hall, and I saw the finery of ages long gone. As the light disappeared from the world, an Anglo-Saxon princess led me far into the forests of a forgotten land, her metal jewellery sparking in the light of the moon. I held her hand, and it was she who brought me to safety. When I awoke I found myself alone. The goggles were in my pocket and the waters of Rutland Water glistened serenely below in the darkness of night. I looked out from the top of a small wooded hill. Through the gloom I could see the tops of grizzled treetops, laced with algae, poking through the water. Towards the edge of the lake, a bedraggled chimney pot rudely stuck out from the depths, a small yacht moored to it by a shimmering rope. I realized then that the waters were retreating and that I had to leave this place.

PART SIX

Rutland

1922, Late October

Perambulations of a Soldier: Autumn to Winter
by John Crowe

And so we turn to the dark and unchanging pinewood. From spring to winter it remains the same while other trees across the land bloom and wither. The onset of autumn means little to the evergreen pine. The thick, menacing shadow that sweeps across as we enter the wood is as deep now as it will be at the height of winter, and were it not for the sweet, delicate scent that suddenly pervades the air, we might be tempted to turn back into light.

Moving through the wood we see the Scots Pine in all its stages of growth. The wood has a preponderance of great pines, towering specimens that shut out the light, causing the death of many saplings. Yet so debilitating is the darkness that even these great pines suffer, their lower branches withering and eventually dropping to the ground so that when you get deep into the wood and look up, there is nothing but naked red trunks, disappearing into the canopy as though columns in some monstrous cathedral. So thick is this canopy that it seems hardly any light can steal through the leafy boughs to play upon the needle-strewn floor. Indeed, as we move into the centre of the wood we find little surface vegetation bar the usual collection of fungi, lichens and mosses, the sole creatures of this strange twilight world in which we suddenly find ourselves.

Look at what lies here, close to the base of this mighty

pine. A young rabbit lies dead upon the blanket of brown needles, no doubt killed by a stoat. As I turn the cadaver over with my cane, a black beetle about an inch long tries to regain cover under the needles. And there! Its mate suddenly scuttles out from within the corpse. They are sexton-beetles, an insect that spends its time seeking out the bodies of dead mammals before attempting to bury them. Tonight, when joined by others, they will sink the entire cadaver below ground level before completely covering it with soil. This stops the flesh from decaying, preserving it for their grubs, which hatch from the eggs that are laid upon the corpse before it is fully interred.

But let us move on, away from this grisly scene. Ahead I see a clearing made by several fallen trees, the great shafts of light luring me as if I were a moth, flitting through this sepulchral place.

Rev Cecil Crowe,
The Vicarage,
Great Glen,
Leicestershire

20th October 1922

FROM: *Captain John Crowe, Railway Hotel,*
Oakham, Rutland

My Dear Father,

I hope this letter finds you well. I am both fit and
healthy, if rather tired. I currently have a room at the
Railway Hotel in Oakham that is adequate for my rather
simple needs. Indeed, it has proven itself to be a veritable
centre of hustle and bustle. I have dim recollections of
visiting a certain relative here many years ago when I was
very young. Would this have been Uncle Julian? I seem to
recall a large man putting me on his shoulders at the
station. I watched as you carried the cases away from the
train. There is no reason why I should remember this
scene. It exists in isolation, for I have no other recollection
of the trip, and I am not even certain that it was Oakham
station. However, I recall from some corner of my mind
that you had a brother resident here, although further
detail eludes me. I presume Uncle Julian must have died
before the War?

Certainly the citizens of Oakham appear very proud of
their little county, Rutland, and their own status as

residents of the county town *par excellence* in the Catmose vale. The streets are jammed full of people – residents and tradesmen all going about their business with a quiet air of confidence and satisfaction. My fellow guests at the hotel appear to be a collection of retired gentlemen and businessmen, many of whom I have just left in the lounge discussing the various events of the day, including the unusually warm weather. The pessimists among them are certain that the tropical conditions will break down tomorrow, although this was strongly opposed by an optimist minority which seemed to be holding out hope that these conditions would last until Guy Fawkes Night, no less!

My room is homely, if rather basic, but at least there is a small table at which I can write. Although the hour is late, there is still the intermittent rumble of traffic outside my window, mingling with the singing that drifts across from a nearby public house. Earlier, I found myself listening to these sounds for some time, allowing them to engulf me with their evocations of calming domesticity, as my single candle guttered and danced. Although my mood was hardly dark, I found these emanations immensely restorative, and it was with an equal sense of tranquillity that I washed, my soul further calmed by the simple tinkle of water against the porcelain bowl in the corner of the room.

Since my last letter, Father, I am pleased to inform you that my mood has more generally improved. Indeed, it is with some embarrassment that I recall the solemnity of my previous correspondence. If anything, I have now settled into the routine of my present endeavour with a certain ease, a process aided by the manifestation of the regenerative effects that I envisaged emanating from this 'tour'.

It has been some minutes since I finished the above paragraph. Yet again I have found myself listening to the cocktail of sounds coming through the open window behind the heavy curtains in front of my desk. Over the last quarter of an hour, the guests of the nearby hostelry have been dutifully leaving, taking their melodies and conversation out beneath the cloudless sky. Some have passed beneath my window, their voices loud and coarse, intruding into my dimly lit room like phantoms of the night, fading away into nothing beneath the still and silent stars. A few minutes ago a motor car came roaring down the street, its engine exploding several times, much to the delight of the late-night revellers, who must have been pressed to the walls as the beast stormed past. The beams of its headlights raced across my curtains as though portents of some cosmic calamity.

I watched the darkness return to my room as the car, and the lights of the buildings outside, faded away into the night. But as I lit a second candle with my woodbine I was forced to conclude that in many ways my journey across the East Midlands is leading me out of the darkness. Although rather fanciful, it is as if I have been stumbling within a giant labyrinth, a device of such construction that only in the last two weeks have I begun to edge towards a return to the world I left many years ago.

In contrast, as Angus and I trudged out of Houghton-on-the-Hill early on the morning of the 16th, it seemed that my mood could not get blacker. Indeed, as I ate breakfast in my room an hour or two before this departure, I must admit that I came close to abandoning the entire venture. As I sat listening to the growing traffic outside, the events of the 14th fell like a suffocating layer across my mind. Had I met with Albert the day before, maybe I could have resolved some of the confusion that befuddled my brain. But he did not come to the public house, although I'm sure he knew that I remained a guest. In truth, however, I also stayed hidden, refusing to leave my room for most of the day. Occasionally a voice from the street would drag me cautiously to the window, but Albert was nowhere to be seen, and, as I pondered over the previous night's events, I came to the conclusion that a further meeting would be both unnecessary and painful.

Thus it was that the following morning the solitary figure of Mr Potter waved me goodbye as Angus and I quietly and unceremoniously left the village. My route naturally took me past Albert's little cottage, and although I gave it a glancing look, the door and net curtains remained unmoved. Pushing my cap further over my head, I directed Angus onto the Peterborough Road, where we began to trudge our way eastwards.

Despite the early hour, the sun was warm in front of us, the fields either side of the road covered in silvery mist and dew. Angus appeared much rested and trotted along at a healthy pace. Occasionally a motor vehicle would pass at high speed and Angus would jolt, but soon he became used to such technological intrusion. Given the flatness of the land, dare I say the bleakness of the fields, I found such distraction welcome, even waving at those motor cars that loomed towards us from out of the misty east.

I had spent some time the previous evening planning my route. Mrs Potter kindly brought up a modern road map when she came to collect my plate for the evening meal, and so I was able to fix a route with some degree of accuracy. My passage would take me through Tilton-on-the-Hill and thence to Oakham, from where it would be but a short hop to Nether Hambleton. I expected the journey to take no more than four or five hours at most, dependent of course on how often Angus and I decided to view the scenery. But as we proceeded along the Peterborough Road, and then off along a country lane that would lead us into Tilton, it soon became clear that there would not be much to detain us in terms of panorama. This area is justifiably known as High Leicestershire, and to my eyes, on that sunlit morning, the surrounding country was most bleak and lonely. Distant farmhouses shimmered through the lifting haze, exposing tracks of limitless fields that vanished over the horizon. Deserted villages lay in ruins, crumbling into the soil; mysterious earthworks, moats, mottes, baileys, castle foundations and other remains, echoes from a time now long gone, cover this forgotten part of the country; the Melton to Market Harborough line, snuggled deep in its cutting, follows an ancient track that led across the county; and all around, in constant companionship, the remote and empty hills stared stoically down at our silent progression. It was indeed a most solemn approach to Tilton.

The village was sleepy when we arrived. There was a small public house where the landlord was kind enough to fill a bucket of water for Angus, but all else in Tilton was deserted. Once Angus was refreshed, we moved on through the village and passed out once more into the forlorn landscape. To the south stood a lonely earthwork, perhaps a moat of some sort that once encircled a Bronze Age palace. But Angus and I had no time for such desolation, and we moved out of the village heading due west.

Much of the mist and fog was now gone and, with the village behind us, it was as though we had entered a great chalice of undulating fields, intermittently broken by rippling hills and wooded outcrops. The sun had risen into the sky, its heat causing both Angus and me to sweat profusely.

Not far from Tilton the lane took us over the rail track that dodged and cut its way deeply through the countryside. As we crossed the bridge a single engine passed beneath our feet and we were consumed in warm smoke. I was momentarily taken back to when both Lizzy and I would stand on that little bridge close to Canal Cottage and shriek with delight as the vaporous breath from the mid-afternoon train consumed us, Lizzy pirouetting as though she were an angel chime, caught in the sooty updraught of a candle. Angus and I continued, the lane taking us between two blunt hills that stood on either side of the road as though eroded sentinels of some long-forgotten kingdom.

By midday we had crossed over into the county of Rutland, the forlorn remains of Sanvey Castle watching us across the invisible boundary. We reached the quiet village of Braunston-in-Rutland soon after. Here I stopped at the

Blue Ball, a most attractive public house. Leaving Angus tethered outside, I went within and ordered lunch. From a table at the front of the establishment I was able to look out across the village. Certainly this appeared to be a most tranquil and beatific spot, the settlement being everything that an English village should be, with thatched cottages and broad green oaks. As I stared out, a horse-drawn cart slowly made its way past the low church across the lane, the driver huddled beneath a large straw hat pressed firmly down over his face. Such was my contentment I did not want to leave, and it was with difficulty that I gave some thought to the remaining part of the journey.

From Braunston-in-Rutland I estimated that Nether Hambleton was no more than three or four miles away, to the south-east of Oakham. I thus felt confident in reaching 'Weenie' Simpson's cottage by mid to late afternoon. (Simpson's first name was John, but he always appears to have been known as 'Weenie' to his friends.) As before, I had an old letter in my pocket that Weenie had been kind enough to write to me while he was with the regiment in Germany in early 1919. Here he had expressly given his home address in the hope that I would one day pay him a visit 'in better times', as he himself stated. As I looked out of the Blue Ball, I began to believe that maybe those 'better times' were only round the corner.

Weenie had been the brains of the company. I believe he had been a schoolmaster in his early years, perhaps at a school in Oakham. However, at some point he had gained a large inheritance, which included a cottage in Nether Hambleton, and immediately retired to a life of leisured activity. For Weenie this mostly consisted of following his own scientific inquiries. When the War came, he was one of the first to enlist, grateful, as Weenie himself used to say before we arrived in France, to witness the greatest scientific experiment in the history of empirical endeavour. If I picture him in my mind, Father, I invariably see Weenie bent over by a candle in the officers' mess, his black hair neatly combed, reading one of the many books that kept him sane.

There were times in the trenches when faith, or a belief in our cause, could be put under immense strain, Father. The loss of companions could leave one mentally depleted, vulnerable to invidious speculation and doubt. At such times I found Weenie to be a reliable interlocutor. More than any other man in the company, Weenie had a comprehensive and strategic insight into the campaign, through which he could situate our present activity within the greater whole. His own eugenic theorems were frequently wielded to confront any suggestion of failure. I can still remember one particular evening's diatribe in the officers' mess as we prepared for night-time trench work. A couple of officers, perhaps with more than enough drink inside them, had begun to suggest that the tactics employed by the British could only lead to a withering defeat. In the midst of the resulting debate, Weenie revealed his schoolmaster experience by taking some paper, pinning it to the wall, and listing, in two perfect columns, the racial composition of both Allied and Enemy forces. The system he used to quantify such characteristics escapes me now. I remember sitting in the corner of the dugout, holding my mug of cocoa between my hands with Mother's old rug across my knees, occasionally turning back to look up the wooden stairs and out across the trench, hoping to catch the first sight of Sergeant Hill's swinging lantern. While I waited, I peered through the gloom of the mess and watched as Weenie clarified his argument. One of the old candle lanterns that we used a lot of at that time swung above his head, giving Weenie the appearance of a vaudeville star, trapped in a shifting pool of light around which sat the restless audience. As I watched, Weenie assigned each country a racial index, allowing an aggregated total for Allied and Enemy forces to be somehow achieved. Using a large campaign map that a fellow officer had obtained from one of the British newspapers, Weenie was then able to indicate how vital theatres of the War across the Empire could only end in victory for the racially superior British forces. As I recall it was a most impressive piece of reasoning that certainly induced a round of applause from some of the more supportive officers that sat around the dugout on that particular evening.

Of course I can recall many such instances that demonstrated Weenie's intellectual prowess, and I must admit that as I stared out across the idyllic scene from the window of the Blue Ball, I indulged myself in their recollection. It would not be too much of an exaggeration to state that during the War itself, Weenie became a great support and comfort to me. The long drawn out campaign was a perfect breeding ground for doubt and speculation, as I have already indicated; the brutality of the War could also weigh heavily on the mind. The paradox was that comradeship offered some initial resistance to these emotions. The relationship between officer and men in these conditions could become strong, as my own experience would testify, but equally it was such attachment that made the inevitable losses and mutilations of battle hard to take. I know of officers who deliberately affected a most haughty and distant manner with their men, so that when the inevitable happened, they would not be unnecessarily tortured. This was not my own way, I hasten to add, although there were moments when I came close to wishing it had been. At these dark times it was Weenie who was able to best console me, almost inadvertently. His own confidence in the forward progression of mankind, as explicated by the great scientific endeavours that, even as we fought, were emanating from laboratories across the civilized world, became a sturdy buttress for my own fragile emotions. Of course I prayed, Father, but it should come as no surprise to you that my own faith was a far humbler version of your own. In the midst of War we were in the very teeth of a great secular, rationalist campaign. Technology was all around us – from the aeroplanes and airships in the skies, the tanks and machine guns on the land, to the submarines in the sea. And so perhaps it was not surprising that it was Weenie's technocratic visions that were the greatest consolation to me.

And Weenie spoke of other things, scientific breakthroughs that were changing the way we understood the world. One occasion I remember vividly and I hope you will indulge me, dear Father. Weenie and I found ourselves together in a small outside toilet by a row of cottages on the edge of Villeret, in the Somme region, early spring 1917. It was night and through the wooden door we could see the German searchlights scouring the village, the enemy machine gunners seeding the arch of light with bullets. We had bayoneted two German soldiers outside one of the cottages but had been fired on from an unknown location. It was Weenie who found the small outhouse in which we took shelter, his arm bleeding from a bullet that had grazed his skin. As we stood listening to the sounds of battle around us, Weenie pointed out the various constellations that could be seen clearly over the top of the door. It was then that he mentioned a book that was to feature in many of his conversations throughout the War, a book which, being written in German, few had been able or inclined to read at that time. Albert Einstein has since become a household name but back then, standing together in that limited space, the name was a great unknown. Even now his theories mean little to me and I struggle to recall exactly what they are. But I do remember that special and general relativity were concepts that Weenie spoke about with almost messianic fervour. As we gazed up at the stars during that evening at Villeret, Weenie stated that Einstein had proven that time and space were not absolute constructs, but were dependent on the motion of the observer. He also stated that other theories had demonstrated that gravity itself can affect or warp time and space. We had killed a soldier in the outhouse who was now sat on the latrine between us, his limp head bent to his knees, blood seeping out from the bullet hole in his face. His eyes lay on the floor like pickled eggs. Weenie was using the corpse's back as a convenient table on which to rest his helmet. Weenie must have recognized my difficulty with the situation for he stated in rather more simplistic terms that time and space are different depending on where you are in the universe. I recall his eyes shining in the moonlight as he conceived a most fabulous experiment in which he would be propelled towards the sun in a great rocket, circumnavigating the planets many times. On returning home he would find that though his journey had been but a matter of months, for those left on Earth it had lasted thousands of years, where all trace of his venture had long ago passed into oblivion. Of course, the famous eclipse in 1919 has since proved these theories correct. A Frenchman came out of one of the cottages towards us but was shot almost immediately and so we were not able to leave our position for some time.

Oakham lies not more than two miles from Braunston-in-Rutland and is approached by a most pleasant lane. As I have already written, Oakham itself is a bustling little town, and as we passed through at what must have been two in the afternoon, Angus and I found ourselves surrounded by motor cars and bikes. Progressing eastwards with due haste, we quickly found sanctuary from such technological intrusion on a quieter road that meandered through a deciduous wood. As we emerged back out into the sunshine, the village of Upper Hambleton could be seen in front of us, the low spire of its church most clearly visible.

The village is situated on an isolated hill that looks northwards to the ridge where Burley-on-the-Hill can be seen in its park. The vale of Catmose extends westwards, with Oakham spire in the middle distance, while to the south lays the shallow valley of the Gwash flowing eastward towards Stamford. As Angus and I surveyed the scene, one could well understand why the Anglo-Saxon kings had made Hambleton their capital in Rutland.

We plodded past St Andrew's and the public house, and then dropped down the steep hill to the south that took us alongside Hambleton Hall, a fine late-nineteenth century Gothic building that squats in its estate by the side of the village. The air was very still and peaceful – so peaceful in fact that one could not mistake the tinny squeal of gramophone music drifting across from the Hall. Angus and I momentarily stopped to listen to the strange sound before moving on.

After descending for a short time, I came across a track by some idyllic cottages that led off to the left. Mistakenly I decided to take this route and soon came upon another, more ancient hall, alone amid green rolling fields bar a few farm buildings. Realizing that I had made a mistake in my navigation, I brought Angus to a halt and looked about me. I was in the process of admiring the wonderful views when a farm hand appeared from the shrubberies by the side of the track and asked me if I was a guest of Mrs Astley-Cooper. If so, he explained I should proceed back to Hambleton Hall where the other guests had already arrived. I explained that I appeared to be momentarily lost in my search for Nether Hambleton and was immediately given fresh directions. Thus armed, I bid my friend goodbye and brought Angus about – for the moment at least – turning my back on the old hall and the mysterious happenings of Hambleton Hall.

Nether Hambleton was not far away, nestling further

down in the Gwash valley. The village itself is tiny, consisting of no more than a handful of cottages and farm buildings. This rather took me by surprise to the extent that, before I could gather my thoughts, I found myself outside Weenie's cottage. Even as I dismounted I heard the door open and there in the doorway appeared Weenie. He was exactly as I had last seen him – as wiry as a racehorse, thinning black hair hanging down over large, wild, staring eyes. At first I feared that he hadn't recognized me but as I tethered Angus to the gatepost, I heard a gasp of recognition as Weenie rushed towards me. The memory of that occasion still leaves me weak and emotional. All I will say here, Father, is that the subsequent embrace will be something I recall until my dying day.

Weenie's cottage is a wondrous place. The roof is thatched with golden straw and the gardens left untended, but the overall effect is of a disarming beauty. Weenie was most amused that I was still wearing remnants of my army uniform, even commenting that he wished he had kept certain articles of clothing himself. Inside, all was cool and dark. I placed my old coat and cap on a rocking chair that stood by the door, but kept my trusty camera slung across my back. A black cat that had been asleep on the chair quickly jumped off and ran out into the kitchen. Weenie explained that Alice was his sole companion. He commented that she could disappear for days, despite being almost totally blind.

Weenie, as I have already explained, had been in the lucky position of being able to retire from his former employment as schoolmaster before the outbreak of the

War. His subsequent life of solitary academic pursuits permeated the entire cottage. Numerous bookcases loomed from the shadows of each room, even the kitchen. Books and magazines littered the floor, and strange scientific instruments could be found discarded on tabletops, along with bones, stuffed animals, charts and other mysterious jottings in yellowing journals. As we sat on two wooden chairs outside his kitchen, overlooking the delightful anarchy of his cottage garden, Weenie appeared most eager to learn of my experiences since my enforced hospitalization. I remember we drank several glasses of elderberry wine that Weenie had brewed himself. It was late afternoon and the shadows were lengthening. In the shade it quickly became cold and reminded me that the winter season was not that far away. Still, sitting there, in that little pool of sunlight, with Alice swishing her tail beneath our chairs, her eyes as glazed as marbles, one could believe that the Indian summer was going to continue for ever.

Weenie had stayed with me after my injury during the attack on 26th September. He explained that it had been impossible to move me that night. The shelling on Hill Thirty-seven had become intense. Consequently, Weenie had dragged me into a nearby shell hole where we stayed all night. He explained that another private had helped in taking me to the Rear the following evening. Apparently, not long after this incident, the private had been beheaded by a shell on the Wieltje Road.

Despite my condition, I do remember some of these experiences. I confirmed with Weenie that at the bottom of the shell hole had been an overturned British tank. I remember a night-time gas attack, during which I watched the lights of the whiz-bangs through the lenses of my goggle-eyed mask. Weenie recalled with a smile the difficulty that he had had in getting me to wear that gas mask. He stated that as the gas drifted into our shell hole he was forced to manually press the goggles against my face.

From the Front, I was taken to the Stationary Hospital at Boulogne by ambulance train. The hospital was right on the harbour side, in huge requisitioned sheds, normally used for storing those materials passing through the port. Men were laid out across the stone floor on makeshift beds or stretchers as if they were kippers. A smell of carbolic pervaded the atmosphere, that and the taste of the sea that could be heard constantly through the thin wooden walls. It was here that my leg wound was attended to amid the clouds of flies.

While I recalled these details, Weenie sat quietly and watched the leaves gently falling from the sycamore tree that leaned precariously over the pond to our right. The large yellow and red leaves covered the surface of the jet-black water, forming a stunning spectacle. There was not a breath of wind – all was motionless in the hot, treacly autumnal brew.

It was pleasing to see that Weenie was happy to hear my story. None of the awkwardness that Albert had displayed when recalling past events was evident. And yet I did not want to dominate proceedings with my own recollections, and so I tried to invite my companion to comment on his own activity since he had returned from

Germany. Perhaps I had forgotten how bashful Weenie could be. However, my memory of him is of someone who was always most forthright with his views and opinions. Indeed, this was his most prepossessing characteristic, often saving me from the dark gloom that could all too easily consume those days spent at the Front. And yet now he seemed disinclined to discuss those things that were uppermost in his mind. I say disinclined, but perhaps a sense of embarrassment would be closer to the mark, because as I pressed him for the direction of his current researches, he threw his cigarette to the ground and disappeared into the kitchen without so much as a word.

I took a sip of my wine and looked at the cat, who had fallen asleep underneath my companion's chair. At the sudden departure of her master, Alice woke up and stared back at me with a degree of confusion that must have been reflected in my own eyes, could she see them. Some minutes passed before Weenie appeared once more in the doorway. He was holding a copy of *Perambulations*, fetched presumably from his library. He was smiling broadly.

'I've read this several times since I bought it last summer,' he explained as he stood in the doorway of the kitchen. 'It is a very special book.'

Those were the very words he used: 'a very special book'. Such praise from one so eminent in the world of scientific endeavour affected me deeply, and I was forced to look away to hide my blushes.

'Never been much good at that sort of thing myself, of course,' he continued. 'Still can't tell my geranium from my aspidistra.' Weenie moved in front of me and faced his garden as though he were Dr Livingstone before the first tropical lands. 'Do you fancy a stroll round my own humble Eden?'

And so it was that I left my chair to accompany Weenie on a voyage through the undergrowth! Much of the garden was overgrown, as I have already indicated, and so we had to wade through the long, yellowing grass as if we were indeed on an African plain. Throughout our journey my companion would point to a tree or shrub and suggest a name. More often than not this proved to be accurate and only occasionally did I have to offer a correction. At other times we would stand before a certain specimen and Weenie would read out the accompanying description from my book. On one or two occasions after these renditions, Weenie would strike an appropriate pose so that his picture could be taken and his name entered on the back of the film with my little stylus. He would then snap the book closed and we would march off again through the vegetation.

The garden was far longer than I had originally supposed and in a short space of time we found ourselves lost amid the tall grasses, shrubs and trees that constituted the estate, the cottage now completely lost to us. As we moved further into the unknown, we occasionally came across overgrown statues, often half smothered by lichen and ivy, many leaning precariously, some lying broken and prostrate across the ground. They were all cast in the style of ancient times and would not have been inappropriate in the grounds of some of the larger estates that dominated this part of the world. When I asked Weenie about this rather incongruous statuary, he stated that the pieces had been with the cottage when he had inherited it and had seen no reason to remove them.

Towards the end of the garden we came across an overgrown summerhouse. Thick ivy had almost swallowed it whole, and there appeared to be no obvious entrance. Weenie pushed some ivy aside, low down on the wall facing us, to reveal a hole that had rotted through the timber. We crawled inside. It took some time for my eyes to adjust, for although shafts of light pierced through the ivy that hung across the large glass doors, it was generally dark and dank. In the centre was a single chair. Weenie explained that he often came here.

We came back out into the garden. Though it must have been five o'clock, the heat was still oppressive. The grasses rustled hypnotically in the gentle breeze beneath a blue cloudless sky. Large mature oaks casting long, chilling shadows over the summerhouse dominated this part of the garden. We moved out to where the sun fell on the grass and found a long, low stone plinth buried in the undergrowth, covered with strange yellow lichen. We both sat down on the warm stone surface. For a few minutes we did nothing but watch the smoke from our cigarettes rise through the gnat-speckled bands of light above our heads. There was no sound; apart from the smoke and the occasional falling leaf, all else was frozen in time. I remember Weenie leaning back so that he was prostrate upon the stone, his head propped up on one arm. I thought he looked rather classical and insisted on taking his picture. As I did so, Weenie enquired where my

interest in photography came from, as he could not
remember me ever mentioning such a hobby while I had
been at the Front.

'It was a hobby that was suggested to me by my doctor
at Quex, a Doctor Worthington. Arriving at Quex Park in
Kent from the ambulance ship, I believe the staff were at a
loss what to do with me. The hospital was small, holding
no more than between forty and fifty men. Most of these
patients had physical afflictions upon which the staff were
more than sufficiently trained to dispense treatment.
Watching the lame hobbling on their walking sticks and
crutches, I came to almost jealously regard the
unproblematic status of their condition. In terms of
diagnosis and treatment, the parameters of their affliction
appeared to be clearly demarcated in the medical journals,
which in turn made the role of 'patient' that much easier.
For those such as me, however, the situation was fraught
with imponderables. Diseases of the mind are something
that few doctors have much interest in, and I still have the
feeling that those who do are opportunistic dilettantes. Dr
Worthington, although a consummate professional, was
little more than a local general practitioner overwhelmed
by the slaughter.'

Although these may not have been my exact words, I
feel they have captured the essence of what I said that
afternoon. I recall Weenie staring intently at me as I
recounted the details of my stay at the Auxiliary Military
Hospital.

'Although no doctor, I recognized elements of hysteria
in your condition while I was with you in the shell hole,'
he commented at last. 'Many times you threatened to

simply walk out into open fire or drown yourself in the gas. It was all I could do to pin you to the mud.' Weenie said these things with his usual languid charm, one arm hung down to the ground, the cigarette smoke rising up from the grass. Although my memory of these events at the Front is vague at best, it was with some incongruity that I found myself contemplating such profound happenings amid the idyllic circumstances of my present situation.

'By the time I arrived at Quex I was suffering from what was classed as hysterical mutism. I was placed in "B" Ward, where I could gaze upon the monstrous animal exhibits that stared down from the walls or jabbered behind the boarded-up dioramas.' I informed Weenie of the strange collections of fauna that had been brought together by Major Powell Cotton. 'His thirst for knowledge was immense, and on special days we would wake from our nightmares to find the shutters removed and the major, hat held above his head, astride a tiger or leopard, his shouts muffled by the thick, heavy glass around him.'

I remember Weenie suddenly grabbing my arm and looking over at the summerhouse, where a pair of greenfinches flitted in and out of the ivy. We watched their frantic motion for some moments. The sun disappeared behind a cloud and the birds flew away. 'And it was here that you attempted to regain some sanity?' he asked as he watched the birds soar over the oak trees.

Weenie's question was facetious, of course. I continued: 'Dr Worthington tried a number of cures. The electric shock treatment was dispensed in the Billiard Room, which was being used as the quartermaster's stores at that time. The two billiard tables had been dragged to one side of the room, and numerous boxes and makeshift shelving had been added in progressive layers from the doorway. In the centre of this maze was placed a chair with thick leather straps, and it was while seated here that the faradic currents were passed through my neck in the vain attempt to break my mutism.'

I realize these details are new to you, Father. The chloroform and electric treatments were seen at first as being of some value. I recall standing to 'attention' by the side of my bed, along with all the other men, at least those that could move sufficiently, as Dr Worthington and Sister Cotton did the rounds. I remember them smiling as I pointed to some of my pencil drawings while my neck throbbed with the electric burns.

At some point after this event I found myself living in a glorified shed in the grounds of the hospital. The building must have been an old summerhouse, similar in some ways to that which now faced me from the bottom of Weenie's garden, although luckily my abode was not nearly so dilapidated. There was a bed and enough space for the most rudimentary furniture. For all my other needs I was allowed to enter the house.

'A classic response by your physician: isolation. Take away any opportunity to recall those experiences engendering the trauma.'

'I spent much of the autumn and winter of 1917 wandering the grounds of the estate. I believe there was some respite in my condition. I have clear memories of waving to those tubercular men whose beds had been moved out of 'A' Ward and onto the adjoining veranda.

'As my condition stabilized I was given small tasks. I think it was Major Powell who suggested I should work on the gardens. I was presented a strange bronze key that I carried for many days without knowing through which door it allowed access. When no one was looking I would try the key in any door that I came across, whether it be in a wall or on the outside of a building. It was Camille who eventually found the small shed, lost amid the undergrowth of the gardens, where we found a treasure trove of old tools and gardening implements. From that moment on, I spent much time tending the grounds, pushing my wheelbarrow across the lawns, stacked high with various tools. The other men were told to ignore me and I, in turn, tended to disregard them, often finding the most secluded and obscure parts of the gardens, which extended over many hundreds of acres, in which to work. Such was the appreciation of my efforts that Dr Worthington brought me a small book on horticulture that I at once set about reading. My present knowledge of the vegetable kingdom was germinated at that moment.'

Weenie wondered whether this was an unbearably lonely existence.

'The solitude did allow my trauma to recede into the darker corners of my mind. Camille was often at my side, of course. He had been at the hospital since the early part of the War. I was told that he was from Belgium. Like me he was dumb, and though he did much work in the house as an orderly, he was also more than happy to help out in the garden with a spade or rake. I often wonder how little Camille has fared in these post-war years.'

'And it was Dr Worthington who also gave you the camera?' asked Weenie as he flicked his spent cigarette across the long grass.

'Yes. I remember him bringing it out to me as I tended a large rhododendron by the Winter Gardens, the tropical conservatory that had been taken over as the staff mess room. By then the more intense period of treatment had come to an end and my relationship with Dr Worthington had begun to ease. However, I still had not uttered a sound. I remember how the camera swung at his side as he marched briskly towards me. As always, he was impeccably dressed in his dark-grey suit that gradually began to glisten in the morning drizzle. I straightened up and leaned on my spade as he came to stand before me, pulling the camera strap over his head while announcing that this was a gift. He pushed a latch on the front of the black box and out popped the main lens. With a further flourish, the viewfinder was brought up into position. He told me it was called a Kodak Autograph because, through the Wonders of Science, it was possible to individually inscribe each negative with a suitable description. Here Dr Worthington showed me a little door at the back of the camera to which was attached a thin metal stylus. The doctor explained that after taking a picture one could open this door and, using the stylus, inscribe a few words onto the film.'

Weenie peered forward as I demonstrated these features to him. Opening the little door and pulling out the stylus, I felt the keen eye of a scientist upon the camera. In the

sun the stylus glinted like a sliver of silver. I offered
Weenie the opportunity to inspect the instrument himself,
but he declined.

'A most generous offer. He seems to have been a rather
odd individual.'

'One evening I found Dr Worthington at the top of the
Waterloo Tower. It was a foul winter night, clouds
scuttling across a full moon. I was out walking through the
gardens as wind and rain tore through the trees. The
Waterloo Tower is not near the house. During Quex's
period as a hospital the tower was deliberately kept out of
bounds, with the doors firmly locked. It was thus with
some surprise that, as I passed underneath the great
monument and looked up, the sudden appearance of the
moon from behind a dark bank of cloud revealed the form
of Dr Worthington perched perilously on top of the metal
spire many feet above me.'

'Metal spire?'

'An iron spire that rests on top of the red brick edifice
via four beautifully curved legs. It's painted pure white and
rises for a further seventy feet beyond the top of the
tower. Major Cotton once caught me gazing up at it and
told me that he called it his little Eiffel Tower. And
indeed, as I surveyed the spire through a pair of binoculars
one day, I could not help but recall the French
monstrosity. Yet whereas the French tower is all bombast
and Gallic arrogance, there is a subtlety and nuance that
graces the Quex spire.'

I could see that this digression into architectural matters
had seized the attention of Weenie so I ventured to discuss
the finer detail. 'In the centre of the spire is a platform,

which is accessed by a ladder. From here I was assured by Major Cotton that the finest views could be attained across the Kentish countryside. On the night in question, Dr Worthington had obviously made his way up the spire and was now leaning precariously over the railings that ran round the tiny metal platform. For a moment I remained perfectly still as the wind roared past me, bending the great trees almost double. As I stared up into the heavens, the moon disappeared behind some cloud and the white spire immediately lost its eerie phosphorescence. With the returning shadows, the fragile form of Dr Worthington disappeared from view. I did not move. I think in all honesty I was incapable of leaving the scene. When the moon appeared once more, the nocturnal light found Dr Worthington perched on top of the railings, one arm held out, the other holding firmly to one of the spire's bowed legs that disappeared over his head towards a natural apex. As the wind dipped, an owl glided over my head, its wings beating out a low, rhythmical throb that seized my heart.

'I rushed to the entrance to the tower. The wooden door, normally locked, was now open. All was dark inside and after some hesitation, I found myself in the ringing room. Loosening one of the bell ropes, I pulled hard and felt the mechanism above slowly respond. After a short delay a booming sound echoed from the top, shaking the small room to its foundation. I pulled again, and then again, the rhythm of the peal increasing as I mastered weight and tension. After several minutes of this I secured the rope back against the wall and found a set of stone stairs that wound their way upwards to the top. At the top of the stairs was an opened door that was banging against its frame in the fierce winds. I emerged onto the roof with the white spire disappearing off into the firmament above me, its huge steel legs set down on each corner of the crenulated edifice. Once more there was a booming sound overhead and for a minute I wondered if some unseen force was now pulling down on the bell ropes far below in that tiny room. The heavens lit up with a flash of lightning and another peal of thunder roared. In the light I saw Dr Worthington still gripped to the side of the spire, crouching on top of the railings as though about to leap out into the electric storm and fly up towards the moon.

'I tried to shout but my voice, if voice there was, was taken away by the gale. Around me the world was submerged in darkness. From this supreme vantage point there were no buildings, villages or cities. Dr Worthington and I were alone, clinging to the tower amid the Devil's blackest Abyss. I moved towards the spire and found the ladder that ascended up to the platform. The rain by this time, and at this height, was intense, so that it was difficult to see much further than the rung in front of my face.'

'You must also have been worried about being hit by lightning, or the spire being struck when you were on it? Electrocution isn't a nice way to go.'

'These thoughts did not come into my head until much later, when I was safely back on the ground.' At this moment a large Red Admiral, fooled by the unseasonably warm weather, fluttered past us. Weenie and I watched its chaotic path over the swaying grasses until it disappeared from view. I then continued.

'As I climbed on to the platform in the centre of the spire, I almost fell over on the wet metal. Dr Worthington, alerted to my presence by this sudden movement, turned round and eyed me with some suspicion.

' "I hear there are fine views to be had from here," I shouted out, my voice sounding strange after so many weeks of inactivity.

'Dr Worthington appeared to consider this statement for some time. "Indeed there are," he replied, turning to face the blackness before him. "There are none finer. I have been here many a time on a clear summer's day."

'I stayed on the far side of the platform, fearing that any approach would lead to calamity. "Do you know how high we are?" I asked.

'Again, Dr Worthington considered his reply as the rain fell off his face to be carried away in the storm. "I believe the tower is approximately sixty-six feet high, with the spire another sixty-five. That makes a combined height of one hundred and twenty-five feet."

' "So it does. Astounding. And when exactly was she built, sir?"

'With this question, Dr Worthington edged round and gingerly lowered himself back onto the platform. He stood before me, arms by his side, back straight as a die. Only his face betrayed his utter exhaustion. We were now no more than six feet away from each other upon the delicately perforated metal floor, both drenched and stricken with fear.

' "She was built in 1819 by John Powell Powell. Look here.' Dr Worthington pointed to a plate on one of the metal legs. In the dim light I could not read the faint words forged upon it. "It says 'John Clark Ramsgate 1820'. He worked on the estate and oversaw the construction. It was all built with local skill and materials. An amazing feat."

'Never have I been more grateful to parochial architectural competence as on that stormy night. Though the wind roared and the thunder bellowed, the spire stood firm. Dr Worthington eyed me for some time. "The Tower was named after the famous battle, Waterloo."

'I nodded in agreement.

'"It's a hobby of mine." A quizzical look must have fluttered over my face. "The Battle of Waterloo. I've done much reading around the subject."

'"Ah, yes. The Duke of Wellington and all that."

'"Indeed. But don't forget General Blücher from Prussia, the world-weary seventy-two-year-old." Dr Worthington turned round, grasped the dripping handrail and gazed out into the darkness. "It rained all night then, as well."

'"When, sir?"

'"The night of 18th June. The night before the battle. Waterloo. You can imagine the scene as the sun rose fresh over the Forest of Soignes: the soaked bivouacs, the heaps of piled muskets, the horses tethered to sunken bayonets, the fields of men smothered in sodden blankets, with their heads on their knapsacks. Behind them, the vast ranks of cavalry, hundreds of horses picketed line after line, and then the artillery, cannon, limbers and ammunition wagons."

'Dr Worthington was standing up on his toes as he said these things. He suddenly spun round. "You men speak of heavy artillery." His eyes flashed in the darkness. "I've experienced that too, you know. Ladysmith, waiting for

Buller while Long John had his little fun. Oh yes, my friend, you're not the only one with things that you'd rather forget."

'And then, as the storm passed over us and disappeared out to sea, Dr Worthington began to relate the details of the great Battle of Waterloo, from the French attack on Hougoumont, to the merciless artillery barrage and fighting around La Haye Sainte. With the storm spent, the clouds melted away and we found ourselves under a million twinkling stars. The air temperature plummeted and since Dr Worthington was naked, I took it upon myself to cover him in my trusty regimental long coat. Dr Worthington, it would have to be said, remained unconcerned by his condition, and continued talking of the battle until he slipped into a sudden sleep upon the cold metal platform. In the early morning I was able to shout for help to a passing groundsman who dutifully helped lead my companion back to terra firma, where we found the doctor's clothes neatly folded in one of the tower's side rooms.'

Weenie took a deep breath and sat up on the stone plinth just as the sun disappeared behind a cloud. 'A most amazing story. And what became of the good doctor?'

'He left very soon after. I saw him only once after the incident, when he handed me the camera. He had inadvertently cured my mutism, of course.'

PART SEVEN

Durham Category 'A' Prison

Present Day, Late October

As I recall, it was only a few weeks after the attack at
Rutland Water that I heard Julie had died peacefully in her
sleep. I must categorically state that at this point I had not
seen Jim since the incident. For obvious reasons I was
avoiding his presence. I have recently read that Julie must
have known what Jim was up to, that before she died she
had somehow been able to link Jim to the attempted rape
at Rutland Water. My lawyer has also said as much. And
that, as a consequence, Jim had been forced to murder her.

I've been told that Jim has denied this. Initially I thought
the suggestion to be nothing more than fanciful newspaper
talk. But just recently, during the long sleepless nights, I
have taken to wondering about the last days of Julie's life.
Apparently few saw her after the attack at Rutland. Maybe
she did put the scanty bits of evidence together and lie
awake at night just as I was doing at that time across the
road. Perhaps it was a certain look, a glance in a mirror
that told Jim what her suspicions were. If that had been the
case, from that moment on, her life would have been in his
hands. The folded blanket, the hot water bottle still warm

on her rigid lap, would not have begun to tell the doctor the terror of her final days behind the prison of those abominable lace curtains.

But this is all conjecture.

Thinking back, the first time Jim and I spoke after the attack was when he came up to me in the street and stated that Julie had passed away. It was four weeks since I had last seen him and I noted how tired and desperate he looked. We were standing in the main street of Great Glen. I remember feeling very exposed.

I waited a day or so after the funeral. I also waited until it was dark. The downstairs lights of the lounge shone out across Jim's driveway. The curtains were closed. The evening was surprisingly cold.

Jim let me in and I hurried inside. In truth it was a rather strained first meeting. At first sight the house appeared unchanged – I almost expected to see Julie. But then I noticed that her bed in the corner of the lounge had gone, as had the potted plants with which she had surrounded herself. Yet elsewhere her feminine touches remained – the knitting basket by the side of the settee, her magazines on the coffee table, and her make-up bag on top of the TV. I was led upstairs with hardly a word spoken. I stood on the landing and watched as Jim brought down the loft ladder. He glanced only momentarily at me before disappearing into the black hole above in that rather ungainly fashion of his. With only half his body enveloped in the blackness, I watched him reach across to the light switch. There was an audible power surge, a hum, before the strip lighting clattered into life. I followed Jim into the light.

Soldiers were massed on the shelves around us. Cavalry and horses blinked in the light. Canons and lances glinted. Jim walked across to the centre of the room where the large table sat, and placed both his hands on the tabletop as if preparing to address a board of governors. The table was completely bare. For the first time since I could remember there were no troops or hills, trees or buildings.

Jim must have seen me looking at the vacuum. I've not felt like war gaming, he said.

The table squatted before us like a large blank rectangle of canvas. I hesitate to say that Jim was the frustrated artist, but in this context perhaps he was.

No, I suppose not.

In my mind I can picture Jim standing by the table. This is one level. But at another level I see the images of what subsequently happened peering over his shoulder like succubae – I see him hunched over the body, I see his quick movements with the tape and binding, I see his picture in the newspaper. And there, in the centre of the scene, is the table – that blank surface upon which so much grotesqueness was to happen in that tiny, suffocating room.

We must play again, I remember stating as I watched Jim walk round the loft. I've been reading up on the tactics of war gaming.

Really?

I continued to stand by the table and watched as Jim

circled me. He paused as he passed the small window in the sloping ceiling. I remember him tapping the glass inquisitively as if testing it in some way before continuing.

It's fascinating. I've been studying how attempts were made to reduce war to a series of discrete mathematical laws or rules.

Yes? Truly fascinating Herr Doktor.

I continued. Just as Newton unearthed the basic laws that explained physical phenomena, so scientists wanted to discover if similar mathematical principles underpinned human behaviour. Interestingly, much of this work was done straight after the Great War, the First World War. The war to end all wars.

I remember Jim suddenly stopping in his stride. He picked one or two soldiers off a nearby shelf, holding them in his palm as if they were a couple of beans. With his other hand, he picked each soldier up individually, holding it to the light as if inspecting a diamond, before placing it on the bare surface of the table. He reached for more of the soldiers neatly arrayed on the shelf behind him. I watched as, on the opposite corner of the table from me, a small party of Second World War American soldiers gathered.

Jim suddenly noticed that I had finished speaking. Do please go on, I'm all ears, he said.

In order to predict warfare it was recognized that some mathematical way was needed by which conflict could be replicated.

Jim continued placing his warriors on the table, squinting in the crude white light as he made minute changes to their positions. I paused and he looked up. He saw me staring at the soldiers and immediately returned his gaze to the figures in front of him.

I suppose it's one of life's ironies that war gaming is derived from scientific endeavours intended to wrestle peace from the jaws of chaos.

Have you noticed how quiet it is? asked Jim after I had fallen silent for some time. With Julie gone, we're completely alone. At this point Jim looked up from his troops, which were now massed in two phalanxes, and stared hard at me. I remember that stare. Even then I recall thinking that this was the beginning. The beginning of the end.

It must be strange without her, I ventured, trying to disperse the growing sense of gloom with an appeal to sentiment.

I want to buy a computer.

I grabbed two dice from the shelf behind me and dramatically rolled them across the board, knocking down a number of his American soldiers as if they were pins in a bowling alley. I can still picture the surprise on Jim's face as his little army collapsed.

PART EIGHT

PART EIGHT

Rutland

1922, Late October

Perambulations of a Soldier: Autumn to Winter
by John Crowe

The cold, damp air of this majestic oak wood reminds us that winter will not be long in coming. Yet if we place our bare hands upon the soil we find it surprisingly warm, for the ground still holds the heat of a long, hot summer. In these conditions it should not surprise us that fungus, the invisible, undetectable flora of our wooded universe, proliferate. What we now see around us, the bracket-shaped polypores by the logs to our right for instance, those bright yellow chanterelles, and the boletes and red fly agarics that are scattered amongst the trees, are no more than the fruiting bodies of a vast network of roots, or mycelium as is their scientific name, that spread out for hundreds of acres across the forest floor, a dark unseen presence that has never left us on our rambles. Saprophytic fungi feast only on the dead, the mycelium penetrating the rotting wood to form an invisible capillary system around which the host disintegrates; mycorrhizal fungi remain integral components of a live system, each one dependent upon the other. Certain plants, such as orchids, are totally dependent on this sort of symbiotic relationship.

Look up! It appears our autumnal sojourn through the oak trees has upset one of its fondest residents, a bushy-tailed red squirrel. In a few weeks these busy little characters will disappear as though a Pied Piper had come through the land, but fear not, for they will be merely sleeping in the nooks and crannies of the trees, their great protectors, and when the sun warms the earth, they will once more rise up to delight the eye and satisfy the soul.

As we plunge into the twilight of the wood, it is not long before we encounter a low hillock, composed of dead twigs and leaves. Getting closer, we can see that in fact it is the home of the largest British ant, the red or wood ant. The mound is about three or four feet in height and is probably home to hundreds of thousands of ants. Even now at this late time of the year, streams of workers can be seen setting off with empty jaws, alongside others returning with insects they have caught. Much of the activity of an ant nest is centred on the rearing of the grubs, and, like wasps and bees, the ants consider the safety and welfare of the young before everything else. If we get too close and the colony thinks it is under attack then the soldiers can even spit minute drops of acid that burn your skin.

Bending over the nest even now, on this perishing cold autumnal afternoon, we can still feel and smell the acid vapour rising up to brush our faces and clot our throats.

Continuation of letter to:
Rev Cecil Crowe,
The Vicarage,
Great Glen,
Leicestershire

20th October 1922

FROM: *Captain John Crowe, Railway Hotel,*
Oakham, Rutland

It is some hours since I wrote the above pages concerning my visit to Weenie's cottage. Tiredness suddenly came over me, Father, and it was all I could do to stop myself falling asleep at the desk. As it was, I was able to roll over on top of my bed. Though I have been asleep for only two or three hours I feel refreshed. It is still dark outside as I once more take up my pen.

While asleep, my strange visit to Weenie danced across my restless mind. It is a curious aspect of dreams that things that remain hidden or obscured during the waking hours can suddenly be exposed as though a curtain across our minds is pulled back. It certainly now seems clear to me that Weenie's behaviour during my visit was rather coy, Father, perhaps even evasive. As I sat once more at my little table and lit a fresh candle I reflected that this was a most unexpected circumstance. As I have already stated, my recollection of Weenie was of a forthright and engaging personality, a man to whom there was seemingly no subject on which he did not have an opinion. Indeed, I believe that as we entered the kitchen after our tour of the garden I made a special point of describing to him just how I had valued his companionship and support during those difficult months at the Front. I even went as far as to say that his supreme belief in the British cause was a major crutch both to me and to the other officers of the company. I went on to recall one particular incident to illustrate this. It took place at Fermoy in August 1916, after we had successfully put down the Easter Rising. In readiness for France, the battalion was undergoing training using specially constructed trenches on Corrin Mountain. Many days were spent scrabbling amongst the gorse while live ammunition was fired over our heads. We knew a big push was underway in France and the men were keen to get over there as quickly as possible. In the meantime Weenie, who had never shown the fondest inclinations towards the indigenous population, provided much entertainment in his constant lampooning of the Irish character.

At the Fermoy barracks Weenie inspired many a heated discussion with our fellow officers. One particular discussion comes to mind. Weenie had been reading *Mars* by the American Mr Perceval Lowell. One night, lying on his bunk bed, he provided a fascinating introduction to Mr Lowell's theories, which are now so well known. I remember the company had spent much of the day receiving wiring instruction, and all the men were tired. In fact it was all I could do to stay awake. Perhaps I even dozed off momentarily, but in my dreams I saw the most wondrous vision, no doubt inspired by Weenie's words, drifting across from his bunk. Although there were some men who demonstrated a degree of scepticism, I was not the only man to find Weenie's descriptions a most wondrous and enlightening experience. Even a non-believer such as you, Father, would, I'm sure, have been moved by the passion and energy of those Martian scenes painted for us that evening.

And what astonishing scenes they were! I can recall them, even now: that cold, lonely planet, so much like our world and yet so alien! And so much older, eons older than Earth – so ancient in fact, the cooling process has left the surface cracked and pitted, and the great oceans that once glinted in the light of a young sun have trickled away. The storms of the Great Polar Bay, the rolling shores of Mare Erythraeum, and the monstrous sea creatures that lurked in the deepest depths of the Hour-glass Sea, are now no more than whispers in the harsh winds that scold the never-ending wilderness.

For those poor beings left on the surface there is but one subject that must occupy their minds: water – water to drink, bathe and to grow their crops. Certainly there is water upon the planet. Much of it, however, spends its time trapped in the huge glaciers of the southern polar ice cap. As the Martian seasons tumble across the windswept plains, this great wall of ice fattens and retreats in synchronicity with an alien calendar.

And here the canals come into their own. For in the spring, as the ice begins to groan and crack, a huge polar sea forms. From this great pool, water is fed northwards across the parched vastnesses of the planet until there is not one part of the surface left untouched. Such is the level of scarcity, not a drop is wasted but instead is carefully sent on its way through the most intricate of mazes that can ever be imagined by the human mind. Only the Russian Tsars, with their great Siberian railway projects, have ever got close to what our Martian neighbours have effected to stay alive upon their world. The Gorgon, the Titan, and the Brontes run for thousands of miles, linking up great planetary oases hundreds of miles across, where luscious vegetation grows, ripens and dies with the advancing Martian winters. From the Earth, we do not see the canals directly, for the thin threads of water are far too small to be observed, even with the most powerful of telescopes. Instead we observe only the after-effects of the pure, cool water running through them: the darkening shadow as vegetation eagerly grows and clamours along their sides, as though the banks of the Nile.

I remember Weenie pausing to draw on his cigarette, an action that allowed my companions time to reply. Charles Moore was particularly vociferous in calling such theories the delusions of an amateur crank. He tried to argue that the canals were nothing more than ripples in the sand, hallucinations of a fevered imagination. Before he left the mess for his night duty, Moore categorically stated that there was no water on Mars and that life on other planets was an impossibility.

After the door had been slammed shut Weenie explained that life on other planets was anything but an impossibility. Theories of evolution had proved that life can adapt to the harshest of conditions, and that if one accepts that Mars has a polar ice cap, it is not too fanciful to assume that life, similar to our own, could have emerged.

I remember Weenie noting that the canals reveal something of the people who constructed them, their trigonometric exactitude suggesting a most intelligent race, and their global nature pointing to the lack of inter-racial dispute and confrontation. In short, Weenie concluded that the Martian people had reached a stage of racial equilibrium for which we on Earth have no equal and are still in open struggle for. Technologically they must be as gods, possessing inventions beyond our dreams, a place where our great airships and aeroplanes would be confined to obscure, dusty museums.

I do not remember how the conversation progressed from this point. It is certain that my companions continued to question the wisdom of Weenie's theories. Although I may have fallen asleep, the vision that Weenie drew did not leave me. Months later while at Quex, Camille and I often stared up at the tiny red planet through the lenses of my binoculars, desperate to see just one sign that someone was looking back at us. But deep down I knew that no buildings or railway lines, not even the blasts from the bloodiest of our battles, had rippled the serenity of the Earth's tranquil veil, and that if there were Martians, the presence of humankind had yet to make itself known.

As an aside, the very night of Weenie's Martian lecture saw a great deluge descend upon Fermoy as the River Blackwater burst its banks. It came with an immense roar that forced us from our dreams. We jumped from our bunks to find the floor of the mess and the town itself submerged under three feet of water that didn't subside for some days. Charles Moore's body was never found. It was assumed he had been carried away by the first surge of water that had silently come upon him beneath the stars, in the cold of the night.

Back at the cottage Weenie made a pot of tea. He appeared completely unmoved by my recollection, to the point where I even considered that its retelling had in some way offended him. He moved back into the garden with the teapot and together we watched the sun sink low as the temperature fell. We spoke little until after I had checked on Angus, when Weenie kindly offered me one of his spare rooms for the night. In return he was keen to understand more about my journey. And so, yet again, I explained the details of my sojourn from Husbands Bosworth and how I had visited Albert Furrows at Houghton-on-the-Hill. After asking about Albert, Weenie wondered who else I intended to visit, supposing that I had a pre-arranged itinerary. Instead, I explained that my journey was more of an organic event and that I had several possible destinations for the next part of my trip, all neatly stored in the bundle of letters shoved down in one of my saddle bags. As my companion stared across his garden he asked when my journey would be finished. I explained that it would probably be the winter storms rather than my own enthusiasm that would bring the venture to a close.

Much later I removed the saddlebags from Angus and took them upstairs to a little room at the front of the cottage. Weenie explained that he would take Angus across to a nearby field. As we ventured upstairs I couldn't help but notice two large travel bags through the opened door of one of the guest rooms, from which a profusion of assorted clothes lay strewn across the bare floorboards. Weenie saw me looking at these objects and immediately stopped by the open door and leaned against the frame.

'Oh, I forgot to say. You're not the only guest staying tonight. I have a friend staying over as well. His name is Lewis Richardson.'

It was rather gloomy in the corridor where we stood and I recall a distinct smell of peppermint. The name Richardson meant nothing to me at all, although Weenie's eyes shone out in the dark, perhaps searching for a reaction. Forced by my companion to stop, I peered more closely into the tiny room.

'Have I met him before?' I enquired with some concern.

'I should think not. Not really your sort, old chap. He's from Newcastle-upon-Tyne. We were both students together at Cambridge. Mind you, I wasn't in his league, of course.' I noticed how Weenie rubbed his hand along the smooth surface of the door frame. 'He was, or should I say, is a genius. A mathematician like me, but that's where the similarity ends. I'm not being demure. He really is a genius. Upon my word . . . Well, look at this!'

The saddlebags were rather heavy and so I hitched them up higher with my knee before poking my head around the door of the mysterious guest's room. 'A fifth edition. Came out last year.' Weenie must have seen my bemused expression as I attempted to draw meaning from the book held in his hand. *'Elements of the Mathematical Theory of*

Electricity and Magnetism by J. J. Thomson. Found it lying on the bed here. Old Lewis must be doing a bit of homework.'

'Is it important?'

'The old man taught us both while we were at Cambridge.' The book was dropped unceremoniously onto the bed. 'You must have heard of him? Discoverer of the electron and all that?'

I told Weenie that I hadn't but that the hidden world of these atomic crystalline objects was a most fascinating one.

'It was Thomson that first postulated the idea of negatively charged particles within the atomic structure.' Weenie walked out of the room and continued along the dark corridor. I followed, still struggling with my bags. 'He did this wonderful experiment where he used a cathode ray tube to prove that there was a stream of negatively charged atomic particles. He recreated the experiment for us one afternoon. Of course, we were only students and most of it went over our heads, but it was really fascinating stuff.' We came to a closed wooden door that Weenie threw open. 'I remember Lewis being especially interested. Here we are. This will be your room.'

'Has Lewis been staying long?' I enquired as I walked over to the little window and looked out. The sun was now dropping quickly behind the trees, although streams of sunlight still pierced the darkening heavens.

'He arrived last night. Apparently he's on his way down to Cambridge and thought he'd drop in to see his old chum. I think you'll find him an interesting fellow.' Turning back into the room I found that my eyes were now not adjusted to the darkness – Weenie was no more than a shadowy outline in the corridor. However, in this semi-blind state, the emphasis of Weenie's final remark was not easily ignored. But before I had time to respond, Weenie disappeared from the doorway and I heard his voice receding down the corridor. 'I'll light the candles so we can see what we're doing.'

The house was dark as I moved down the bare wooden stairs to arrive once more into the hallway. The sun had now disappeared and the ground floor of the house appeared to be in total darkness. Well, almost total darkness – from the half-opened door of the kitchen I could see the flicker of a sickly yellow light. As I stood there in the gloom I also discerned the faint sounds of a gramophone drifting across from the kitchen. The lone female voice was one I had heard many times while at the Front, and, for a second or two, I was unable to move. One of my fellow officers, I think Burrows, had possessed a portable gramophone which presumably his manservant conscientiously lugged around. Burrows was with us at Ypres in late 1917 until he went west early on, but I remember quite clearly the contraption sitting in the corner of a dugout in the reserve trenches at St Jean. Burrows had been a most high-spirited sort of fellow, and as the gloom and desperation of the Salient overwhelmed us, we came more and more to depend on those three or four scratchy recordings kept in a biscuit tin. I remember returning to the billet after one difficult night on duty. The faint sounds and light from the quarters drifted down the trench as I approached, and on this particular occasion I stopped and listened until the needle disappeared off the end and the light in the billet was blown out.

Burrows had not lasted long. He was caught by a shell that dropped straight on top of three horses. Shrapnel had seared his face in half and plucked off a leg and arm. His body remained half buried in the mud until we were moved up to the Front Line. Each time we struggled along the duckboards I would glance over and watch as his body grew bigger and bigger.

I walked towards the kitchen door and gently eased it open. Weenie was sitting at the kitchen table, a lit candle and a glass of wine by his side. As I entered, he looked up and smiled. 'Fancy a glass, old chap?'

I said that I did, and pulled out a chair from underneath the table as my companion reached over and grabbed hold of a bottle and an empty wine glass from the cupboards opposite. I looked round and noticed that the gramophone was on a small trolley in the darkest corner of the room.

'There's a meat and potato pie in the oven. Should be ready in an hour or so. Hope you don't mind a bit of music?'

'Of course not. It's a voice I haven't heard for a number of years now.'

'I can play something else if you'd rather.'

'No, please. This is perfect.'

For a moment or two we both sat at the table, listening to the ghostly voice and the crackle of the coals in the oven from which seeped a rich orange glow.

'If you want my advice, I think you should go home after this and continue with your nature books.'

I looked across at my companion. The candle was

between us. One side of Weenie's face was brilliantly lit by the yellow flame, the wine in his glass sparkling luxuriantly as he swirled it round and round in front of his eyes. Yet beyond this illuminated foreground yawned the utter darkness of a crypt. The scene was at once homely and terrible.

'What have you against my little sojourn?'

'John, people want to *forget*. They want to move on.' As he said this, Weenie turned from his wine and faced me over the flickering flame. His eyes shone out against the blackness beyond him. '*And so do I.*'

Perhaps Weenie sympathized with my confused state, for at least he added, in no more than a whisper, 'Things change; people change.'

I watched as he poured himself some more wine.

'Have you changed, Weenie?'

'We've all changed.' He took a large sip of his drink. There was another long pause. 'You're like a ghost returning from a lost world. The past has gone, John, and so has everyone that inhabited it. They exist only in your mind. In your dreams. It's us, the survivors, who dwell in the real nightmare, crawling amongst the half-buried ruins of what once was.' And then, in the faintest of whispers, 'Look upon my works, ye mighty, and despair.'

Weenie's wine glass was slammed onto the table top with such force that the sound of the front door closing was almost inaudible. When Lewis Richardson peered round the kitchen door we were both somewhat taken by surprise.

I immediately saw that Richardson was a tall, lean man, almost ecclesiastical in demeanour. His large forehead spoke of the intellectual powers alluded to by Weenie, and his hair was already grey. As he emerged from the shadows the lenses of his round glasses flashed in the candlelight. His left hand held a large hat and in his right a scarf trailed limply along the floor. He was wearing a long coat and his shoes were covered in mud. 'Hello,' he offered.

Without a moment's hesitation Weenie rose out of his seat. 'Ah, Richardson. Glad you're back. I was beginning to get a bit concerned.' Weenie's dark mood had suddenly evaporated.

'I'm afraid my shoes are a bit muddy. I got lost in the gloom and ended up crawling across a field.'

Weenie moved across the kitchen to the new arrival. 'Oh dear. We'll soon have those clean again.' Richardson began undoing his shoelaces. 'While you were out, I had a most pleasant surprise – John here, a friend from my army days, popped in to see me.'

With his shoes off, Richardson once more straightened to his full height. I got up out of my chair and shook his hand.

'I haven't seen John in over five years now, so this was something of a shock. He's staying here tonight. I've put him in the small room next to yours.'

Richardson had a firm handshake. I noticed his large nose and thin mouth. He looked into my eyes. 'I'm pleased to meet you.' I tried to return his gaze. 'Have you travelled far?'

Before I had a chance, Weenie responded. 'John lives in south-west Leicestershire. He's come up from Houghton-on-the-Hill, which is a village not too far away. He's in the process of visiting some of his old mates from the army days. I was next on the list, as it were.' He held up his wine glass to me as some sort of salute before taking a sip.

With our hands disengaged there was now an awkwardness in our proximity. Richardson appeared to view me with a certain degree of suspicion. 'Really,' was, I believe, his only comment before he turned round to take off his coat and wrap his scarf around the peg on the back of the kitchen door, over which he placed his hat.

I took this opportunity to sit back down at the kitchen table with Weenie. Richardson joined us and was immediately presented with a glass of wine. I offered him a cigarette but he declined. The smell of baking pie was slowly spreading throughout the room as the sound of the gramophone enveloped us like an autumnal mist.

'So, tell us of your explorations today,' urged Weenie to Richardson after we had quietly sipped at our drinks.

'Well, I don't think there's much to say. I went roaming rather aimlessly and have no sense of the path that I took.'

Weenie had spotted that Richardson was trembling with the cold, and quietly moved over to the hearth, where he began to light the coals.

'I came across a stream at the bottom of the valley and then moved on up the other side. Here I found an old estate, with a church. I think I may have been trespassing but I didn't meet anybody, and as I moved through the grounds I realized that the estate was rather overgrown. When I came upon the house I found that it too was disused. By this time the sun was declining rapidly and so I attempted to find my way home. Unfortunately I got rather lost.'

Weenie turned round from the hearth. 'That's the old Normanton Estate. It's currently being sold off. They were a powerful family in their time, but seem to have withered away. I'm not sure what will happen to the old hall, but we're hoping another family will take it on.'

Weenie stood up, brushed the coal dust from off his trousers and joined us at the table.

'What struck me most about the land here is just how isolated it feels from the rest of society. Standing in Normanton Park, looking back across the valley, I felt that time had in some way stood still. There were no visible roads, no rail lines or houses, hardly. As the sun dropped, all I could see was an endless canopy of autumnal leaves. And here we are in a house with no gas, and certainly no electricity. It feels most . . . tranquil.' Richardson had only the faintest of northern accents. As he spoke he lowered his eyes with a degree of modesty.

'What do you say, John? Are we all Luddites here?'

'There is a certain charm to this area that I recognize in Richardson's description.'

'Well that's good enough for me. John here is something of an expert in these parts. He's published a book on flora and is in the process of extending the series; is that not right?'

With the wine, Weenie's manner had become rather direct, a change that left me feeling distinctly uncomfortable. I decided I should respond to this new tempo by simply stating the facts as cleanly and directly as possible. 'Yes, that is true. I published a book called *Perambulations of a Soldier*, which was based on my own

naturalistic studies through the spring and summer of
1918. One purpose of my current sojourn is to research a
companion study for the seasons autumn and winter.'

'Indeed. A most interesting study and rather romantic.
Is this a long-term interest?'

'Not really. After I went into hospital I was introduced
to gardening as a therapeutic exercise. I was sent on a
short walking tour in the spring of 1918 to help recover
my senses, and so it felt natural that I should in some way
combine this with my new-found love of English flora.'

'John served with me in the 2nd Leicesters.'

'Oh yes.' Richardson's eyes again dropped.

'And your regiment?' I inquired quite naturally.

'Richardson is a Quaker.' Weenie's interjection was
immediate. On reflection I feel that he had been waiting to
defend his friend since the moment Richardson had
walked into the kitchen. I must have looked rather puzzled
because Weenie added, 'A conscientious objector.'

Some of the bits of wood and paper that Weenie had
used to start the fire suddenly flared up in the hearth. I felt
a wave of warmth rush across my face and I suddenly
realized how cold the cottage had become.

Richardson looked across at me. 'I joined the Friends
Ambulance Unit and served in France. I was assigned to
the 16th French Infantry Division.'

We all sipped our drinks and watched as the flames
climbed up into the chimney. A cold draught of air was
now blowing on my neck. I noticed that the opened page
of a book left on the side of the kitchen was rustling as
though some poltergeist was making merry. It was Weenie

who ended the silence: 'I was telling John here about old Thomson.' Richardson frowned. 'Old Jo Thomson at Cambridge.'

'Oh yes,' responded Richardson with a certain forced civility.

'We saw *Elements of the Mathematical Theory of Electricity and Magnetism* on your bed. I was telling John about those early experiments with the cathode rays.'

'Indeed, the new 5th edition.' Richardson turned to me. For a second the reflection of the dwindling flames in the hearth flashed across his glasses. 'Are you a scientific man as well?'

'I'm afraid not. Much of what I have picked up has come through books and magazines. And what Weenie has told me.'

'Ah yes.' A slight pause ensued. 'Thomson was a most inspiring man. You can't imagine what it was like to hear him talk. You see, at that time his discovery of the electron was still very much uppermost in people's minds. It was a most amazing piece of scientific endeavour – to actually peer into the sub-atomic structure.' Despite Richardson's rather laconic style, he had suddenly become animated as he recalled his days as a student at Cambridge. 'Thomson was able to prove that the centre of the atom must consist of a quantity of negatively charged electrons embedded in a sphere of positive electricity, the subsequent charges cancelling each other out.' And then, after a second's hesitation, 'In many ways it is hard not to think of the atomic world as an infinitesimal Newtonian universe, with myriad suns and planets spinning through the void that is at the heart of all matter.'

Again I thought of those crystalline particles orbiting gracefully in the remote vastness of the atomic plane. 'But you didn't go into physics yourself,' I enquired.

'No, mathematics was always my first love.'

The record on the gramophone had at last reached the end. As Weenie walked over to rescue the needle, he slapped Richardson on the back. 'He's being rather modest, John. Richardson is a genius, believe me.' Weenie carefully removed the record and placed it in its cardboard sleeve. He then slipped another record out from its casing and placed it on the deck. The needle was dropped down unceremoniously before sweet music once more filled the kitchen. Weenie pretended to dance, holding his arms out as though embracing a partner, twirling round and round, his feet gliding across the stone floor. He sang along with the words. Richardson and I both looked across at each other in some embarrassment as our host pirouetted through the flickering light.

Weenie stopped, rather breathless. 'If ever you want to know about algorithms for solving ordinary and partial differential equations then Richardson's your man.'

'I know nothing of these things,' I responded.

'Of course you don't. Why should you? You stick with your mushrooms and liverworts.' Weenie began to waltz gently around the room again. As he passed the oven he quickly opened the small metal door, peered in and then kicked it closed with his foot before waltzing off once more.

'I find the practical side of my work the most satisfying,' I retorted, eyeing Richardson rather than the bizarre form that was circling about us in the shadows.

'I'm a scientist, not a theoretician,' replied Richardson. 'I also work in the real world.'

'Indeed you do. Tell John about your weather forecasting. Fascinating.'

There was a slight cough before he began. 'I'm not sure you know about this, but my real interest lies in the use of mathematical modelling to achieve statistically accurate forecasts and predictions. Before the War I began work on the application of numerical techniques to weather forecasting.' Richardson stopped. He appeared reluctant to divulge anything further.

'Go on,' cried Weenie, 'you can't stop there! What about your Scottish work and the book?'

Richardson shuffled nervously in his chair as Weenie joined us at the table again. There was another cough. 'In 1913 I became Director of the Eskdalemuir Observatory of the British Meteorological Office—'

'Before that you worked with peat,' interjected Weenie.

Richardson smiled painfully at this rude interruption. 'National Peat Industries Limited, if you must know. The cutting of drains is a most precise art.' I assumed this to be a joke so I smiled before emptying the contents of my glass. 'It was while I was at Eskdalemuir that I began to use the approximation techniques developed with National Peat Industries. This became the basis of my numerical weather prediction technique.' There was a slight pause as Richardson removed his glasses and rubbed his eyes as if the work from his days in Scotland still lay heavy on his shoulders. 'I was dealing with huge amounts of information and an incomplete understanding of differential equations. In some instances I was forced to develop new differential approaches from first principles.'

'Much of the research for this was carried out while Richardson was at the Front.'

'Yes, indeed. I took with me as much of my equipment as I could. Most importantly this included a set of detailed meteorological recordings that had been made for Western Europe on 20th May 1910. Using this data I was able to test the predictive capabilities of my methodologies.'

'Indeed,' I responded with some interest.

'Taking the data that had been recorded at 7 a.m. on 20th May 1910, I then attempted to predict what the weather had been at 1 p.m. on the same day – exactly six hours later. A rather modest endeavour, one would assume.'

'I won't stake my life on predicting what will happen with the English weather one hour in advance!' I replied.

'Perhaps wise. But I had to test my predictive calculations. In fact the effort took me the best part of six weeks and the conclusion was less than satisfactory.' After a quick glance at Weenie, Richardson added, 'In fact the prediction was wildly inaccurate – a most depressing result for me, of course.'

'There goes the Enlightenment.'

I couldn't help but note the increasing flippancy of Weenie's behaviour. Richardson was right to ignore his sarcasm. 'The quality of the data was poor, of course. Due to the limited distribution of meteorological observing stations across Europe, I was often forced to deduce wind strengths across key geographical areas. This naturally introduced large degrees of error into the mathematical modelling that was reflected in the result. But the actual predictive technique has yet to be proved ineffective.'

'And while all this is going on, Richardson's dodging the shells with the rest of us!' Weenie again slapped Richardson on the shoulder.

'It sounds fascinating. Have you managed to extend this prototype?' I asked.

Richardson drew a deep breath. 'The experiment in France proved that unless the predictive model could be fed with reliable and up-to-date information, it would have little to offer. I say as much in my book.'

Weenie leaned back on his chair, picked up a small volume that had been lying on top of the cupboards, close to a rack of unwashed test tubes, and slid it across the table to me. It was called *Weather Forecasting by Numerical Process*. The name Lewis Fry Richardson was also on the front. 'Just happen to have a copy here, signed of course.'

I began to glance through the contents, letting the pages run across my fingers.

'In the book I describe a global weather-forecasting factory. A bit of fantasy, if you will, but perhaps one day, who knows?' Richardson took a sip of wine before continuing. 'To capture changing conditions across the planet one would need a network of weather balloons, no more than one hundred miles apart. The information recorded by each of them would then be sent back to the forecasting factory.

'One would need a large auditorium, of course, spherical in shape just like the Earth. The inner walls of the auditorium would be painted to reflect the oceans and landmasses of the planet, each in its correct position. Standing in the room would be like standing within the globe itself, looking out – the darkness of the interior cut only by the brilliant shafts of red and blue light beamed onto the landscape, indicating climatic change.' He looked across at me for confirmation of his vision. 'A column would rise up into the central space of the factory, a thin sliver of wood, hovering between the north and south poles represented at the top and bottom of the auditorium. At the top of this command post would sit the controller, ensuring that the computational readings for every aspect of the globe were up to date and coterminous. Around this central column, upon great circular platforms spanning the entire room, would be arrayed countless clerks and computationalists, working as teams specializing in a fixed part of the global map. With slide rules and other computational equipment they would undertake the task of completing the predictive equations, updating the global map in a perpetual process. Pneumatic communication would ensure that these results could be quickly dispatched across the factory complex, perhaps even distributed globally through the means of radio.'

Weenie opened another bottle of wine and we talked some more during the meal. The meat and potato pie was delicious but all three of us were very tired and we had retreated to bed by ten o'clock. Before we did, however, I brought down my camera and took a picture of Richardson and Weenie together in the candlelit gloom of the kitchen. Observed through the viewfinder, my two companions took on an ethereal, ghost-like quality, their drawn, grim faces seemingly coming to me from ages past. As we departed from the kitchen Weenie came and whispered to me that Richardson's service with an ambulance unit had enabled him to witness the full range of injuries inflicted by the War. But Weenie also stated that the job had allowed him to further his inquiries into mathematical explanations of the conflict itself. From this work Richardson hoped that it might well be possible to derive the explanatory mechanisms that underpin all conflicts, a general principal of warfare. Richardson had already published a short monograph on the subject, *Mathematical Psychology of War*, in which these theories were discussed. He was in no doubt that he would soon be in possession of a series of mathematical laws that would enable him to model basic conflict patterns, with the potential benefit that the twentieth century could become the most peaceful ever recorded.

I fell to sleep pondering these wondrous ideas.

The following day began rather overcast. Although I am not a late riser, as you know, Father, I found that when I came down from my room both Weenie and Richardson were out, although I had no inkling as to where they had gone. The cottage was still and quiet, as was the tiny lane outside. I made myself a pot of tea and sat in the kitchen with my little notebook, the cat circling me. I had many things to consider, of course, not least the theories of Weenie's strange friend. I profess I had been deeply moved by the pious earnestness that underpinned his work, to the extent that visions of his great meteorological machine had drifted through my dreams the previous night. The great hall, crammed with clerks forever calculating global data, to be relayed back across the planet through a network of wires and beacons, was an idea that affected me acutely, and I found that I had emptied Weenie's tea pot before I realized I had entered nothing in my notebook!

Much as I was enjoying the hospitality offered by my host, I realized it was time to once again think about the continuation of my journey. There were a number of options that lay before me and I spent some time considering each with care. By the end of these deliberations I had decided upon a course of action and knew that the next leg of the journey would take me into the heart of Leicester itself. But there were other things to consider, of course. I had a book to write which, despite my best intentions, was rather floundering. I thought of the kind words and enthusiasm offered by Uncle George and Aunt Beth and realized how much I now needed their horticultural expertise and support. What I craved was inspiration, and that could not be gained by sitting at a table drinking tea. I thus grabbed my coat and camera and duly left the house, tucking the notebook into the pocket of my Burberry. Alice's glassy stare followed me up the garden path from her position in the bay window.

The countryside is wonderful in these parts, as Richardson had alluded to the previous night. The Gwash valley gently slopes down to the river and then rises again as one continues south. As I meandered along the lanes, the low autumnal sun appeared as the clouds broke, cutting through the canopy of yellow and orange leaves intertwined above my head. There are now great heaps of such leaves upon the floor – I'm sure it is the same at home, Father! – and it was with a childish joy that I waded through the mounds of this golden and bronze precipitation, releasing the most gorgeous earthy smells in my wake. It reminded me of the one autumn that I spent at Quex, and how I had helped my dumb friend Camille sweep up and burn the leaves from the Bothy. As I continued down the little lane it suddenly occurred to me that Camille might still be at Quex, now surely transformed back into a family estate, and was perhaps at this very minute raking the leaves just as we had done together four years before.

I wandered further away from the cottage, the sun warm enough for me to undo my coat. As I progressed along the empty lanes that crisscross this part of the world, I was suddenly overcome with a memory of my walking tour in the spring of 1918. Then my mind had been besieged by darkness. It is the walking that is always the most evocative, the trudge across open land, the slow march ever onwards. In those early spring days, fresh from my time at Quex, it was not just my imagination that convinced me the tremor in my legs was caused by the field artillery across the Channel. Then as now, I suddenly saw the veil of mud and felt the blasted air of a creeping barrage.

The sun peeked out from behind a large apple tree that grew by the side of the lane. Flies and bemused wasps stumbled across the rotting fruit that littered the grass verge. It is certainly very late for such insects, but nonetheless, there they were. I stopped to kick at the fruit and reflected that, unlike the terrain of my earlier walking tour, Rutland has its fair share of country estates and bucolic hideaways, reminding me very much of that small area of Belgium I came to know so well in the summer of 1917 – although by the time our company arrived at the Salient, the chateaux, farms and idyllic villages were nothing but scattered rubble and earthworks amid a sea of mud.

The chateau atop Bellewarde Ridge had once been a country retreat of the highest order. Situated just off the Menin Road, it had possessed many rooms and servants, with grounds that boasted a large lake stocked with carp. As I crept over the land one night in early September 1917, nudging through the carcasses of previous assaults, it was hard to picture what the place had once been. With Very lights streaming down from the stars above us and enemy fire disembowelling the monstrous cadavers over which we crawled, I had imagined those huge fish, now gone, slipping lazily through the banks of rich green algae.

It was with some surprise that I at last came across the singular Romanesque church of Normanton, practically submerged beneath an advancing tide of foliage. It stood all alone, bereft of any attendant village, and gave no suggestion that it was presently used or indeed that it had been for some time. This was rather a shame as even my poor architectural interest was excited by the pretty design that lay hidden beneath the encroaching weeds. I forced my way around the entire edifice, noting its chancel, nave and western tower, around which stood several impressive gravestones that were now unrecoverable beneath a tangle of ivy, nettles and lichen. The door of the church was not locked and I was able to creep inside. However, so little light penetrated the interior, and such was the pall of death upon the place, that I stayed for a few seconds only, held momentarily spellbound by the torpor of abandoned antiquity that emanated from the chancel and out across the frozen lines of stone pews.

I moved away from the church through what I recognized to be the Normanton Estate. As Richardson noted the previous night, this was now a most distraught and broken property. The grounds suggested they had been left unattended for several years – I emerged onto an overgrown lawn through a rampant ivy that was steadily engulfing an entire border. I could see a large house ahead of me, in front of which three black cars were parked. I stood and watched as two men emerged, carrying a large painting that was carefully placed on the back seat of one of the automobiles. The house itself seemed to be in reasonable shape although its large black windows were curiously soulless on such a splendid afternoon.

As I stared out from my secret position I noticed that not far from me, underneath a large oak tree in the centre of the lawn, were two squirrels, their red fur contrasting markedly with the pigment of the grass upon which they lay. It was clear that these animals had been shot, their tiny bodies clinically ripped open and left to dry beneath the autumn sun. Still visible were the two sets of tracks that the animals had made in the dew that coated the grass in the shade of the large trees to the east. I anxiously looked about me for the sniper but could see nothing to disrupt the peace of this English scene.

A bullet entering bone can make a most extraordinary sound – terrible to hear. Before the victim has time to scream, the shell whines and screeches like a red-hot drill bit, spinning its way through into the marrow. I remained for some time on the edge of the lawn, watching these animals until my distraction was broken by the sound of a car's engine spurting into life. The car loaded with the picture drove away. I noticed that the large wooden door at the front of the house was now closed. I moved back into the undergrowth and retraced my steps through the knee-high grass.

Further into the woods I came upon an untidy heap of leaves and twigs. I plunged my stick into the pile, rather fancifully expecting to arouse the wood ants, whose home this almost certainly had been. However, it seemed clear that this nest had long been abandoned.

On my way out of the estate, as the sun dropped low and the chill of impending night rose from the ground, I found myself pondering on the thoughts and insights revealed to me the previous night. In particular I reflected upon the words of Richardson. I had already experienced at first hand the advantages that a kite balloon could apply to the battlefield, providing observations for field artillery while also illuminating an archaeological tapestry of strange undulations and earthworks lost to the earthbound human eye. Indeed, as part of battle preparation I had been taken up in such an observatory balloon in early September 1917. As I rose into the air from behind the front line I remember how extraordinary it had been to see one's perspective change. What had been chaos and confusion on the ground gradually became ordered and rational as I ascended into the air. I recall holding on to the basket and watching as the frenzied battle preparations below were compressed and stripped down until they resembled nothing more than detail in a two-dimensional photograph. At the same time as this minutiae was lost, a greater clarity was achieved whereby the endless vista of cratered wasteland became as but a cartographical aid beneath the gaze of a general. To the west stood the gates of Ypres, framing the smouldering ruins of the once great cathedral and Cloth Hall. To the north lay the rolling heights of Passchendaele and Zonnebeke, and to the south the blasted nothingness of Hill Sixty and the Messines Ridge.

As we climbed further into the air, the Allied front line became a monstrous thing – a deep scar of trenches and earthworks tearing Flanders asunder, beyond which, to the west, seethed a sprawling army of countless men. There was now no uncertainty that the salient on which they stood had indeed become one enormous sponge. Yet from our vantage point in the balloon those water-filled craters below took on a rarefied beauty in the bright midday sun, their surfaces serene and still as though laid with crystal glass. Streams of ooze and detritus meandered from flooded shell hole to flooded shell hole as if they were rivulets joyously exploring the home counties. Occasionally these gossamer surfaces and surrounding land were infused with a crimson colour of such iridescence that I was reminded of the red glass in the chancel of St Cuthbert's on a hot summer's afternoon.

I recall that as my fellow officer and I climbed further into the sky all sounds from the ground slowly withered away, to be replaced by nothing but the creak of the basket straining at its tether and the flap of the balloon over our heads. Even the pounding of enemy guns appeared to have momentarily ceased as we made our way up alongside our companion balloons. Perhaps at that moment I too fancifully thought I could leap from the basket and propel myself higher into the clouds.

We stood and watched the scene below for some time, my fellow aeronaut occasionally shouting across to those balloonists closest by or signalling to the ground with the aid of the flags. It was only as enemy fire resumed, rippling the surface of the stilled ocean below like pebbles idly dropped from Olympus, that we were winched back down to terra firma.

I returned to Weenie's cottage late in the afternoon. The front door was ajar but inside all was quiet and apparently unoccupied. I crept through the hall and stuck my head round the kitchen door. Weenie was sitting at the table, his delicate reading glasses perched on the end of his nose and a book held aloft in one hand. He looked over the top of his glasses.

'The wanderer returns. How did you find my little valley?'

'A most rewarding landscape. It has a timeless, lost-world quality that is quite haunting, as Richardson noted yesterday.' I took the camera from around my neck and placed it on the table alongside a large pestle and mortar before unbuttoning my coat and hanging it on the back of the door.

Weenie put his book down before carefully removing

his glasses and placing them on top. I looked at the cover of the book: *Relativity: The Special and General Theory.*

'I came across the Normanton Estate. I understand what Richardson said yesterday when he described it as rather run-down. The gardens have certainly seen better days.'

'The estate is being sold off. I have no idea what will become of it.'

'I came upon a little church all by itself within the grounds. I was able to peep inside.'

'That's Normanton church – the only remnant of a village cleared in the 1760s to make way for the expansion of the Heathcote estate. There's a rather fine old hall.'

'I watched as two men removed a large picture from it. It appears the building is being gutted.'

This seemed to upset Weenie. He got up and filled the kettle before placing it on his stove. 'It's not all doom and gloom. Did you come across the Marshall Estate and Hambleton Hall?'

'Indeed I did. Yesterday, as I came in through Upper Hambleton a strange man asked me if I was a guest at the house. I'm sure I could hear music and laughter from the grounds.'

Weenie tittered. 'I'm sure you did. The house is now owned by Mrs Astley-Cooper, who tends to keep, shall we say, the queerest company in the county.'

I did not question Weenie any further on this point but rather attempted to question him about his current researches. Yet it would be misleading of me if I didn't say that Weenie appeared less than enthused with this direction in the conversation.

'I suppose this is another book I should be reading,' I stated, sitting down at the table.

My companion appeared to scoff before sliding the book across the table. 'Give it a go.' I randomly flicked through the pages, an act that offered Weenie enough time to explain his problem. He gave it a certain name, what he called the *relativity of simultaneity*. He explained it thus: Newtonian certainties were now out of the window. Doctor Einstein's theories were suggesting that there was no absolute measure of time against which events could be ordered. That is only the essence of what my companion said, of course. Weenie spent many minutes describing, in the most scientific ways, the true depth of his despair over this issue. It was such a fundamental principle, and was explained with such vibrancy, that as I sat in that little room surrounded by darkness, it appeared that the very pillars of the universe were crumbling beneath my feet.

It is now early morning of the 23rd. I have just heard the milk cart rumble past below my window. Soon it will be light. I find it hard to believe I have been up most of the night writing this letter but that must be the case. I will be able to sleep for the rest of the day – I will set out tomorrow for Leicester.

Weenie appeared genuinely upset when I informed him of my decision to move on. Perhaps the situation wasn't helped by the fact that Richardson was also intending to depart that same morning.

Weenie prepared a wonderful breakfast of egg, bacon and toast after which I went off to reclaim dear old Angus.

After packing my saddlebags it was with much emotion that I finally waved goodbye to Weenie and set off up the tiny lane that would take me towards Upper Hambleton and thence Oakham, the empty gaze of Alice silently tracking my departing form as I made my way up out of the valley.

The intention is to move towards the end of my journey, Father. And for me the journey's end lies in Leicester, at an address at the very heart of the city. This will offer a contrast with little old Oakham, as I'm sure you are aware, and even more of a comparison with the Gwash Valley of the Hambletons, which, more than any other place I have been to, seemed to exist in its own time and space, where the beat of modernity is kept at the door.

And so today (yes, there is now light under the curtains) I shall recuperate, continue with my notes for *Perambulations* and then set off again tomorrow on perhaps what will be the final leg of this odyssey. And then I will be homeward bound, Father. Back to my home, where I belong.

Your devoted son,
    John

PART NINE

Durham Category 'A' Prison

Present Day, November

– 1 –

I am rapidly losing sense of time and place. This diary remains my only anchor.

Time is the biggest distortion. In here things are totally reversed, a strange mirror reflection of what goes for normality outside. An hour is a day and a day an hour, or rather a minute or even a second. The short term becomes an immeasurable gulf, the next hour the tallest crest against which both wit and common sense can snap like a hawser. It is the ticking of the minute hand that sends men insane. Contrarily, the days and weeks are as nothing while months and even seasons remain as faceless as the walls of my cell. At times I feel as though I were becalmed within the centre of the darkest of storms, the black hole in the centre of the cosmos. From here time itself ceases to exist, yet for those outside the event horizon, years, centuries, even eons, fall through the fingers like sand.

It is completely understandable that Jim was almost able to hang himself. To the guards, he must hardly have moved, a granite Buddha no less, while around him, in his lonely cell, the strips of torn bedding came together with the imperceptibility of tectonic plates.

I have told Dr Sanders of these things and he seems immensely impressed with my fortitude. Since the governor appears deaf to my pleas to attend the prison garden, I am in the process of bringing Dr Sanders onto my side. It was for this reason that earlier today I explained to him the wonders of the English puffball (*Lycoperdon giganteum*). The fruit are certainly edible, especially when young, and when ripe the merest touch will send tens of thousands of spores into the air to be carried away on invisible currents. Autumn is such a wonderful time of year, particularly for the fungologist such as me. I have decided to call this period Opora in honour of those botanists who have gone before me. Opora – the time of death but also of revival and hope for the New Year. My own hope for the future is undiminished.

– 2 –

Dark Matter. Behaviour can only be explained by what can't be seen – by the missing ninety per cent. Invisible, unseen, existing outside the realm of equations and mathematical models. The stuff of black holes. The non-empty emptiness behind his eyes.

Karl Schwarzschild was born in Frankfurt am Main, Germany, in October 1873. A gifted child, he had already published two papers on the theory of orbits of double stars by the time he was seventeen. After studying at the universities of Strasbourg and Munich, Schwarzschild worked as an assistant at the Kufner Sternwarte in Vienna, where he developed a formula to calculate the properties of photographic material.

On the outbreak of war in August 1914 Schwarzschild volunteered for military service. Given his technical training perhaps it should not come as a surprise that the Imperial Army thought it best he was put in charge of a weather station. This seems perfectly sensible. The German master plan relied on speed and surprise, puncturing through Belgium, knocking out Paris before turning to deal with the east. The Schlieffen Plan indeed! One of the great unknowns in warfare is the weather, of course. Battles, perhaps even empires, have been won or lost on the whim of an anticyclone. The advance of the German armies in August 1914 depended on a gathering and unrelenting momentum. Delay of any kind could seriously jeopardize the entire war effort, as Herr Doktor Schwarzschild, bouncing from side to side with his barometers, thermometers and astronomical telescopes in the baggage train, would have known only too well. I picture him as the necromancers and soothsayers of old, parting the canvas skin of his wagon to decode the great fortunes written in the sky, the massed ranks of the invading army spreading out before him beneath an unrelenting summer sun.

The army soon ground to a halt in France, the speed and surprise of the charge replaced by the attrition of trench warfare. And likewise the fortunes of Schwarzschild changed also. Since the weather was now of secondary interest to the strategists, the good doktor found himself part of an artillery unit. Here his great mathematical lore was invaluable, capturing the exquisite tracery of German shells arcing over no-man's-land.

With stalemate in the west, Schwarzschild was transferred to the frigid outlands of the Eastern Front. It seems almost beyond comprehension now but from 1915, while serving in Russia, Schwarzschild continued with his pioneering mathematical work. Just months after Einstein published his General Theory of Relativity in 1915,

Schwarzschild worked out the effect of this theory for the gravitational fields of stars. He came to the extraordinary conclusion that objects with sufficient mass would actually be able to curve spacetime, to distort the known universe. Further, he postulated that bodies of sufficiently large mass would effect a spacetime curvature of such a degree that even light could not return once it had entered the vortex. These truly startling entities would be unseeable, invisible to those with mortal sight, their only physicality being the utter void their presence punctured in the exquisite tapestry of the heavens.

It seems apt to me that as Schwarzschild drew together these remarkably pioneering ideas, he himself was set within the midst of the greatest terrestrial behemoth, Mother Russia, into which whole armies, even time itself, had been known to disappear. Staring out across the limitless grasslands of the steppes, it must have seemed a cruel irony that as he described the ultimate desolation of the singularity, he too was lost, cut off from home, invisible, unknowable to those he loved many thousands of miles away, beyond the slow curve of the limitless space stretched out before him.

What price is there for staring into the heart of the beast? For Schwarzschild, at least his moment of triumph was shortlived. His body quickly set about destroying itself. Pemphigus was diagnosed, a rare disease even in 1916, by which the body's immune system attacks the skin. When invalided home in March 1916, his family was shocked by his appearance, so aged had he become. It was as if

Schwarzschild had experienced twenty years when but two had passed for those in Germany. He was dead within two months.

At his funeral a colleague noted that though he had died so young and with such promise, the name of Karl Schwarzschild would live long after memories of the War had dissolved into dust.

As I sat in a corner of the library reading these things, the nasal expirations of Tuckman growing and receding as he shuffled round his tiny world, I recalled the time I mentioned quantum mechanics to Jim. It was not long after he had bought his computer, with Internet access of course. A Saturday morning. A few weeks after Rutland Water, not long after the death of Julie. By the time Jim came knocking at my door with tales of the Lolitas I had been up since four reading several important academic papers published on the Internet. Before reaching the lounge Jim had also mentioned the hardcore and the ebonies. With excited gesturing that I recognized only too well, he talked about the she-men and the Russians. As Jim huddled around my computer I explained the purpose of my new line of scientific endeavour.

The theories of Newton and Einstein proved capable of explaining not only the everyday world – men and clouds and trees – but also the very large, the world of cosmological giants such as stars, planets and galaxies. Yet not long after the end of the Great War it was clear that these theories did not fit so well with the atomic world.

Electrons had been discovered at the turn of the century by Thomson. It was believed that these strange particles circled the nucleus like planets around the sun, forever orbiting within their invisible crystalline spheres.

I recall that Jim showed no interest in my elucidation of these complex theories. But he told me how shocked he had been by the amateurs.

I continued. It was quickly realized that this atomic model could not in fact be explained by classical theory: according to Newtonian physics, the electrons should crash into the nucleus like minuscule comets. The fact that this didn't happen was the clearest indication that something was deeply amiss with our classical theories of the physical world.

What about teens? And what about pre-teens? Let me show you, offered Jim.

In 1927 it was discovered that electrons have both particle and wavelike properties, underpinning the need for two quite different and contradictory theories to explain the physical behaviour of light. Jim grunted and moved his face closer to the screen. I mean, light could either be understood as a wave or as a stream of particles, but not both. But this is what the studies of electrons suggested.

Animals, can you believe animals? With a pig or horse. They'll send you as many of these babies as you want. Just a monthly fee. Interested?

Light behaves as both a particle and a wave, depending on what method of observation you use. Each explanation fundamentally opposes the other – light can either be a particle or a wave; it can't be both. Or can it? I recall moving over to the bedroom window to add a certain gravitas to what I was saying. In truth, light and matter do exist as particles; what behaves like a wave is the probability of where that particle will be. I could see Jim's hunched form in the reflection of the window. Everything has a wavelength, a wave-particle duality; even you, Jim. For things other than at the atomic level, however, this duality is so small as to be practically non-existent. That's what the scientists say.

Lesbians, have you seen what those girls do to each other? Young girls, I mean schoolgirls, like you see on the street. The answer is at my fingertips.

At the sub-atomic level, the everyday physical rules that govern our world are thrown out of the window. Have you heard of the Heisenberg uncertainty principle?

Jim's reflection in the window refused to move. Shaved, that's how Jim liked them. That's one thing he did know.

It appears that the position and energy of a sub-atomic particle cannot be known simultaneously. Both exist only as probabilities, and the very act of measuring itself intrinsically changes the properties so that its current position can never be known with any certainty.

Here we go. Have you got your credit card there?

I have no idea why Jim was insistent on signing me up for these services. The pictures of young girls were nothing but obscenities; I deleted them all as they arrived in my inbox. The police will confirm this – they found nothing of ill repute in my email account. But as Jim sat in front of my computer on that day, it was all very new to him. He was a kid with a new toy.

Shall we print a few of these off?

I don't want anything to do with them, I replied.

Jim seemed content with this and the printer remained inactive. However, I could tell that something else was on his mind. I looked outside. And then it came.

I've made a friend in a chat room. Just like your little friend.

I watched as my neighbour assiduously mowed his rear lawn. He adamantly refused to purchase an electric mower, claiming the old push mowers produced a better finish. His face was red. Occasionally he wiped it with a white handkerchief.

I don't want to know.

Oh yes you do.

These words hung in the air, lingering above the delicate moan of the computer. I rested my forehead against the cold pane of glass, gripping the windowsill. In my mind I saw the great crystalline spheres of electrons and neutrons spinning round the fiery nucleus of the atom.

I don't, I whispered, my strength suddenly deserting me. I've had enough.

3

When I was arrested my first reaction was to think of my fish. Does that surprise you? Looking after fish is no simple matter, you see. Even the most capable aquarist cannot establish a self-sustaining aquarium: the fish need to be fed, the plants tended to, the glass sides regularly cleaned. Temperature and filtration units need to be regularly monitored. The onslaught of disease keenly contested. I hope it should not now come as a surprise that my first question to the arresting officer was that I should be allowed to feed the fish. It still hurts me, of course, that my aquariums have all been closed down, the fish given away by all accounts. I was not allowed to get involved in the process.

Jim's talk had disturbed me. I found it difficult to sleep that night. I remember getting up early the following morning to clean my tanks. Let me repeat: keeping an aquarium clean and tidy is not a simple matter. It is something that cannot be left to pure chance. The longer the aquariums are left in their natural state, the worse they become, until the plants are ragged and eaten, and the glass sides thick with algae. If this is not to your liking then you have little option but to roll up your sleeves and begin the cleaning process.

Looking back, perhaps I tried to lose myself in this task. It must be admitted that once the cleaning process is begun, there is little time to consider anything else. I seem to recall that I had nearly finished capturing the fish when Jim unexpectedly came round. I answered the door with my sleeves rolled up. My arms were wet, and there was water over my jumper and down my jeans.

I'm in the middle of cleaning aquarium one, I said. I looked exasperated, hoping he would come back at a more opportune moment.

Good for you. He walked past me into the kitchen. We need to talk.

I still had the net in my hand. Water was dripping from it onto the floor tiles. I closed the door and returned to the lounge. Jim followed.

I can't stop, I informed him. I have to get this done quickly.

Jim stood by me and watched as I caught the last of the fish. There was a plop sound as I placed them into the bucket squatting at Jim's feet. Their companions were all there, crammed into that tiny globule of water, as vulnerable as micro-organisms within a droplet of water. Jim looked down at them like some monstrous Tellos. The bucket was practically between his feet, as vulnerable as the Argonaut.

How long can you keep them alive in there?

They should be OK for about an hour. That gives me enough time to clean their home.

Jim watched as I started to rub the algae off the glass sides with my cloth. Although he remained quiet I was aware that there was something of importance he wished to share with me. It was only when I began siphoning the dirt off the bottom of the aquarium that he explained what this was.

I'm going to need your help.

With what?

There was a further pause. Some loose gravel was sucked up into the pipe. Moments later it rattled into the second bucket that I was using to collect the detritus.

I've already told you, I've met someone on the Internet.

Jim, it's far too dangerous. I've told you about the risks.

I've taken all precautions. All the things you said. It can't be traced.

I was less than convinced, of course. The bucket had become full. I pulled the pipe out of the water and took the bucket into the kitchen where I emptied its contents down the sink. When I returned I found Jim unmoved, staring down into the container of fish that was still trembling at his feet.

I don't want to be a part of this any more. It's too dangerous.

I've arranged to meet her next Saturday. I'll bring tape and rope.

This has got out of control.

We'll bring her back to my place. Keep her in the loft for as long as we can.

The siphon slipped to the floor, its contents spilling out across the carpet. The room was filled with the rot of fish shit.

This is madness, Jim. You can't possibly think you're going to get away with it.

He stared down at the fish again. You leave that to me, he said.

Later on that day I went over to Jim's. The afternoon sun was hot and, as I walked out of my driveway, I could feel it burning the back of my neck. Every front garden that I passed was brimming with flowers of one sort or another. Several people were even out with wheelbarrows and spades, their backs bent and their heads submerged within shrubberies or flowerbeds. I was able to quickly slip by without causing any distraction; in fact I doubt whether anyone actually observed my short journey. I kept myself to myself, as did many others on the street.

I noticed that Jim had put out a number of hanging baskets. They were attached to the side of his house. They gently swayed in the breeze as though part of a Newton's cradle. I walked up Jim's driveway and knocked on the kitchen door. There was a hanging basket here as well. It had great festoons of colour cascading down in the manner of a Technicolor beard. I tapped on the frosted-glass pane and watched as Jim's distorted shape drew towards me.

I'm going to bring her back here.

We were in the kitchen now and I was watching Jim making a pot of tea.

But why? I asked. What will you achieve? The risks are enormous. If she escapes, she'll know you and where you live. There'll be no way out this time round.

Jim poured the boiling water over the leaves in the bottom of the ceramic teapot. I was sitting at the breakfast bar, my legs dangling stupidly from the stool.

But she won't escape, will she? We'll both see to that. She'll be upstairs, out of sight, in the loft.

I just don't understand. This is too much, beyond anything imaginable.

It's very simple, actually. The details are all on the Internet, the relevant case histories and diagrams. We simply keep her tied down and sedated. The loft is the perfect place. There's the large table.

Jim gently rocked and swung the pot as if it were a miniature baby in his embrace. The tea was then poured into two china cups through the strainer. The spout knocked against the sides of the cups, producing the most delicate ringing sound that hung in the air for several seconds.

But this is no game. What you're suggesting is, is not right. An abhorrence.

Jim remained standing at the bar. He raised a cup to his lips and then abruptly lowered it back to the saucer. Again, there was the golden sound of angels' voices.

That's why I need you, he said. I need your expertise. It

will be your job to keep her alive. You do it with your fish every day. You maintain them, feed them, sustain them. It will be your job to do the same to the girl. Think of this as your biggest, most important project.

It was difficult not to be swayed by such flattery. Jim was right, of course. If the girl was to be kept alive, artificially as it were, confined in that small room, for the pleasure of Jim and his friends, then my skills would be critical. Indeed, I would be the central pin upon which the whole project revolved. The girl would be kidnapped, that much was already pre-determined. My intervention could not stop this. Yet I could ensure that the girl's last days were of a suitably humane character, given the circumstances. I would be the expert adviser, exerting his influence to keep the worst of the debaucheries at the door.

By the Friday of that week I was gaining some sense of the difficulties that lay ahead. My initial hopes and ambitions were certainly floundering. To put it bluntly, my scientific researches were proving less than satisfactory. For several days I had not been able to read any of my books, such was the disturbed state of my mind. I felt the frustration that the great scientist must feel when he is denied access to his laboratories. On the Friday I had got up early because I knew that Jim would be coming round at 10 a.m. to take me to Bradgate Park. Both of us had taken a day off work. He was not late.

Jim stood in the kitchen and watched as I grabbed my coat. It's warm out there. You won't need that, he said.

I feel better with it on if you don't mind. Have you hired the van?

We pick it up tomorrow.

Our experiences at Rutland Water had encouraged the hiring of a van for Saturday. Given the fact that the girl was coming back with us, I deemed a van to be essential.

What about the rope and sedatives?

I've managed to get everything we need. Don't worry, everything's in hand.

Have you made contact with the girl recently?

I was in a chat room with her yesterday evening. She's still up for it. She doesn't suspect anything at all.

I picked up my plastic bag from the kitchen table. Jim smiled. What's in there? he asked. I drew out my notebook and a tourist's guide to Bradgate Park. Jim shook his head. Come on then. Let's get going.

I do not remember much about the journey through the countryside. We took Jim's car and parked in the main car park. The teashop over the road was not very busy, although you could tell that this would not last for long. The car park was only a quarter full. But then, it was still a weekday. Tomorrow would be very different.

After the engine had fallen silent we both remained in the car. We did not speak initially but instead watched and observed as people came and went. Jim reached down for a bag of boiled sweets that were kept in the pocket on the driver's door. He took one himself before shaking the bag under my nose. I declined the offer.

There were dogs everywhere. A family was having a

picnic by their car. A football was being kicked to and fro. And always there was the movement of people into the park itself, through the gate or over the steps that went up and down the stone wall.

It's busy, I remarked after some time.

It'll be busier than this tomorrow. I looked across at Jim. But that's a good thing. The more people there are, the less significant we will be.

I followed the logic of what Jim had said but still felt distinctly uneasy. A Frisbee landed close to the car. A small boy ran across and picked it up. Before running back to his family he looked up at us and smiled. I smiled back.

She'll be here tomorrow at 10 a.m., said Jim. She'll be on time, I'm sure – she's coming on the bus from Loughborough. I've already told her that my car, or should I say my character's car, is a bit dodgy. When she arrives we tell her that his car has broken down and that we've come to pick her up and take her to him. She steps into the back of the van and wham! We've got her.

And we're meant to be his older brothers.

That's right. Again, I've already slipped them into the conversation so she should be aware of us.

And I drive back?

Yes, unless you want to do the nasty work in the back?

And afterwards I take the van back to the garage?

You do *all* the driving. That gives me time to deal with the girl. You then come back. Remember, you've got to keep her going.

It was such an odious scheme that it was difficult to

summon up the effort to remain positive about our chances. But with no real option but to go along with Jim's madcap plans, I remained quiet and instead meekly followed my companion as he got out of the car and strolled around the car park.

The weakest point will be when she gets into the back of the van. I'll have to get in behind her and hold her down while I use the sedatives. You get into the van and immediately drive away. If she does put up a struggle I'm hoping the sound of the engine will smother it.

And if it doesn't?

I've got alternative strategies. Jim looked at me with a slight smile. He then looked across the car park. Do you want an ice-cream?

We had come to the far side. An ice-cream van was standing before us. There was no queue.

No thanks.

Jim bought an ice-cream cornet and ate it as we walked back. At the car we stood on opposite sides, he on the driver's side and me on the passenger's. We looked across at each other over the roof.

So you know what you're doing?

I think so, I replied. I drive the van.

4

Bradgate Park stands on the remains of an ancient volcano. Charnwood Forest lies all around, although it has not been a forest as such for many centuries. The park itself is a rather bleak place, with rocky outcrops, ancient trees and herds of deer. At the park's centre lie the redbrick remains of Bradgate House. To walk amongst its ruins on a dark winter morning is to experience the greatest solitude that the county can provide. The house had been built by the Grey family at the end of the fifteenth century, and here in October 1537 Lady Frances gave birth to Jane, the first of three. From an early age this erudite little girl was caught up in the dark schemes of Tudor politics.

I had hoped to find some time to visit the house on the Saturday morning. The early sunshine was bright and clear, and as we drove silently to the park through the empty streets I began to visualize myself wandering through the redbrick remains of that once important domicile. After only nine days as Queen, Jane was thrown into the Tower, from where she and her husband were executed for high treason. It is reported that as the poor girl went to her execution, she passed the decapitated body of her husband being brought back from the block. The head and body of Jane were buried in the chapel of St Peter-ad-Vincula, and it is said that, many years later, when the coffin was opened, the remains were found in perfect condition, the ivory skin of Lady Jane Grey miraculously preserved just as it had been when she was led to her death at the age of seventeen. But within seconds of the wonder being seen, the remains, both body and clothes, crumbled to dust.

We were at the car park by 9.15, stationary against the perimeter wall, the rear doors of the van facing out. I argued there was time to visit the house but Jim was in vehement disagreement. I couldn't help but notice that he was in a very nervous state. The relaxed figure of the previous trip was certainly gone. His face was red and he was sweating. We both sat in the van and waited. I had brought my book with me. It was in the pocket of my coat. I took it out and found my familiar bookmark. Twentieth-century philosophers, chapter three, Bertrand Russell. Jim pretended not to notice.

The radio was on but the volume was so low that it was impossible to tell what the man was saying. On arriving, the car park had been almost empty, but as we waited cars began to appear. Dogs and wax-coated owners too. Jim's fingers drummed on the wheel as he looked out at the side mirrors. In the back of the van I could see some carefully folded sheets and a plastic bag. There was a smell of disinfectant.

What was Russell doing, scribbling away during the

Great War, refusing to fight? Analytic philosophy, that's what: the belief in the centrality of the scientific method. Getting to the logical core of our existence, unearthing the logical forms hidden within our natural language. Like an alchemist, slowly distilling the ambiguity and vagueness of the spoken words, releasing the bird from the bell jar.

You let me do the talking, OK, I remember Jim saying at one point, as we sat there.

I looked up from the book and nodded.

You just look as inconspicuous as you can. She mustn't suspect a thing.

I recall thinking that we both looked rather suspicious and that I wouldn't be surprised if the girl simply fled. That would be the ideal solution, of course. If the girl had anything about her at all she would run away and we could both go home and forget about this sad adventure. I even remember thinking that I could give the girl a signal, perhaps a slight shaking of my head that would make her think twice about stepping into the back of the van.

As it got close to 10 a.m. Jim opened his door and got out. He had picked a rather obscure spot in the car park, and, as yet, no one had parked near us. I could tell that Jim was pleased with this. As he climbed out he told me to stay in the van. I watched him circle the vehicle, constantly glancing back at the car park entrance. I began reading the book again.

So there was a truth, that most holy of holy, the objective fact. Russell is right, words are the lenses through which knowledge is attained, but can he be right also that the logical forms of that knowledge are equally sequestered within the structures of those very words? And if not, how is the truth attained?

Suddenly I noticed Jim stop and stare. I could tell immediately that he had seen her. He came round and stuck his head through the open driver's side.

I think this is her. You had better get into the driver's seat.

This I did by shuffling across. Jim stayed outside. I watched him through the windows. I watched him hover, uncertain at first. I leaned forward and glanced back at the entrance. I saw a girl in the distance walking into the park. She had long blonde hair. She kept looking round. This had to be her. And then she clasped something to her ear – a mobile phone! She was talking to someone. Jim hadn't thought of that! I tried to catch Jim's expression but I couldn't find him, he was obviously standing at the back of the van where there were no windows. I glanced back at the girl and noticed that she had now stopped, presumably at the prearranged meeting place. She was still talking into the phone. I couldn't see Jim. He had not moved from his position. He must have been watching her, waiting for his opportunity. I was about to lean out and suggest that we go when, in the side mirror, I suddenly saw him strolling away from the van towards the girl. Obviously this was the moment. The girl hadn't seen him. Her hair fluttered in the slight breeze. She was wearing jeans and a pink top, laughing into the phone. Such confidence and charm! Who was it on the other end? Her dad, her friend? Jim was now close to her, no more than ten feet away and yet still she hadn't seen him. What would he say to her? Perhaps he would walk straight past and come back to the van. I prayed that that would be the case. I leaned across the passenger seat and stared out of the window. He had stopped in front of her and was obviously talking. The mobile phone had been put away. Jim pointed back to the van and I quickly dropped down. When my gaze returned I saw that the two of them were slowly walking towards me. Jim seemed to be talking earnestly. The girl was passive, listening but showing no emotion. As they approached I could hear Jim's voice. He mentioned something about the sea, or a holiday. She would not fall for it.

They stopped at the back of the van. I heard Jim say, I'll take you to him now. He's waiting for you.

There was a pause, and then the girl said, I'd rather not. If you give me his number I'll phone him.

There was now another pause and then Jim said, OK, I've got it here in the back of the van.

And then I heard the door open. And at that point it all happened.

He must have pushed her into the back. I heard a scream but it was quickly muffled. The van shook on its suspension springs as though a boat buffeted by a sudden squall. There was another muffled cry and then I heard the rear door slam shut. I did not look behind me. I refused to look back. The sound of scrabbling was too much, of hair pulling, of biting, of sharp, concentrated heavy breathing. And of the punch, like an iron bar, that brought bile to my throat.

The atomic structure is one familiar to us, but in philosophy too? Why yes, of course, because while the guns still pounded Flanders fields didn't Russell introduce his theory of logical atomism. Logical atomism?

The girl screamed again. She had loosened Jim's hold on her. I heard him shuffling in the carrier bag. The van lurched to the right and then the left. I looked out of the window and in the side mirrors. All was still and serene as if I was staring out at the gentle undulations of a sea bed while the mightiest tsunami raged many leagues above.

Logical atomism, that the world consists of logical atoms, irreducible points of non-inferential knowledge. Foci of true certainty in a subjective void! Little atomic structures of pure logic, known only through our sensations, the very building blocks upon which molecular facts are created. And language too must be used to represent this underlying logical form; it must not muddle or confuse, but rather it should lay bare the logical components upon which its propositions are based.

I heard the girl's muffled voice again: No, no, no.

Jim was saying, Yes, yes, yes. I then heard the girl's voice disappear, fade away, as though she had fallen down into a large black hole, like Alice chasing the White Rabbit. Goodnight, my dear. Drive, drive you bastard. Get us out of here.

We carried the girl into Jim's house. Jim had wrapped her up in his sheets so that we wouldn't arouse suspicion. She was Cleopatra being brought before her Caesar. We closed the curtains and unwrapped her on the lounge carpet. Jim returned to the van and brought back his plastic bag. He reapplied the anaesthetic and then removed the rest of her clothes. I was very afraid now. Jim's hands were shaking. They were scratched and bleeding. He worked frantically, like a man possessed.

We both carried her upstairs. Jim brought down the loft ladder and told me to go up. He carried her on his shoulders as far as he could, and then I reached down and helped to drag her unceremoniously as Jim pushed from below.

The girl was moved quickly on to the waiting table, and at this point I seem to remember that she began to gain consciousness again. Jim had a supply of the anaesthetic already in the loft, and another dose was duly applied. While he was doing this I was told to tie her legs and arms. Nylon clothes line was used to secure each limb to a table leg so that once I had finished the poor girl was strung out in an 'X' shape.

It was only then that both Jim and I were able to stop. The girl lay stretched out on the table before us, her ivory skin beautifully defined in the light through the overhead window. Jim and I were sweating profusely. Our clothes stank with perspiration. Jim's scratch marks were still bleeding. His hair was all over the place, but his eyes shone with a light that I had not seen before. Neither of us moved but just stood on either side of the table. It was now 11.30; we had been on the go for an hour and a half. I hardly had the energy to breathe. Neither of us spoke. We just looked.

And in that suffocating silence I could not stop the greatest doubts entering my mind.

She's shivering, I said at last. And it was true, the girl was trembling all over. What have we done, Jim? I remembered whispering as we both watched the girl trembling in the morning light. I'll get a sheet from downstairs and put it over her.

Don't be daft. You know what you've got to do. Jim looked across at me maniacally. He must have seen my confusion. You've got to clean the van. Take it back. We can't have the van sitting on the drive. That's the first thing the police will start to look for.

I started to move towards the ladder. *For God's sake, Jim, look after her.*

5

As arranged, I spent some time cleaning out the van. Jim did not emerge from the loft. When satisfied, I loaded the six bags of rubbish that Jim had left in his garage. It was his opinion that we should use the van in a legitimate way, as a cover story, just in case we were investigated by the police. So I was forced to take bags of garden refuse to the council refuse tip, and it was only then that I was allowed to return the van to the hire place before catching the bus to Great Glen.

It was late afternoon when I arrived back. On my way home I walked past Jim's house. I recall two strange cars parked on his driveway. I had certainly not seen them before and I wondered whom they belonged to. The house itself was still and seemingly lifeless. I walked on and disappeared into my house.

There was nothing on the news yet about the abduction. I wondered whether the girl's family had even reported her missing. Perhaps it would be only now, as mealtime approached, that her empty room would raise concern.

Whatever happened, I vowed that this was the last time

I would get involved with Jim. His end seemed fairly certain: Jim would take more and more risks until capture became inevitable, if not with this girl, then with another. And once arrested, it wouldn't be long before Jim led the police straight to my front door. I remember thinking even then that perhaps the end was now inevitable, for both of us, that there was little any of us could do to try and trick Fate. I think it was during that very evening that I first contemplated the effects of a long prison sentence on my life. I remember watching my fish, wondering who would look after them. My house would be mothballed until my early release. The neighbours would talk and perhaps I would be forced to sell up and move on to another part of the county. It was a blessing my mother was dead. I couldn't have endured her satisfied look.

Sleep was difficult. Instead I spent prolonged hours scanning the Internet, the TV news broadcasts and radio shows. But when I finally succumbed to tiredness, the disappearance of the girl had still not been reported.

Early Sunday morning was bright and sunny. I listened to the news before feeding my fish. There was still no mention of the girl. I went back upstairs and looked out of the window in the master bedroom. There were no cars outside Jim's house. I looked at the tiles of his roof and wondered what was going on behind them. Was the girl still alive?

The phone call came at just after ten that morning. It was Jim. He just said two words: Come round. As I held the phone in my right hand, my sleeve rolled high, the warm liquid ran down my arm and dripped off the elbow onto the kitchen tiles. I did not put the phone down immediately, but stood completely still for several minutes, disturbed only by the smell of the fish flakes that were smeared across my naked arm like some exotic eczema.

I returned to fish tank three and put down its metal hood. Most of the food was now gone, although I noted that there were still one or two scraps left on the bottom. These would have to be removed but there was no time now. I washed my arms, put on my coat and then set off across the street to Jim's.

Unsurprisingly, it was quiet. The street was devoid of people. Not even a car passed by as I negotiated the short distance to Jim's ordered front garden. I tapped on the kitchen door and opened it. Jim was sitting at the breakfast bar with a cup of coffee. The radio was on. It was playing some music. The volume had been adjusted so that it would not disturb the sensibilities.

Come in and close the door. Jim pushed a stool out with his foot. Underneath his dressing gown he was still wearing his pyjamas. Do you want a coffee? I nodded and then watched as he reached over to the cafetière and poured out the last of the black liquid into a clean cup. I sat next to Jim and put both my hands round the cup as though we were on top of a mountain and this was our only warmth. There was a short period of silence, disturbed only by the soft music.

She's still upstairs.

I looked up at Jim and nodded. Jim took a sip of his

coffee but his eyes did not leave my face. You can go up and see her if you want. I held tightly to the cup. She's been as good as gold.

There's been nothing on the radio?

Nothing yet, but there will be today. The police will have given her a few hours to return home. I nodded slowly, my fingers slipping further round the little cup in my grasp. I want you to have a look at her, make sure that she's OK.

I slipped off the stool and put down my coffee. I waited for Jim.

You know where she is.

I nodded again and slowly moved out of the kitchen and up the stairs. Jim stayed where he was. The loft ladder was down. I remember standing underneath the hatchway. I could hear nothing. Above was shadow, lit only by the skylight. I placed a foot on the first rung. The metal ladder shrieked. I inflicted the agony again as I lifted my remaining foot off the ground and my full weight was transferred. I moved my left foot up to the next rung. Again there was a squeal of pain. Above me, from the loft, I caught the slightest of noises – a muffled movement, quick and sharp, as though a startled deer had sprung from a clearing. I slowly advanced further up the ladder until my head entered the loft. The table was in the same place. That was unchanged. Stretched out, the naked form of the girl was clearly visible. She was not moving, still and silent, and yet I knew that she was wide awake and listening. I moved further up the ladder before climbing onto the wooden floor. The sight of the girl made me gasp. Her face was bound with thick masking tape, wrapped tight around eyes, ears and nose. A narrow slit had been left across the mouth. Underneath the table I could see a discarded pair of handcuffs, chloroform, vaginal cream and a gynaecological mirror.

Suddenly I heard a loud exhale and the gentle flutter of the tape as the girl began a series of frantic, desperate cries. She had obviously been holding her breath. Unable to see the intruder, she began to shake with fear. I moved closer and saw how the tape had been crudely spun around her head, the girl's long hair sticking out from the top in a blonde plume. Her head suddenly turned to face me, and although I could not see her eyes, I felt that deep beneath the layers of tape they were now surveying me, reaching out in some primitive fashion. I touched her arm, but it was as if I had placed a live electrode to her soft flesh, such was the resultant convulsion that twisted her body. I immediately moved away.

There was much to be done. Clearly my first job was to remove the mess that she had naturally caused. I went back downstairs and returned with a mop and bucket. The detritus was quickly cleared away. I left the loft again only to come back with a glass of water. I attempted to place my hand underneath her head so that it could be elevated into a drinking position. But as my fingers slipped beneath her skull, her body once again convulsed, and there emanated a muffled scream from beneath the narrow slit. I did not desist but let my fingers continue on their journey until I was able to slowly raise her head.

I'm only trying to give you a glass of water.

With these words I placed the cold glass to the edge of the slit and then gently poured the contents into the darkness. Some of the water tumbled out over the top while a stream sprang from beneath the chin. Yet despite her gargled coughing, I am sure my crude attention proffered some valuable succour.

Once the frantic motions of her body had ended, I returned to the kitchen where I found Jim reading the paper. A fresh cup of coffee was in front of him and the radio was still warbling quietly in the corner.

I've given her some water.

Jim nodded slowly. He took a sip of his coffee. I did not sit on a stool. The bright morning light came through the kitchen window. It was blinding.

Is there anything else you want me to do?

Jim looked straight back at me with his deadeye look. I guess not. Did the van go back OK?

I nodded. Has there been anything on the radio?

Not yet.

My stomach tightened and I suddenly felt very sick. Perhaps it was the heat. And the light pouring through the window. Oh God, I whispered, and reached out to the breakfast bar for support.

The police won't be able to trace anything back to us.

We've been too smart. You've seen to that. Everything's OK.

Everything's OK, that's exactly what he said. And on reflection I agreed – yes, I suppose we had thought of everything. My skills were important here. Jim couldn't have pulled it off by himself.

The ring started again. The little electronic ditty. The catchy little number that perhaps was in the charts. Jim fumbled in one of the pockets of his dressing gown. The phone was brought out and placed on the breakfast bar. It was very small, bright red in colour. It looked so vulnerable on the table, as though it were a tiny creature sheltering in its plastic shell. We both stared as it bleated out its painful melody. I felt the girl squirm and shake to the beat. It was calling her, her parents were calling her, even as we sipped our coffee in Jim's kitchen. And then it fell silent and the phone was returned to the darkness of the pocket.

It's been ringing all night. I turned it off and then switched it back on this morning.

Don't answer it. It can be traced.

I know. It'll be out of power soon, anyway.

You haven't used it, have you?

No, don't worry. I just like to hear the tune. And Jim began to hum it out loud, very loud as though he had lost all senses.

I left very soon after this strange incident. I could not take being in that house any longer. But once home I felt equally uncomfortable, to the point where I found myself continually returning to the upstairs bedroom window to look across at Jim's. What I expected to find, I have no idea, perhaps a police car, but nothing untoward was apparent throughout the day, apart from the arrival of a single blue car that remained parked outside Jim's house. I did not see the visitors arrive and nor did I see them depart later on that afternoon.

I knew it would eventually happen, of course. It was the six o'clock news bulletin. I was boiling an egg in the kitchen. It was the local news, the first story. A girl had gone missing from Bradgate Park. Lizzy Butler. Lizzy – what a wonderful name. Short for Elizabeth, my own Queen Elizabeth! The police were appealing for information.

I checked Ceefax. Nothing yet, but I knew there soon would be. By tomorrow morning it would be headline news across the country. I went back to the window. All was quiet and serene. The evening light glanced off the blue tiles of Jim's house in a most majestic way. A deep yellowy-red light that you only got at that time of the year. A man walked along the street with his dog. He stopped outside a house to consider some flowers before moving on.

At eight o'clock that evening Jim rang to say that the girl's disappearance had been reported on a local news broadcast on the TV.

Do you want me to come over? I enquired.

No. And make sure you go to work tomorrow. Do

everything just as you normally would. Come over to-morrow evening.

I put the phone down and began the process of closing my aquariums down for the night.

Lizzy Butler was national news the next morning. Her face greeted me when I switched on the television. It was a picture of her standing in a garden, holding a tennis racket. It was not a particularly good picture, presumably taken with a cheap instamatic. The colours were too rich, almost obscene, while the composition was too ad hoc to warrant any praise. The girl's mouth was open and her eyes focused on something to the left of the picture, out of shot. Behind her, completely out of focus, was an orange ball lying peacefully on the lawn. I remember thinking that it seemed a strange picture to use. It certainly did not capture the likeness of the girl I briefly saw in the car park of Bradgate Park. The girl I saw then was a young woman, confident and at ease with the world. The photograph was of a young girl, someone who still played tennis in the garden with her dad.

I went into work. The disappearance of Lizzy Butler followed me in my car through the radio. But at work I was able to settle into my usual routine. I hardly said a word, and no one mentioned the disappearance to me. Why should they? It was just a quiet Monday at work. I left slightly earlier than normal in the afternoon but no one said anything.

Outside it was another hot day. The news bulletins

informed me that the hunt for Lizzy Butler was ongoing, and that the police were still appealing for information. I surmised that little headway had been made.

After I had eaten my tea I received a phone call from Jim asking me to come round. Before doing so I picked up the length of transparent plastic tubing that I had taken from work. I also collected my plastic water bottle into the lid of which I had already drilled a small hole.

Jim was watering his roses on the front garden. A box of plant food stood by his feet. He put the watering can down and followed me into the kitchen. His earlier savoir faire was now gone. I could tell he was getting nervous. He closed the kitchen door behind him before turning to me.

The police are looking for a white van.

I nodded slowly and watched Jim move over to the breakfast bar.

You did clean it thoroughly, didn't you?

I nodded again. They might not think of looking for rented vans, I suggested.

Maybe not, but we can't take any risks.

How is she?

Jim pulled out a stool and sat down. She's still alive, if that's what you mean. He suddenly noticed the piping and water bottle. What have you got there?

This'll help her to drink.

Jim nodded with little interest. She's a lot weaker, he said.

Upstairs I found the loft ladder still down. I squeezed by

it into the bathroom where I filled the plastic bottle with water. I then climbed up into the loft.

The girl was not moving. Her body was still spread out across the table. In the red evening light she looked more beautiful than ever. At first I feared she might be dead, but as I approached, her head moved slightly and I thought I heard a distinct groan.

I've got some water for you.

One end of the piping was secured into the lid of the bottle. The other was then pushed through the small slit in the tape. I remember that as the plastic touched her mouth the girl suddenly began to writhe as if I had driven a red-hot poker through the gap.

Just suck the end of the pipe for water.

Again, this failed to get a reaction so instead I squeezed the bottle, pushing water through the piping and into the mask. The girl coughed and gurgled.

Drink.

With my other hand I lifted the girl's head. I squeezed the bottle again. Water oozed out from behind the tape and splashed down onto the floor. Once satisfied that the girl had at least taken a mouthful, I carefully lowered her head and pulled the tubing out from her mouth. I then cleaned up the table and sponged her legs before retreating back down to the ground floor. I couldn't help but notice the deep scratch marks on her thighs.

I'll start to put the loft ladder away when we don't need it. We can't take any risks.

She's very weak, I commented.

I told you.

Perhaps you could let her go. She hasn't seen the house and I doubt she could recall either you or me.

There's only one way she's leaving here.

The kettle clicked off and the steam rolled up over the kitchen window.

Jim rang me soon after I got back from work the following day. This was now Wednesday. On entering his kitchen he exploded with a pent-up fury that I had seen only rarely.

Listen, and here Jim walked straight up to me and peered menacingly into my face, the police were here this morning. He jammed my chest with his finger. Just before I went to work.

The shock and fear on my face must have been obvious. Jim evidently extracted some satisfaction from seeing the effect his news had on me.

Now, what do you make of that?

Good God! What did they want?

It appeared to be a routine check-up on all those who had hired a white van last Saturday. They'd got my details from the hire firm.

Did they suspect anything?

Jim stared hard at me for several seconds before responding. I don't think so, but they asked a lot of questions. I had to mention you, of course.

Why? Why did you do that?

Because you were helping me, remember? That was our

story. People will have seen us together in the van. We've got to stick to what we agreed.

Yes, yes.

His finger was again hammering against my chest. Jim turned away and looked out of the kitchen window. We've got to get rid of her tonight. We can't keep her here now.

I remember how shocked I was at the casual way Jim spoke about the girl, as though he was referring to a bag of rubbish that needed removing. Get rid of her. How?

Leave that to me. But we need somewhere to put her body. Jim turned from the window. Got any ideas?

My head was spinning. What have we got ourselves into? My words must have been no more than a whisper.

Jim remained silent.

I'll go up to her, I said at last.

As I left the kitchen Jim called after me, Well, you just offer your sweet goodbyes 'cause she won't be here tomorrow.

The loft ladder had been retracted. The girl was completely sealed in. I took the stick, opened the hatchway and then dragged the ladder down. The smell of faeces and urine escaped from the hatchway as I climbed the ladder. In truth I recall being unsure what I was going to find. What condition would the girl be in? Would she even be alive? At first, in the modest light, it appeared her condition had changed little since my last visit. Indeed, as I looked across at her from the ladder, my first feelings were of awe: in the soft evening light her body had become iridescent. As clouds raced across the sky, individual shafts of sunlight carouselled through the tiny window in the ceiling and lay about her as attendant angels. Yet, as I came to stand on the floorboards and move towards the table, it was obvious that all was not well. The iridescence of the skin was now clearly seen to be the product of a sickly film of grey sweat that covered her completely. The rope had cut into both her wrists and legs, and there was much bleeding, most of it old and dried. Cuts on other parts of her body had also bled, and the wooden table had begun to resemble a butcher's slaughtering block. I ran my hand across her stomach. She did not flinch or move. Tape had been re-applied to her head making it difficult to gauge whether or not she was drawing breath. It was only by placing my ear up against the tiny slit that I was able to make out the faintest signs of life. As I listened, my eyes closed, ears straining for the merest flicker, I felt as though I were a rescuer atop a mountain of rubble, directing all my energies to the crippled body that lay many miles below. Was it my imagination or did the head not make a slight movement in my direction, and then, as my ear lay against the slit, did I not hear the faintest of whispers, a garbled echo from the larynx of the dead?

What have they done to you?

Despite the fact that her fate was now sealed, an enormous sense of compassion welled up within me. I left the loft only to return with a bucket of warm water and a cloth. As I sponged her body I waited for the slightest movement to indicate that she was aware of my presence.

But she remained completely still, as though her consciousness had retracted from the external world. After clearing her mess I came back with a beaker of fresh water, which I once more attempted to pour into her mouth. The convulsions and vomiting that ensued were the clearest indications of life that I had seen.

I was with her about an hour and when I finally returned downstairs I found Jim sitting in his lounge, watching television.

Have you put the ladder back? His eyes did not leave the screen.

Yes.

What do you think?

About what?

About her.

She's very weak. She hardly moved.

Jim nodded and turned to face me. I'll give you a call tomorrow.

Jim would strangle her. I knew that was how he would do it. I didn't need to be there. But what would he do with the corpse? Now that was the real conundrum. If the police found the body then who knows what would ensue? Forensic investigation seemed such a science these days that they would be bound to find a giveaway hair or a telltale flake of skin. DNA. That was the latest thing. And Jim was all over the body, his skin, his fluids. The only safe way was to destroy all the evidence, to obliterate it from the face of the earth.

I left work at the usual time and drove straight home. As I pulled into my driveway I noted that Jim's car was in its usual place, outside his garage. He was home. There was no sign of any police. Perhaps Jim was watching me as I arrived, peering through the net curtains in the front bedroom. I walked straight to my front door and disappeared inside.

I went round and fed all my fish. It was as I was doing so that I found that the water in aquarium four in the second bedroom had become cloudy, like a thin white milk. I had seen this before, of course. It was normally a symptom of an unhealthy filtration system, or perhaps excessive detritus on the gravel bottom. I immediately went downstairs for my bucket and plastic tubing. I siphoned off half the water, hoovering up any debris from the gravel as I did so. I then topped up the aquarium with fresh tap water, slightly warmed. A few drops of a dechlorinating agent were added before I replaced the hood, rolled down my sleeves and dried my hands on the bathroom towel.

I recall that it was as I walked down the stairs with my bucket and piping that the phone went. I picked up the receiver. Immediately there was the usual precursive draw of breath before Jim's guttural voice spluttered across the line.

Get over here.

The line then went dead. I had not said a word. I briefly checked my computer to make sure that he had not been stupid enough to send me an email. But there was nothing from him, just the usual hordes of spam.

I placed the bucket and piping under the sink and left the house. My knees were trembling, if the truth be told. Although Jim had said little, the tone of his voice had been enough to confirm that some monstrosity had occurred, that the girl was dead. So now there was no way back, no way out of this mess. The darkest of events were unravelling around us, pulling us further into a world of madness and depravity. But, as I walked up Jim's driveway, I reflected that it was a world I had entered undeservingly. As I'm sure you will now agree, I had done nothing but try and restrain the beast at my side. It was I who had tried to dissuade Jim from his monstrous path of destruction, and it was I who had mopped the fevered brow of his saddest victim.

6

It is a well-known truism that an Englishman needs his garden. And thanks to the governor I now have mine. Yes, it's true. I have been given access to the prison garden. One hour a week, when the other prisoners are having dinner.

It was McGuire who showed me the puffball growing in front of the privet hedge by the eastern wall. It was McGuire who walked me round the garden on that first morning. He didn't need to speak. I was able to sum up what needed to be done immediately. The rows of decaying vegetables, of unkempt bushes and plants – it was a sorry sight, as I knew it would be before I even left my cell. I shook my head slowly as I followed McGuire round the concrete path. I think he was aware of my disapproval. The puffball was offered as a placatory gift. He stood straight as a rod, pointing his trowel at it, like a policeman directing traffic. I nodded, knelt down, and inspected the specimen for several minutes. McGuire stood and watched.

A calvatia, of course. They belong to a most curious genus do they not? I remember saying to my companion, as he stood above me in the quickening shade of another dreary autumnal evening.

Although McGuire could not talk, an acknowledged mute within this bizarre community, I expected at least some reaction, however cursory. Instead he continued to stare down at me, as though a barbaric native on the shores of the Ivory Coast.

This here is merely the ephemeral fruit of the fungi, I continued. The fungi themselves exist as a complex structure of roots, or mycelium as is the proper scientific name. Fascinating, is it not?

I stood up, shook the soil off my knees and looked across at McGuire. If he was the dumb native then I was surely the scientifically trained explorer upon the sands of a foreign shore! It seems strange that out of all the prisoners in this madhouse, only the mute is allowed to join me in my horticultural endeavours. While the others eat their dinner, McGuire and I have the garden to ourselves. Indeed, I have been told that McGuire is rarely out of the garden, presumably helping the other prisoners in their horticultural dalliances when I'm not around. He is a slight man, not much more than five and a half feet in height, with mousey hair plastered onto an angular skull. He stared back at me with unblinking eyes.

Show me the rest, I exclaimed eventually and like a diligent dog, he spun on his heels and led me into the vegetable patch.

As I say, I was not impressed with what I saw on that first day. It was evident that those responsible for the garden had limited botanical experience or training. Many of the vegetables, for instance, had been left to grow in their own wilful way, and I spent most of that first session simply tearing up the hardened, enveloping stalks of cabbage, lettuce and potato.

Those prisoners that have subsequently complained of my clearance programme are simply the dullards responsible for the poor state of the garden in the first place, and thus do not deserve the respect bestowed on them by the governor. As I explained to McGuire when I saw him again the following day, it is important that the scientific principles of botany and horticulture are adhered to at all times. The path of scientific endeavour may not be easy, but neither is it without reward, I said. McGuire, of course, simply chewed on his twig with no interest in my aphorism.

I instructed McGuire that the rhododendron should be pruned and prepared for the winter. We spent some time removing the bronzed flower stalks using the scissors. While McGuire finished this off I selected a disused area and began the arduous task of digging over the heavy soil in preparation for the spring bulbs that I hoped I could persuade the governor to buy. A display of tulips, daffodils, crocuses and snowdrops was forming in my mind as I lifted the heavy sods.

I did not expect the governor to agree to my request with such speed. Today I met McGuire holding a small bag of daffodil bulbs that he had been allowed to take from the stores. I was informed by one of the guards later that other bulbs would be ordered on my recommendations. McGuire and I spent our hour together carefully burying each bulb, my fingers delighting in the exquisite dampness of the soil.

Despite my miserable surroundings, I can honestly say that since arriving here, I have never been happier. I therefore find it abhorrent that they have started to drug me. Not only does the prison doctor drug me each night, but also I am sure certain powders are sprinkled over my food. With the two guards holding me down, the doctor feels safe to stick the needle into my arm with an unwarranted roughness. There is really no need for such depravity. I have too many thoughts flooding through my mind, and the drugs bring a sleep that is most appreciated, but who are they to decide when my anguish is beyond the pale?

7

We both drank too much coffee in an attempt to stay awake. Jim was restless and made repeated trips to his kitchen for food and drink. Mostly, I remained seated, watching whatever was on the television. It was only as the clock approached half one in the morning that I agreed we should bring down the body. We both put on the gloves as agreed. Jim lowered the ladder and disappeared into the loft. I slowly followed.

The stench was sickening, the smell of death of course, but also the crude flavours of piss and shit that still lingered. The body lay untethered on the table. I remember how the skin glistened in the brilliant light, a cold bluish effect that reminded one of a shop window dummy. I walked over to the table and stared down at her. I had forgotten how small she had been. Her head was still wrapped in tape. There was no evidence to suggest how she had died.

We should take the tape off her head. We mustn't leave any incriminating evidence.

Jim nodded in agreement but did not move. In the end

it was I who had to reach over and run my fingers across the mask until a suitably loose bit could be found. It was with some effort that I then began to strip this back, lifting the head as I did so, and slowly unravelling. It took some time to do this as Jim had done a most thorough job. I started at the neck and gradually worked upwards. We both watched as first the chin and then the mouth were revealed. The skin was in a poor condition, blotchy and distended, her lips dark blue, curled into an agonized grimace that preserved the horror of her final moments. I went on unravelling until her wide, staring eyes emerged at last from the prison of their enforced darkness. It was only then that I had to look away.

I had forgotten how beautiful she had been, you see. The enormity of what had been done suddenly engulfed us and we both stood about her as silent sentinels for several seconds, struggling with our thoughts. Her ears were purple as well, I remember that.

Let's get her downstairs. Jim moved round and picked up her arms. You grab her legs.

The body was cold, heavy and cumbersome. We lifted her from the table and moved to the ladder. I retreated backwards, slowly easing her down the metal structure. Inevitable fluids, escaping from the corpse, ran across my arms and onto my shirt. Jim stood behind her, grunting mercilessly. Together we inched down the rungs, Jim also exiting in reverse fashion, one hand anchored to the ladder while the other held both the girl's arms above her head.

We left the body in the hallway while we collapsed onto

the sofa. The darkness outside contrasted starkly with the gaudy illumination of the living-room lights. Despite the early morning chill, both Jim and I had sweat pouring down our faces. Jim in particular appeared to be in some discomfort, struggling for breath as his hands clasped and unclasped a tiny round cushion.

There's a sheet in the garage, he said. The key's by the door in the kitchen. His words came in gasps as though he were a fish struggling on the side of a bank.

I nodded, picked up the key and opened the back door. The silence of Great Glen at this darkest of hours was overwhelming. Bathed in their orange glow, the streets were silent, undisturbed by even the slightest flicker from the countless numbers of blank, colourless windows. Apart from ours of course. I walked over to the garage, unlocked the door, and found the sheet on top of the chest freezer, neatly folded.

When I returned to the house, Jim was standing by the body in the hallway.

Lay it on the floor and we'll roll her onto it.

This we did before carefully wrapping the sheet about her so that she was completely enveloped. We picked her up as though she was a roll of carpet and took her outside, replicating the indignity of her arrival. We lowered her onto the driveway and I waited as Jim fumbled with his keys. The street was still empty, the vacant stare of the houses bearing the only testimony to our terrible activities. With the rear door of the car open, both Jim and I slid the girl across the back seat as best we could, continually adjusting the sheet so that no part of her flesh was revealed. As quietly as possible we clicked the door shut.

I got into the passenger seat while Jim returned to the house to switch off the lights and lock the doors. He returned carrying something.

We might need this. As he seated himself next to me he threw across a small bicycle lamp. I nodded.

The screech of the engine was unbearable. Jim reversed out onto the road. I nervously peered out, watching for twitching curtains, but all remained frozen and dark.

We did not have far to go. I don't think we even saw another car. Once out of Great Glen the darkness became absolute as the unlit countryside engulfed us. Across the fields a thickening mist could be seen, but on the road, with no disturbance from street lights, the stars suddenly appeared in the cloudless heavens, the majestic swirl of the Milky Way faintly visible in Serpens Cauda, Scorpius and Sagittarius. It was as if a protective roof had been removed, revealing the great wonders of the Eternity above us. As we meandered through the blackness of the Leicestershire countryside I stared out of the car and into the distant heart of the galaxy.

We turned left onto Gartree Road. The distant lights of Leicester swung out before us as we drove over the tiny bridge that spans the River Sence. I turned my eyes from the heavens to the skyline in front of us. I recall that St Giles could be made out dimly against the lights of the city, its miniature tower pointing up to the Crab nebula faintly visible in Taurus.

The body did not move, was not even delicately rocked by the pitch and roll of the car as it furrowed its way through the night. Gartree Road was as black as pitch. Trees and bushes loomed out, starkly defined in the crude, penetrating beams of the car's headlights. Sometimes the glint of two eyes would sparkle from the hedgerows, a terrified animal caught for a moment in our monstrous embrace. We dipped down and then rose again, drawing level to the church on our left.

I can picture the car coming to a halt at the smallest of laybys. The car engine died and the headlights dowsed, the blackness of the night suddenly rushing in upon us. In that pool of nothingness Jim and I sat still, barely moving, hardly breathing. The body remained stretched out behind us. Overhead the stars continued their unceasing revolution as the earth spun on its orbit.

OK, let's go.

The night air was cold and damp, the fields covered in a fine white mist that gleamed silvery in the moonlight. I walked over to the nearby gate that led into the field. It was firmly secured with a chain.

We're going to have to get her over the gate. I pointed to the chain.

Jim nodded.

We brought the body out and laid it carefully on the gravel floor of the layby while Jim locked the car. Gartree Road remained dark and empty, the silence disturbed only by the occasional hooting of an owl and far, far away, barely perceptible, the guttural exhalations of the distant city.

We carried the body away from the car, Jim and I at each end. We slid half the body over the gate so that it rested with some equilibrium over the top bar. I then climbed over and held the body as Jim clambered over to join me. We then slid the body across the bar and continued on our way up the small hillock to the church.

The church of Great Stretton.

Before us St Giles rose up into the sky, seemingly floating amid a sea of mist and fog. The water vapour clung to our clothes and skin, quickly enveloping us as we proceeded up to the sacred site.

With some effort we at last came to the low hedge that surrounded the church. I led the way to the small gap through which entry could be gained. It had always been a tight squeeze but with such an encumbrance as we had that night it would not be easy. And so it proved, the twigs and branches of the hedgerow cruelly scratching our flesh and tearing at the sheet as if desperate to reveal the sinister secret of its contents to the stars.

We both pulled the body through the gap, a leg and arm now clearly visible, and collapsed by a gravestone. The shrouded corpse lay at our feet. After regaining my breath I began to explain to Jim the detail of the other gravestones, as revealed to me during my extensive researches. Jim, who was busy applying a handkerchief to his cuts and bruises, merely looked up and hissed, Shut up.

And so silence once more descended on the lonely

churchyard of St Giles. Although deeply offended, I was not surprised by my companion's ignorance and merely lay back on the damp grass and stared up at the heavens, noting as best I could all the constellations that I had committed to memory. It never ceases to amaze me how such a chaotic mess of stars can so easily be brought into order and routine through the simple application of astrological symbols. There is Libra, the great scales, and next to it Virgo. Moving further east is Leo and then Cancer, and so on and so on. I can name them all.

By the time I had finished, Jim had recovered.

Where's the entrance?

I pointed to a patch of grass not far away. Just over there.

He nodded and looked nervously about him. This is bloody barmy, he said.

We sat amongst the derelict gravestones like two ghouls, clawing at our wounds. About us, the darkened land was smothered by mist, disturbed only by treetops and the lonely hillock on which we sat. Indeed, as we both gazed out over the countryside, it was as if we sat upon the back of a great whale, becalmed amid the strangest waters of the Sargasso Sea. At one point the moon disappeared behind a cloud and all about us the haunting iridescence of the mist blinked out as though a monstrous life force had suddenly departed the land.

I got up and walked over to the place I had indicated, moving carefully through the graveyard in the darkness. Although my vision was impaired, I had performed the task often enough to successfully find the edge of the wooden board and raise it up. As usual, grass and earth were wrenched free in the process until the board finally fell back to one side, revealing a patch of absolute nothingness amid the blankness of night. A draught of freezing air rose up, brushing my face, as a deep moan emanated from the slumbering foundations of the church.

I stood up and looked across at Jim. As I did so the moon reappeared, covering him in silver light, and all around us, out across the immeasurable fields, it was as though the lights of a besieged city had suddenly been turned on and the bells of victory rung.

I took out the bicycle lamp from my trouser pocket and quickly scanned the hole before switching it off and returning it to my pocket. Everything looked just as I'd left it when I was last here, some time ago.

I'll drop down and then you pass me the body.

Jim nodded. Together the two of us dragged the girl over the grass until her covered feet stuck out over the lip of the hole. I then carefully lowered myself down into the darkness. For a second or two, I remained suspended in the great subterranean womb, albeit a womb that was now as barren and forgotten as the church under which it lay. The acoustics were those of a small cave, the intimacy of my breathing, and of every other sound I made, being suddenly amplified as the cold, damp air of the antechamber enveloped me, chasing away all sound from the world above.

I closed my eyes and released my grip. Almost immediately my legs buckled as I hit the stony floor, my exhalation briefly reverberating around the tiny room. I looked up and saw the familiar face of Cassiopeia in the sky above me. Yet even as I picked out this familiar shape amid the chaos, a black object moved across, blotting out the light, and a familiar voice drifted down to me as if from a long-forgotten nightmare. Are you OK? The barest whisper, but discernible nonetheless. I took out the torch and switched it on.

OK.

In the sickly white light the chamber took on a macabre character. I placed the torch on the floor by one wall and watched as Jim slowly lowered the body down through the hole. I could hear his grunting as he struggled with the weight. The sheet had fallen loose and the girl's naked feet came down to me from the stars.

Gradually I took hold of more and more of the body.

I'm going to let go from this end. Ready?

I was under the girl's thighs and buttocks. Jim was leaning into the chamber as much as he dared, holding on to her arms. The sheet had practically fallen away, much of it lying draped across the floor.

OK.

Jim let go of one arm and then the other. The full weight of the girl fell against my body, and I momentarily stumbled. Bending my knees, I was able to bring the body down to the floor with some decorum, the two of us finishing prostrate on the ground.

Out of the way, came the hiss.

Slowly Jim lowered himself into the chamber, dropping with a loud grunt before lying on the floor.

While he recovered, I pulled myself up into the church and lay on the cold floor. The stone interior was now awash with moonlight, transforming the nave and chancel into a luminescent grotto. The inside was so cold my breath could clearly be seen coiling out away from me, through the shafts of silver. The blackness beyond the tiny windows was immense, yet around me, across the empty fields, I could make out the muffled noise of a bustling village. I listened for several minutes before a harsh rasp from the crypt below dispelled it.

Are you there?

Unfortunately I was, and with much effort Jim lifted up the corpse so that I could drag it into the church. The body slid up over the lip of the hole with relative ease. Jim stayed below in the dark while I dragged it over to the darkest corner of the east-facing chancel. Jim threw up the sheet, which I carefully wrapped around the body once again. Only once I had done all this did we retrace our steps, Jim's heavy breathing following me all the way as a rasping dirge.

Having pulled Jim back up into the churchyard, I used the torch to ensure that the wooden board was replaced with precision. We then returned to the car. And so the queen is laid to rest, I remember whispering.

8

Great God! My senses are gone! No more drugs! There is no return. I am writing this under my bed, where I have been for many hours. An eternity!

Let me tell you immediately that the garden is ruined, the daffodil bulbs dug up and burnt, McGuire slashed with blades in the greenhouse. The rhododendron, privet and apple all gone, and outside I hear their braying voices, crying my name. Locked into my cell, with no food or light, I at last see my fate before me.

When Jim was taken (I saw it from my window!) I knew that a greater force would be turned upon me. And so it was that I left my house, my home for the sweetest years of my life, a tranquil and pleasurable interlude between the darkness of what came before and what was to follow. Into each of my aquariums I placed the tablets of food that I always used when going away; I took no bag but rather went as I came, with nothing but what could be squeezed into the pockets of my anorak.

I stole away into the hot night, disappearing in the

darkness while those around me slept soundly in the comfort of their beds. I left Great Glen through the fields to the north, along the little track that runs parallel to the River Sence. The wheat was high on either side of me, shimmering in the moonlight as the wind moved across it. Ahead of me I could make out the short tower of St Giles, while to my left, some distance away, the lights of Leicester gleamed. I moved quickly along the path as though I had been born for this moment. The wheat sighed and heaved, its undulations falling like a wave across the land. I passed the hidden remains of Stretton Magna; I passed Great Stretton until I hit the Roman Road. I was passing through time, a golden time gilded by the stars and moon. I fumbled for my goggles and watched as the men and women of St Giles once more returned to the land, their little houses sprouting like mushrooms from the soil.

I dropped down onto Via Devana and joined the heavy traffic that was making its way towards Ratae in the west. Companies of troops marched back and forth along the road, interspersed with tradesmen and their carts. The road was alive as I had never seen it! There was much talk amongst the people as they journeyed, and their words came to me as though they were conversing in my own language. As we marched down towards the settlement, a company of soldiers ran past us in the other direction, scattering a small flock of sheep being taken to market. For a moment there was pandemonium as the farmer tried to regain control of his goods, despite the protestations from the soldiers and the mongrel dogs. I used this distraction to quietly slip away off the road and on to the hidden tracks that I knew would now lead me safely into Ratae.

And into the city I went, invisibly as though I were no more than a shadow. Like a great superhero I was unstoppable; I was beyond the understanding of normal people. Through the golf course and onwards into the houses. Even when out on the street I could not be seen. Pensioners with their shopping failed to catch my eye; young mothers pushing prams saw nothing. I moved on undisturbed, getting ever closer. Through Oadby and onwards into the centre. It was busy now but once again I was able to disappear into the gardens and passages where my friends were waiting. Scrabbling over walls and slipping through shrubberies I advanced with all the unstoppable certainty of an invisible Golem. Through the goggles my route was clearly demarcated; the dog bark and cat hiss were nothing to me, and as I neared the heart of the city I drew my coat closer about me.

There in the darkened alleyways I lay hidden beneath the protection of my anorak, draped across me like a great coat, so that even the inquisitive cats could not guess what lurked underneath, while not more than ten metres away pounded the life of the city beneath the hot Flemish sun.

It was only after darkness fell that I was able to leave the communication trench and scurry out across no-man's-land. The trick is to stay flat on your belly, slithering from shell hole to shell hole. That night the Very lights danced in the sky, romancing the waning moon whose sickly beams caressed the blasted landscape. I moved out with my gun in front of me, using my entrenching tool to dig deeper into the side of a shell hole when the machine gun fire grew too fierce. The smell was almost beyond belief. This part of the line had last seen action on the 1st July and many of the bodies over which I now crawled were unmoved from where they had fallen.

I awoke in someone's greenhouse and moved on through the gardens, avoiding machine gun fire at all times. I marched out of Leicester with Richard's troops on the 21st. He had many thousands of men and all had to cross the tiny packhorse bridge. It was early in the morning, long before most were up, the mist from the River Soar rolling eerily over Bow Bridge. Richard moved across the bridge first, his armour shining in the early morning sun. Behind him fluttered the royal standard. Suddenly his spur struck the low wall of the bridge and a flash of sparks fell to the ground. But I could see no old lady as the myth would have us believe, the old hag who on seeing this incident predicted the king's certain death; the immeasurable line of troops, from foot soldiers to longbow men to heavy cavalry, slowly and in utter silence made their way across the tiny bridge.

From Atherstone we marched through Kirkby Mallory to Sutton Cheney on the old Roman Road. After some indecision we then set off for the southern edge of Redmoor Plain. That night we camped close to Ambion Hill, the fires of the army twinkling across the gentle slopes of the land, as if I were witnessing some strange reflection of the Milky Way above us.

As the day broke the troops were stirred, and by mid-morning we found ourselves in position on top of Ambion Hill. Or were we further south? It was difficult to say. The end was close, that much was now obvious. Rumour circulated that Henry had left Watling Street and was approaching on the Roman road from Mancetter; by the end of the day the glow of the enemy's camp fires could be clearly seen.

I had not eaten for many days, and as the sun rose up through the morning mist I shared a simple breakfast of apples with a young blacksmith. I needed my strength, for I knew that I was entering the dying seconds, the final moments of obscurity. For what did happen that morning? Who attacked first and when? Was it the brave Duke of Norfolk, charging down the hill, with hundreds of billmen behind? Or did Henry attack up the hill, cowering beneath a creeping barrage of arrow and cannon shot?

I moved away from the sirens and helicopters to the sanctuary of the visitor's centre, as the first blood of battle drained down the hill. My state of battle readiness caused some consternation amongst the locals but I was able to slip through and gaze upon the many wonders on display there. I saw models of medieval villages and even some full-sized representations of domestic life. I climbed over the barrier into the stone hut where two women were cooking some food. They were plastic dummies that were easily knocked over but their food smelt good. Time was short and so I moved on through the medieval chapel before coming upon the battle model, a diorama showing the final moments of Richard's great charge. The tiny metal figures were exquisitely positioned, and it was with much bewilderment that I walked round the great glass case in which the display was maintained, watching as the unknown multitudes of soldiers swarmed across the green counterpane.

I was about to remove my goggles when two billmen rushed at me. I ran down a corridor, my assailants giving chase, before squeezing through a window that brought me out on to a gravelled path. I spotted the cars and vans around the centre and so lost no time in returning to the battlefield, where I could see Richard's colours still flying on the hilltop. Yet immediately before me the spectacle of medieval conflict raged as Norfolk's army sliced through Oxford's with its thousand swords and axes. I ran onwards through the mutilation, over the bodies and abandoned weapons, as a group of pike men advanced after me. Overhead the arrows whizzed in huge arcs, plunging down into the marauding mass ahead. I now knew what I had to do. I could see Richard even at that moment pointing as Henry became dangerously detached from his army. I was pounding up the slope of Ambion Hill, screaming at the top of my voice, as all around me the desolation of war raged on. Further down the hill the pike men would not relent, howling like dogs as the storm of arrows tracked me mercilessly through the grass. Richard's steed reared up, his standards tugging violently in the wind, as the knights gathered about him.

For God's sake, no! No!

But my voice was lost amid the cacophony of death, and even as those words were leaving my lips, Richard lifted up his sword and together the knights descended the hill, a wall of metal and horseflesh falling upon the Tudor Prince. I watched until I could see them no more amid the mass of men, even the standard itself, initially raised so high, gradually dropping until it too vanished from sight. I collapsed on to the grass, my hands and face soaked in the blood of the bodies that lay about me.

And so yet again it had occurred, the last charge of medieval knights in British history, the very point at which medieval history is said to end. And I was there; I watched it all. But could I have stopped it? Or was Richard's great charge as inevitable as the setting of the sun? As I was pulled up from out of the mud, it should come as no surprise to you that I was lost amid the depths of this most puzzling of academic conundrums.

PART TEN

Leicestershire

1922, Late Autumn

Rev Cecil Crowe,
The Vicarage,
Great Glen,
Leicestershire

1st November 1922

FROM: *Captain John Crowe, Horse and Groom,*
Evington, Leicestershire

My Dear Father,

Time is more precious than I ever realized. Indeed, I
have worked out that it is at least ten days since I last sat
down to write to you. Believe me when I tell you that
these past days wandering across the Leicestershire
countryside have seemed more like a decade to me; or
rather, to be more exact, this last week has come to me as
a timeless thing, in which there is no beginning or end.
I find it hard even now to concentrate on the page before
me, or to hold the pen, slanting as it does away from the
candle. One day I shall describe in the fullest detail what
happened after finding the bones, but that moment is not
now; and it is with some urgency that I draw a veil over
that mysterious sequence of events.

I can say that I am close now to my final destination,
Leicester, a place to which I was always drawn. Did I
not say so in one of my earlier letters? I am fast losing
track of what I have told you and what has remained in
my head. It was always my intention to visit Ritchie

335

Roberts, and my last address for him was in the centre of the sprawling city. And so it was towards the city that I set off when I finally left dear Weenie. As a souvenir of my stay, Weenie allowed me to keep his copy of *The Weather Book: A Manual of Practical Meteorology* by Robert Fitzroy, which he had caught me reading on more than one occasion. I carefully stowed it away in the saddlebags.

'It was written for sailors. Use it to find your way home.'

These were Weenie's very words as he handed the book over. I took a picture of him standing by his gate with arms crossed and pipe hanging out of his mouth, as though at any moment it might lose its delicate equilibrium and drop to the floor. I had seen a picture of him, taken in the trenches, with the same pose. He was trying to smile in that picture as well, and as I watched him through the viewer I could not help wondering if I would see him again.

Angus and I slowly headed south from Oakham, in the direction of Manton, a cloud of flies already following us as though they were circling sea birds and we a tall ship leaving harbour. As I recall, the weather was unseasonably hot and sunny yet again, something I took to be a good omen for the journey ahead.

Sweat soon began to glimmer on Angus's flanks and I even removed my old regimental cap. The sun was on our left, the Midland line on our right, parallel to the road. As I sat there, my greatcoat flapping against my legs, ploughing our way through the autumn mists, I ventured I was a captain standing upon his poop deck. Gently rocked by the rhythm of the tide, I reached into my bags and drew out *The Weather Book*, and thence, with my hands off the tiller, trusting completely the skills of the pilot, I once more acquainted myself with the words of wisdom contained therein.

My eyes eventually settled on a page showing different cloud formations: cirrus, cirronus, stratus, cirritus, nimbus, cirro-stratus, cumulus, cirrito-stratus and so on. Looking up at the sky I could see a number of wispy clouds that suggested cirrus, but then again, after closer inspection, they could also have been cirritus or cirro-stratus. I dropped anchor to make some brief notes before continuing with my observations.

Although the tiny lane on which I travelled was lined with trees and hedges, occasionally I caught a glimpse of a far darker, more menacing band of clouds seeping over the horizon far in the west. It was this possible portent of trouble that began to occupy my attention. Such meteorology, however, was hampered by the fact that, despite my best preparations, the Good Ship Angus would not have satisfied the attention of Rear Admiral Fitzroy. In terms of scientific equipment, for instance, the captain's cabin was distinctly bare. Where Fitzroy spoke of barometric readings, I had simply the seamen's instinct!

And thus spake my good rear admiral: 'When rising: in winter the rise of the barometer presages frost. In wet weather if the mercury rises high and remains so, expect continued fine weather in a day or two. In wet weather if the mercury rises suddenly very high, fine weather will not last long.' I remember the words exactly.

We were rapidly approaching our first port of call, the tiny village of Manton, through which ran the Midland line to Kettering. I looked at my watch and saw that we had been sailing in our southerly direction for less than an hour. To our right a steam train suddenly came into view, thundering on its way to the southern seas. Its great plumes of smoke hung like mist above the head of a whale, and, as we both converged upon the lowly port, it was as if I were Ahab himself and the great white whale was before me! I watched as its vast form dived down under the village into the oceanic depths, only to reappear moments later at a point now south of the settlement but beyond the visibility offered from the deck. Then, far away already, the shrill whistle floated back to me, suddenly muffled, as the engine once more was lost in the depths of a tunnel.

All hands on deck! There was no time to be lost. Although I had originally planned to rest in Manton, the foresail and mainsail were now unfurled and buckets of seawater thrown upon the canvas. Speed was of the essence! We quickly moved through the village, thundering over the tunnel that runs beneath the main thoroughfare, and back out into the open seas, still running south and alongside the track of the Midland. You should have seen me, Father! Clipping the waves of a tiny lane, we advanced over the Chater and down towards the crossroads where the line disappeared beneath us through another tunnel. And as we stopped at this parting of ways I, standing up upon the deck with the great book before me, felt the timbers tremble beneath my feet as another monster of the deep rose and fell through the salty surf on our larboard side. The spew from its awesome exhalations encircled the ship like a winter fog and for a time I could not read the very words that rested but six inches from my nose.

I must confess that as quietude returned to the tiny lane I was puzzled as to the direction in which my voyage should continue. Standing there on the forecastle, with spyglass to my eye, I surveyed the horizon for the telltale indicators of distant land, but neither fowl nor vegetation could I espy. In a methodical manner that would have impressed Richardson, I then set about a reading of the meteorological signs. The weathervane on the foremast indicated a prevailing wind from the south-west. The thermometer secured to the bowsprit displayed a temperature of 68 degrees whereas the Torricelli mercury barometer suggested a pressure of 998 millibars. Finally I brought out the storm glass and held it up so that the morning light pierced the strange green liquid contained within the vial. As the rays penetrated the glass, a green light played across my hand and down onto my greatcoat, and for several seconds I was transfixed. But the words of Rear Admiral Fitzroy could not be avoided, printed as they were on the wooden board to which the vial was mounted. I have lost the instrument now but still recall the words:

Clear liquid . . . Good, fine weather
Crystals at bottom . . . Frost in winter
Turbid liquid (substance rising) . . . Rain
Turbid liquid with crystals . . . Thunder
Large crystals . . . Close weather, cloudy skies, snow
Chains of crystals at the top . . . Windy weather

> Substance lies to one side . . . Storm or wind from
>   other direction

I stared hard into the liquid but could see no turbidity or precipitant crystals.

'Lower the foresails! Unleash the jib my fine fellows. And to starboard it is!'

Angus slowly moved off to the right, along a muddy lane that took us due west, towards the village of Preston, past the deserted village of Martinsthorpe. At Preston I realized that we were now just to the north of Uppingham, and for a brief time we travelled south through the village towards that famous town, but very shortly I swung Angus round again and we set off westward ho! towards the village of Ridlington. The warmth of the late autumnal sun had almost dispersed the mists of the early morning, although heavy dew still clung to the hedgerows, and in the shade, where the sun could not reach, a frozen tinsel of frost wreathed the vegetation.

Ridlington is a beautiful place, a wonderful collection of thatched cottages around a low church. Angus and I passed the tiny post office without catching sight of a soul. At the western end of the village, in a field rolling down the Chater Valley, however, we came across a curious earthwork on its easternmost edge, the sort of mysterious depression that litters this little-known part of the country. It was only because of my elevated position on the back of Angus that I actually spied the construction in the first place, swathed as it was in mist in the centre of the field. I weighed anchor, tying Angus to the rickety gate that led into the field, hopping over it myself after first rescuing my camera and notebook from the saddlebags.

The long grass was heavy with dew, the cow parsnip along the field edge still coated with crystals of shining silver. As I moved away from the lane, the cold mist swirled about me, smothering the sun. I re-buttoned my coat and moved on. There was silence apart from the squelch of my increasingly sodden boots.

And then it began to happen. Although this may seem strange to you, Father, I cannot deny that as I moved through the grass I began to feel the presence of lost spirits circling from within the mist, leading me on to the very edge of the earthwork. From where they came I do not know, mysterious angels perhaps, summoned for some divine purpose beyond my understanding. When I stopped to stare at a collection of boletus mushrooms that I had accidentally crushed beneath my feet, their sweet voices urged me on, and just for a second I caught the flash of a hardened face, crowned by a wreath of shining bronze. I moved on and as I did so there was an audible sigh as the haze before me suddenly lifted and I found myself on the edge of the great earthwork, staring out across the tiny Chater valley.

I do not remember how long I spent standing there, looking out across this ancient land, pondering the great mysteries of Time. When I turned to go I found that the mist had all but gone and that my camera and notebook were lying by the mushrooms where I had dropped them some time before.

I climbed back over the gate to return once more to the sunny lane. Angus displayed his irritation at my extended

absence with the usual stamping of his hoof, a behaviour
that only stopped once I had fed him the carrot taken
from Weenie's kitchen that very morning, now so very
long ago. It must have been approaching midday. I leaned
on the gate and watched as the autumn haze slowly
retreated across the fields to the long, dark areas of
shadow that were now so effortlessly cultivated by the low
arc of the sun.

It was as I stood there that I realized the true direction
of my journey. In many ways I was as a voyager who had
at last run his galley upon the sands of a strange new
island. It was time to grab my spear and strike out on foot
across the uncharted landscape before me!

Although much of this time is covered in its own
autumnal fog, it is with some clarity that I recall opening
the gate and leading Angus into the field. I knew he would
be safe there until my return. I rummaged through the
saddlebags, taking out those few things that I would need
for the remainder of the journey. Much I was able to lose
in the capacious pockets of my coat but my camera I
would have to carry by hand. I patted Angus's warm flank,
scattering my remaining few sugar lumps across the grass
before shutting the gate and moving off down the little
lane, away from the village.

It was not long before the lane meandered its way to
the busy Peterborough Road and I joined the steady
throng of automobiles and carts heading down into the
Soar valley where the great city of Leicester awaited them.
Luckily I had remembered to take with me my storm glass,
whose board I now held under my arm as I traversed along
the grass verge with my Kodak. At times, as the clouds

flitted across the sky in meteorological confusion, I found it necessary to bring out the board, shake the vial and consult Fitzroy's prognostications. At other times I would veer off into a field to make notes on the squirrels at play there, or to photograph an unusual pattern of poaceae. Such things are clear in my mind, but, as I have already alluded to, it is the time after that, after I had discovered the bones, that things become obscure.

I believe it was later that same afternoon I found the bones. I had drifted away from the main road. I recall marching through the village of Houghton on the Hill again, heading south along the same lane on which I had arrived into the village many days before. I did not see Albert but instead ceremonially doffed my cap and saluted as I passed the Black Horse Inn. At some point I must have left the lane and cut across the fields in an easterly direction until I came to the gentle meanderings of the River Sence. As with my previous walking tour, convalescing after my stay at Quex, I began to make copious notes on wild river fowl, noting in particular their strange propensity to emit human-like noises. Although these notes are now lost, I recall drifting slowly southward, amid the cries and screams, following the tiny river as it made its way underneath Gartree Road, towards Great Glen and beyond. My route in reverse! Perhaps it was this unexpected yearning for a return home, back to you my dear Father, that caused me to pause on the northern edge of Great Glen and reflect on the direction of my odyssey.

It was while seated on the banks of the Sence, listening

to the comings and goings of the little village in front of me, that my eye came across the strange objects sticking out from the shallow bank on the opposite side of the stream. I instinctively recognized that they were bones and that they were most likely human in origin.

You may wonder how I could suddenly become an expert on human bones, particularly when presented in such an unpromising light. But I must tell you that the skills of a soldier are not simply limited to those of the parade ground. You must count archaeology as an important brother to rifle drill! It should not come as a surprise that by the time we arrived in Winnezeele, near Passchendaele, in 1917 the bodies of the dead lay across the mud in all directions. One of the first things we did was to sneak out at night under heavy fire and establish some advanced posts forward from our line. I believe we decided to call them the Ashby, Loughborough and Coalville. As my men and I crawled out across the mud, the minenwerfers and eight-inch shells taking out a good number of us as we did so, I couldn't help but notice that underneath us, churned up by past explosions and scrubbed by torrential rain, lay the ruins of a forgotten army, perhaps from the earliest days of the war, a time that, to us then, seemed an eternity away. High-topped boots, pieces of gold-braided uniform, broken fancy-dress helmets and swords were almost all that remained of those French soldiers from another time, that and their shattered fragments of bone.

In the trenches it was not uncommon to come across a rather decayed companion or two. At Ypres I became acquainted with a rather sad individual who had been exposed by the line of British trenches. He was no more than bone really, bone and the occasional shred of cloth. I suspect he had been buried by an explosion only to be subsequently exposed when the Front lurched forwards and our lads came through with their entrenching tools. During the few days I spent at the front at Ypres before the big push at the end of September, I repeatedly covered his skull and various other parts with liquid mud, but such was the rain that by the following day he was always back again to share my morning tea.

I heard tales that other lads found far older remains, deep down at the bottom of trenches, beheaded warriors from pre-Roman times. It seems the Angels of Mons had at least some archaeological basis. That night before zero hour and our attack on Hill thirty-seven, I remember thinking that our bleached bones would soon be taking their place in the stratified remains of this ancient battlefield, a line of calcium that was but one tiny ring in the great tree of human misery. At stand-to, at the ghastly hour of 3 a.m., I dropped my silver ring through my skeletal companion's left eye socket and wished him well.

I am proud of my waterproof army boots, as you know, and so I easily strolled through the shallow waters to reach the other side of the Sence. I dropped down onto my knees and rubbed some of the soil away from the protrusions. Their curved nature immediately suggested ribs, and as I continued to excavate around the bones with my fingers I quickly unearthed a rudimentary rib cage. With further work I was able to reveal seven ribs in total, each delicately curving round to the knobbly remains of an ancient spinal column. Despite further excavation around these singular remains, however, I was unable to find the rest of the body, and was left to conclude that the head, legs and arms had been carried off by the river long ago. I took several pictures of the remains and scrawled onto the film 'Ancient Princess' for, though fanciful, I was of the opinion that here lay the most exotic of Bronze Age rulers, and that at some point her red-haired skull, capped by a crown of gold, had silently waited out the centuries from this very bank. My very own Piltdown man, as it were!

Dr Worthington had encouraged me to record my feelings and experiences when I set out on my first walking tour in the early months of 1918, in order, as he said, to regain my 'neuropathic equilibrium'. And so it was again, for as I moved away from Great Glen, in what can only be described as a haze of mental doubt and uncertainty, I drew out my notebook and continued to record those things that struck me as of particular interest. Yet memories of Burrow's bloated body would not let me rest.

Such was my crippled state that, in hindsight, I now lose sense of both time and space. As I sit before the guttering candle at this little writing table I can remember many things that subsequently happened but have no sense of when or where they occurred. It is certain that I slept in barns and sheds, often sharing the nocturnal hours with horses and cows, their breath streaming out in the silvery moonlight as I drew my greatcoat about me. I am aware that one day I followed a railway line and was almost hit

by a train, the rush of the machine throwing me down the
embankment, smashing my storm glass into a hundred
parts and sending the green liquid spewing over my tunic.
On another occasion I hid as a plane came down,
recreating the attacks that saw so many of my men ripped
to pieces in a fusillade of bullets. I watched from high up
in a tree as the plane circled before flying off into the
clouds.

These things I remember – and more! – but exactly
when and where they occurred I cannot say. It is enough
that I am safe and well here in Evington.

It is a shock to learn that the diary suggests I was out
roaming the countryside for more than six days! I suspect
that Mrs Cayless, the landlord of the public house where I
am staying in the village, would agree that my dishevelled
appearance on Sunday afternoon was enough evidence to
confirm the story. It was she who took pity on me as I
emerged from the graveyard of the local church – a certain
St Denys – and offered me free lodgings. I cannot speak
more highly of her for I had no money and had lost all
those things of value that I had so carefully stowed about
my person on leaving Angus. I had not eaten since leaving
Weenie, and so you can imagine the enthusiasm with
which I attacked the porridge and stew Mrs Cayless
prepared for me.

After the food I told her of my journey from Oakham
through the wilds of the east Leicestershire countryside.
I told her where I had left Angus and expressed the hope
that he was fit and well, in the hands of his adopted
owners. She listened in silence for most of the time,

eventually leading me up to my room where she lit the candle before suggesting that I should wash thoroughly before getting into bed. This I did, the bathroom being only next door. Despite the fact that the water was stone cold, I was able to remove much of the dirt that had ingrained itself onto my face and hands. The delight of finally settling into a soft, warm bed cannot be exaggerated.

The following day Mrs Cayless washed my garments, which were certainly in a state of dereliction. I in turn offered to do as many jobs about the house as she could put my way. I cut logs and repaired the wooden gate, all in some borrowed overalls, while my own army clothes dried on the line. Meanwhile the person I took to be her husband, a quiet, withdrawn sort of fellow, hardly said a word but remained standing lugubriously behind the bar with his pipe.

In the early evening I sat in the kitchen and ate my dinner while Mrs Cayless clanked and banged around me. I explained that I would be gone in the morning, at which Mrs Cayless nodded. Although she had not enquired into my present state, despite our bizarre introduction, I began to explain to her about my little odyssey and my success with *Perambulations*. She was heartily pleased to learn that I was undertaking a journey of real scientific value and promised to buy the new *Autumn and Winter* edition of *Perambulations* as soon as it was available in the shops. This I promised her would be soon. As I finished off the large bowl of apple crumble that had been placed under my nose, I expounded on these details by explaining that I was also using the occasion to visit several of my old pals whom I had last seen at the Front in September 1917, before my enforced stay in hospital at Quex, in southern England. Here she became rather emotional. I believe she wished me God's speed in finding my friends before suddenly leaving me in the darkened solitude of her kitchen.

Once I had finished my cigarette I returned to my room where, after looking over my freshly dried uniform left folded in a neat pile on the end of my bed, I began to write this letter to you, dear Father. And so here we are at last in the present moment, with all that was, now safely recorded as the past, and the unknown events beckoning before me. As I look up I see that it is 10.30 in the evening and the public house is growing silent as its few customers drift away into the coldness of the night. I hear the weather is at last changing for the worse but I can console myself that it won't be long before I once more experience the delights of a soft bed. Mrs Cayless has already been along the corridor, perhaps extinguishing the few candles that illuminate this side of the house, her movements over the floorboards causing the basin of cold water in the corner of my room to ring as though a secret hand slid slowly round its rim. I thought about her behaviour in the kitchen and can only surmise that perhaps she has lost a son in the War, and that my return, stumbling out of the local graveyard, in some way caused submerged emotions to rise to the surface. I suspect I have done little for Mrs Cayless's own neuropathic equilibrium.

But in a strange way I now feel more at ease with myself than I have done at any time in the last two years. Although I have lost almost all material possessions – I have only my tattered notebook with me, having lost even my dear camera in some unknown escapade of the last few days – I am at peace with my conscience. Last night I slept as well as I have in living memory – no cold sweats or nightmares to haunt the witching hour. Perhaps it will not continue, but I am an optimist and instead see this as an indication of a new beginning – that new start that I prophesied at the start of this little journey when I left you on that misty morn in early September.

And what a peculiar adventure thus far! Did it really commence all that time ago, at Uncle George and Aunty Beth's, with Frederick Simms, the strange aeronautist, and then later, Albert, Weenie and Richardson? All of them cast across the pock-marked landscape of these central shires like seed scattered in the wind.

Who knows what the final leg of this journey holds for me. It is off into the heart of Leicester that I go, that much is certain. My doubts and concerns must be ignored, although I would be lying if I said it wasn't with a sense of strange foreboding that I reflect upon what lies ahead. In truth, I long to be home, Father, to have my hand upon your gate and old Jessie barking at my side.

But let us not slip into depression. Although this journey has changed me in ways I've yet to fully comprehend, I'm now sure of one thing, at least. More than ever it seems clear to me that our cynicism about the future is entirely misplaced. Weenie's lament for the certainties of the past is premature, for I truly sense the vibrant potential of the days that lie before us – the *Great Modern Age* as it will surely be, so well encapsulated by Richardson's theories and innovations.

I believe it was Frederick Simms, the aeronautist I met so many days ago, who exclaimed that the Age of Technology was upon us. And in this he was so right. One day he will find his way home, just as I am doing, and we will both rise like Albert's pigeons into the sun. Upwards, upwards, in the arms of the coming dawn . . .

Perambulations of a Soldier: Autumn to Winter
by John Crowe

When the year is advanced well into October, and certainly by the time Guy Fawkes makes his annual return for ritual burning, the countryside in all its many forms and shapes will be displaying many of the signs of the autumnal season. Yet even now, when mists and mellow fruitfulness should be evident in every nook and hollow, the seasons do not act in accordance with scientific law. For this reason, let us invent a new month, a period outside the diktat of science, a time we shall call Opora, to cover this peculiar end time of the year. It is under a glorious Opora sun then that we walk along by the side of this rural railway track. The line is rarely used and believe me when I say that any approaching train would be clearly visible long before it was upon us! Such is the heat I will take my hat off and use the opportunity to investigate the source of that sweet smell that has suddenly enveloped us. There, growing under the protection of the Midland line, is the gentlest of residents, a rare orchid by the name of Autumnal Lady's-tresses. The name is taken from the way the flowering stem grows in a slight spiral twist, bringing to mind amongst country folk now long gone the side curls then in fashion amongst our grandmothers. Notice that the plant differs from the other orchids we have found on our journey: the flowering stem appears to have no leaves coming from the tuber itself. Close by we discover new shoots already poking through the ground. These will feed the tuber until the flower spike begins to develop, when the leaves will shrivel and die, as they surely have done with our more mature specimen.

Something else has just caught my eye. There on the privet bush close to my left elbow is one of the largest of our caterpillars, that of the privet-hawk moth. Although it is about three inches long and half an inch thick it is so well camouflaged that I suspect you have not seen it yet! Take a good look at this handsome creature for soon it will drop to the ground and thence burrow deep down into the soil until it is lost from the sight of mortal men. There, amongst the bones and rock, it will magically change into a large red-brown chrysalis, as though becoming fossilized, a state from which it will not emerge as a moth until many months hence, in the far-off heat of next year's summer.

But I fear I am being diverted. Follow my hand upwards – although the sky is clear above us, notice how the clouds are gathering way up beyond that line of trees on the distant horizon. If I am not mistaken, they are nimbo-stratus, and portend heavy showers. It would be wise to return home before a wintry shower overtakes us.

And so it is towards home that we set off; but, strangely, it is only now, as our journey starts to enter its final moments, that we find, strewn across our path like confetti thrown before the returning soldier, the seedlings of many of the plants we have known only in their flowering stage on our previous walks. By the springtime, when I hope to be here again, we will find that these fragile shoots will have transformed themselves into mature plants, perhaps even with the first hint of flower.

Much more remains beneath the soil of course, seeds and nuts that hold the promise of springtime growth and replenishment, and those darker forces that stay hidden and unseen for the length of their mysterious lives.

And thus the end, or perhaps not. As nimbostratus gathers overhead and my hand is almost on my little gate, I am once more forced to reflect on this most contrary of times, what some folks call 'the dead season'; a period of berries, and ripe nuts and acorns; of fungus, rot and decay; this strange time of Opora.

EPILOGUE

Article in the *Leicester Mercury*
1 November 2004, page 8

An inquest heard today how the body of a tramp was found in a chest of drawers nearly eighteen years after his death in the Leicester studio of artist Peter Lowbetsky.

The artist died in August of a heart attack, and the embalmed body was found ten days later. It is understood that the pair had met when the tramp, who was believed to be at least eighty when he died, was living in a concrete barrel in a disused alleyway in the centre of Leicester. They subsequently became friends.

The coroner, Graham Parker, said yesterday that he had been contacted by the executors of Mr Lowbetsky's estate, who indicated that they were in possession of information which might reveal the location of the tramp's body.

On Tuesday a coroner's officer and an environmental health official searched the studio in the Stoneygate area of Leicester. They recovered an embalmed body from a large drawer in a chest of drawers, along with several notebooks and letters that had been left with the corpse.

The body has now been identifed as that of a tramp known only as Diogenes. The tramp had featured in Mr Lowbetsky's work, most prominently in a life-size metal sculpture called 'Artist's assistant (retired)' that had stood in the artist's garden.

The 'well preserved' body was taken to a local hospital mortuary; it might now be released, but it is unclear who has a right to lawful possession. The tramp remains un-identified, leaving no will.

Mr Parker said letters were sent to the executors of the artist's estate, asking them to prove they had a right to possession. He explained that if no one can come forward with a proper claim the body will be released to the local authority for burial.

It is understood that the council had been informed of the tramp's death some time in the mid 1980s, and had insisted on a burial. Mr Lowbetsky had refused to disclose where the body was kept, saying it was the tramp's wish to be embalmed. When officials visited, all they found was the artist himself, hidden inside a makeshift coffin.